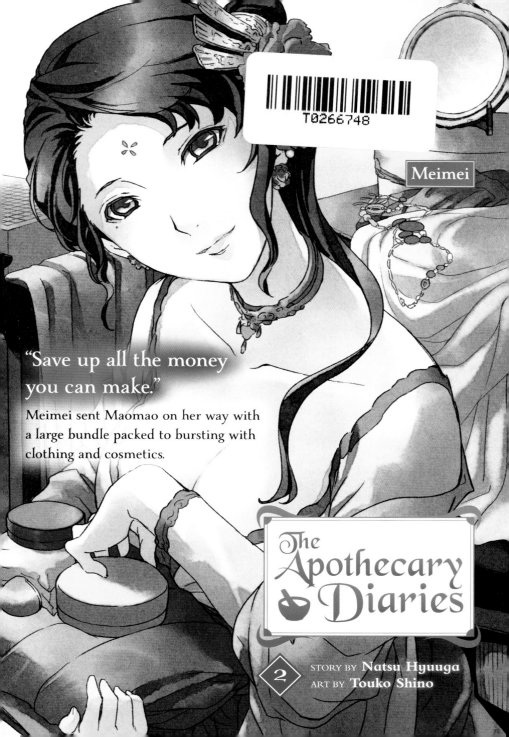

T0266748

Meimei

"Save up all the money
you can make."

Meimei sent Maomao on her way with
a large bundle packed to bursting with
clothing and cosmetics.

The
Apothecary
Diaries

2

STORY BY **Natsu Hyuuga**
ART BY **Touko Shino**

Ailan

Guiyan

When the ladies-in-waiting didn't have much to do, they found themselves chatting in the kitchen.

"I couldn't believe that outfit, could you?"

Yinghua, one of the Jade Pavilion's ladies-in-waiting, said around a mouthful of candy.

"Western clothing is so cool, though, isn't it?"

said Guiyuan in a mild tone.

Yinghua

"Clothes like that choose their own wearers,"

the lanky Ailan observed. "Yeah, sure," Maomao said, nodding and thinking how she hated to get involved in these spats.

Loulan

Consort Lishu

"My cordial greetings to you, honored ladies. I, Maomao, humbly present myself to you as your instructor."

Maomao stood in the center of the hall, then slowly bowed her head.

Consort Gyokuyou was looking as lovely as ever.

Consort Gyokuyou

Consort Lihua

Consort Lihua was watching Maomao placidly.

Consort Lishu exuded the same slight air of nervousness as always.

Finally, the last of the august ladies. A face Maomao hadn't seen before. The young woman who had replaced one of the former high consorts was about Maomao's age. She was Loulan, the new Pure Consort.

She didn't say anything.

Clad in the lovely dress, she called to mind the first steps of the dance she'd been taught so long ago. She'd let her hair down tonight, decorating it with a single rose, a small flower dyed blue. The scarf danced; the skirt rose in time; sleeves and hair fluttered together. Her scarf billowed again—

He didn't say anything.

—and then Maomao found herself looking
directly at a very unwelcome companion.

A NOTE FROM THE AUTHOR

The Apothecary Diaries: a simple story of a young girl, a food taster in a medieval palace who can solve the most perplexing mysteries. People loved it, and so comes the second volume.

In the last volume, our heroine, Maomao, was let go from service in the rear palace. Now, though, she finds somewhere new to belong and gets back to solving cases. We're dialing the thrills up 300%—along with Maomao's Tsundere Ratio!

That's to say nothing of her relationship with the gorgeous eunuch Jinshi, which—well, let's just say you'll find yourself flipping the pages of this hotly anticipated second act as fast as you can!

The Apothecary Diaries

⤙ 2 ⤚

STORY BY NATSU HYUUGA
ART BY TOUKO SHINO

ENGLISH ADAPTATION BY
KEVIN STEINBACH

SQUARE ENIX
BOOKS

The Apothecary Diaries

Volume 2

Story: Natsu Hyuuga
Art: Touko Shino

Translator: Kevin Steinbach
Cover Designer: Sarah Sapang
Interior Designers: Laura K. Corless, Kristin del Rosario
Editor, Print Edition: Jennifer Sherman
Editor, Digital Edition: Sasha McGlynn

KUSURIYA NO HITORIGOTO 2
© Natsu Hyuuga 2015
Originally published in Japan by Imagica Infos Co., Ltd.
Translation rights arranged with Shufunotomo Co., Ltd.
English translation © 2021 by J-Novel Club LLC

Library of Congress Cataloging-in-Publication Data

Names: Hyūga, Natsu, author. | Shino, Tōko, artist. | Steinbach, Kevin, translator.
Title: The apothecary diaries / written by Natsu Hyuuga ; art by Touko Shino ;
  English adaptation by Kevin Steinbach.
Other titles: Kusuriya no hitorigoto. English
Description: First edition. | El Segundo, CA : Square Enix, 2024-
Identifiers: LCCN 2023042712 | ISBN 9781646092727 (v. 01 ; trade paperback) |
  ISBN 9781646092734 (v. 02 ; trade paperback) | ISBN 9781646092741 (v. 03 ; trade paperback)
Subjects: CYAC: Healers--Fiction. | Courts and courtiers--Fiction. | China--History--Fiction. |
  LCGFT: Historical fiction. | Detective and mystery fiction. | Light novels.
Classification: LCC PZ7.1.H97 Ap 2024 | DDC [Fic]--dc23
LC record available at https://lccn.loc.gov/2023042712

Manufactured in the USA
First Edition: August 2024
1st Printing

Published by Square Enix Manga & Books, a division of SQUARE ENIX, INC.
999 N. Pacific Coast Highway, 3rd Floor
El Segundo, CA 90245, USA

SQUARE ENIX
MANGA & BOOKS

square-enix-books.com

TABLE OF CONTENTS

Prologue

A re you quite serious?" Jinshi asked.

Across from him, a man reclined on a couch. The middle-aged ruler with a prodigious beard now nodded slowly.

They were in a particular pavilion in the outer court. Small, but with excellent visibility; a mouse couldn't have crawled in without them seeing it. The ruler leaned on his ivory-bedecked couch and poured grape wine into a glass vessel. Although he was sitting with the most august personage in the nation, Jinshi had also been quite at his ease. At least, until a moment ago.

The emperor stroked his beard and grinned. Would it be rude of Jinshi to suggest he didn't like it? But the beard looked very good on His Majesty. Jinshi couldn't beat him in the facial hair department.

"So, what are you going to do now, O groundskeeper of our garden of lovely blossoms?"

Unwilling to rise to His Majesty's bait, Jinshi held back a wry smile, instead offering one like that of a heavenly nymph—an expression that could have melted any heart he chose. It might not sound very humble, but Jinshi was confident in his own looks if nothing else.

What a great irony, then, that the one thing he truly wanted, he could not get. No matter how he strived, his aptitudes were hardly more than ordinary. Yet outwardly, if in no other way, he was utterly exceptional.

It always used to eat at him, but he had come to accept it. If his intelligence and physical prowess were to be irredeemably average, then he would do all he could with the one advantage he did possess. Thus he came to be the gorgeous overseer of the rear palace. His looks, his voice, seemed too sweet to be those of any man, and he would employ them to the fullest.

"Whatsoever you wish, sire." Jinshi, with a smile at once graceful and determined, bowed to the emperor.

The emperor sipped his wine and grinned in a way that invited Jinshi to do his worst. Jinshi knew full well that he was no more than a child. A child dancing in the emperor's great palm. But he would do it. Oh yes, he would. He would entertain even His Majesty's most outrageous wishes. That was Jinshi's duty, as well as his wager with the emperor.

He had to win that wager. It was the only way Jinshi would be able to choose his own path. Perhaps other ways existed. But a man of ordinary intelligence such as Jinshi couldn't imagine them.

Thus he had chosen the road he now followed.

Jinshi brought his cup to his lips and felt the sweet fruit wine wet his throat, the heavenly smile never slipping from his face.

"Here you go. Take this, and this—oh, and you'll need one of these."

Maomao winced at all the stuff that came veritably flying at her. The one flinging the rouge and whitening powder and clothes in her direction was the courtesan Meimei. They were in her room at the Verdigris House.

"Sis, I don't need any of this," Maomao said, taking the cosmetics one by one and returning them to their various shelves.

"Like fun you don't," Meimei said, exasperated. "Everyone else there is going to have even better stuff than this. The least you could do is try to look decent."

"Only courtesans get this tarted up to go to work."

Maomao had just glanced aside, privately wishing she could go mix those herbs she'd collected the day before, when a bundle of wooden writing strips came flying at her. Her esteemed older sister was solicitous, but sometimes short-tempered. "You finally get a job worth having, and you won't even try to act like you belong there? Listen, the world is full of people who would *kill* to be in your place. If you aren't grateful for what you've got, your hard-won clientele will run out on you!"

"Oh, very well . . ." Maomao said. Whether administered by the madam or Meimei, education in the Verdigris House could be a bit rough. But there was truth to what she said.

Maomao picked up the writing strips sullenly. The wood was dark where it had been written on and then erased over and over; currently, it bore the words of a song, written in a delicate hand. Meimei was old enough to be thinking of retiring from courtesan's work, but her intelligence saw her popularity continue to flourish. She could entertain her clientele by writing songs or playing go and shogi. She was one of those courtesans who sold not so much her body as her accomplishments.

"You've got a plum job now. Save up all the money you can make." The wood-strip-flinging woman of a moment ago was gone, replaced by Maomao's sweet, caring older sister. She stroked Maomao's cheek with a manicured hand, tucking some errant hair behind her ear.

Ten months before, Maomao had been kidnapped and sold into service as a maid in the rear palace. Never in her wildest dreams had she imagined that after successfully making her way back to the pleasure district, she would once again go to work there. To those around her, it must have seemed a once-in-a-lifetime opportunity. Hence the stern look in Meimei's eyes.

"Yes, Sister," Maomao said obediently after a moment, and Meimei smiled her graceful courtesan's smile.

"I hope you'll make more than just money. Make yourself a nice match with a fine man too, eh? There must be plenty of them just bursting with cash there. Oh, and I would be thrilled if you'd bring a few of them by to be my customers." The smile this time wasn't so gracious; there was a distinct element of cold calculation to it. Her chuckling older sister looked a bit like the old madam who ran the place, Maomao reflected. A girl had to look out for herself to survive in this line of work.

Ultimately, Maomao found herself sent on her way with a large bundle packed to bursting with clothing and cosmetics. She worked her way back to her simple house, stumbling under the load.

———◇———

The day when the gorgeous noble had appeared in the pleasure district two weeks after Maomao's departure from the rear palace was still fresh in her memory. The eunuch, with his very particular proclivities, had—thankfully—heard the words Maomao had spoken half in jest and taken them in earnest. He had confronted the madam with more than enough money to cover Maomao's debts and had even had the decency to bring a rare medicinal herb as a gift. It hadn't taken even thirty minutes to stamp the contract.

So it was that Maomao was to resume her employment at that most renowned of workplaces. She was somewhat reluctant to leave her father again to go live in her place of employment, but the conditions imposed by her new contract were, as far as she could tell, much more lenient than before. Moreover, this time, she wouldn't be simply disappearing without a trace. Her father had told her with a gentle smile to do what she wished, but then his face had briefly darkened when he looked at her contract. What had that meant?

Looks like they were very generous," Maomao's father remarked, a large pot of medicinal herbs boiling nearby. Maomao finally put down the cloth-covered bundle and stretched her shoulders. Their ramshackle house was so drafty that it was cold even with the fireplace lit, and she and her father were each wearing several layers. She caught him rubbing his knee, a sure sign that his old wound was paining him.

"I can't take much of it with me," Maomao said, looking at the cargo she'd already prepared. *The mortar and pestle are musts, and I can't do without my notebook. And I'm a little leery of getting rid of any more undergarments . . .*

As Maomao frowned and grumbled, her father took the pot off the fire and came over. "My Maomao, I'm not so sure you can bring these with you," he said, and plucked her mortar and pestle out of her bundle, earning a glare. "You're no doctor. Try bringing these in, and they might figure you're planning to poison someone. Come now, don't look at me like that. You made this decision, and you can't take it back now."

"Are we sure about that?" Maomao slumped down onto the dirt floor. Her father deduced at a glance what she was really trying to say.

"All right now, finish your preparations and then get yourself to bed. You can ask them to let you have your tools, just over time. It'd be rude not to be focused on your work, at least on the first day."

"Yeah, fine . . ." Maomao grudgingly returned the apothecary's implements to the shelf, then picked out a few of the most useful-looking parting gifts she'd received and put them in her bundle. She scowled at the whitening powder and the seashell full of blush, but eventually included the latter, which didn't take up too much room. Among the gifts was an excellent padded cotton jacket. Maybe they'd taken the opportunity to foist something on her that a customer had forgotten; it certainly didn't look like anything a courtesan would wear.

Maomao watched her father stash the pot away and put some wood on the fire. Then he hobbled over to his bed, a simple reed mat, and lay down. His bedclothes consisted only of another mat and a poor outer robe.

"When you're finished, I'll put out the light," he said, pulling the fish-oil lamp close. Maomao packed the rest of her things, then went to tuck herself into her bed on the other side of the room. She was caught by a passing idea, though, and dragged her sleeping mat over toward her father's.

"Well, now, it's been a while since you did that. I thought you weren't a child anymore."

"No, but I *am* cold." Was it a little too obvious, the way Maomao averted her eyes? She'd been, she recalled, about ten when she started sleeping by herself. It had been years. She stuffed the new cotton jacket between herself and her father and let her eyes drift shut. She rolled to one side and rounded her back, assuming a fetal position.

"Ah, it's going to be lonely around here again," her father said calmly.

"Doesn't have to be. This time I can come home whenever I want." Maomao's tone was short, but she couldn't help noticing the warmth of her father's arm against her back.

"Yes, of course. Do come back anytime." A hand tousled her hair. Father, she called him, Dad, Pops, but his appearance was closer to that of an old woman, and everyone agreed that his manner was motherly.

Maomao had no mother. Not as such. But she had her father who cared for her, and the yammering old madam, and her endlessly lively older sisters.

And I can come back and see them whenever I want. She could feel the warmth of her father's hand, withered like an old branch, still stroking her hair as her breathing fell into the steady, even rhythm of sleep.

✦ CHAPTER 1 ✦

Serving in the Outer Court

I was under the distinct impression that I would be going back to the rear palace." Maomao found herself wearing an outfit made of cotton. When she recalled the crude hemp dress she'd been allotted as a maid in the rear palace, it seemed awfully sumptuous.

"You were let go, I'm afraid. You can't go traipsing right back. No, this is where you'll be working from now on." Showing her around the palace was Jinshi's aide, Gaoshun, who was instructing her in the names of the various buildings and the offices that resided within them. Given the size of the palace proper, it was bound to be a dizzying tour.

The rear palace was part of the inner court, where the Imperial family resided. Her workplace now, though, was to be the outer court. In short, the same place as all the many functionaries who staffed all the many administrative organs.

"Over to the east from here you'll find a great many soldiers and military types, so I would suggest steering clear."

Maomao nodded even as she eyed the nearby plant life. *I knew it. Lots more ingredients growing in the rear palace.* She suspected it was her father, Luomen, who had planted the wide variety of useful herbs during his tenure there. It would explain the profusion of medicinal plants in an otherwise limited space.

As they walked along—Gaoshun explaining this, that, and the other thing—Maomao felt a peculiar prickling along her neck. She shot a glance behind her to discover some of the women who served in the outer court looking at her. Or more properly, glaring at her.

Just as there are things among men that only other men understand, there are certain things for which only women have a shared sense. Men have a tendency to resolve their differences physically, whereas women often resort to emotional means. These women seemed to be taking stock of the newcomer.

Don't like this one bit, Maomao thought. She stuck out her tongue at the other women, then scuttled after Gaoshun toward the next building.

It turned out Maomao's duties in the outer court would be much the same as those she had performed in the rear palace: clean the rooms she was told to clean and do odd jobs and little chores when and as she was instructed to do so. Jinshi, she gathered, had had bigger plans for her, but never got the chance to implement them: Maomao had failed the test.

"How could you have failed?!"

Why should I have passed?

Jinshi and Gaoshun had both been stunned. Apparently they had simply assumed that Maomao would succeed. Being brought up in the red-light district, Maomao could read and write, and had received at least a baseline education in singing and playing the erhu. The test in question was not as difficult as the civil service examinations, so they seemed to have figured that with a little studying, she would pass easily.

Gee, excuse me for not living up to your expectations, Maomao thought as she wiped angrily at a window frame. She was in the hallway of Jinshi's office. The architecture was plainer than that on display in the rear palace, though the building was perhaps a little taller. The vermilion-lacquered walls were a brilliant red, evidently refreshed each year.

The truth was, Maomao didn't like studying, and was probably less adept than average at remembering things she wasn't interested in. Drugs, herbs, and medicines were one thing, but why would anyone bother to learn history? What good would it do them? And as for the law, it changed constantly. What was the point of memorizing it? Maomao, sadly, was incapable of investing much effort in that direction. It was only natural she should fail the test.

She had, at least, opened the materials she'd been given to study with every intention of reading them through, but the next thing she knew it was morning. This happened several times in a row. So Maomao consoled herself that the outcome had been inevitable. She nodded in agreement with her own conclusion.

Didn't expect this place to be so dirty.

On the one hand, such a big space had many spots that were hard to reach and easy to miss—but on the other, Maomao didn't *not* suspect that there might have been a little slacking involved. The women who served here earned their place through the test, very much unlike the maids recruited, sold, or stolen to serve the rear palace. The women here had families and educations, and the pride to go with them. They probably saw maids' work as beneath them. Even if they noticed some dust, it was unlikely they would lift a finger to do anything about it.

To be fair, it's not their job, she thought.

The ladies of the outer court were something like secretaries. Cleaning was certainly not part of their portfolio, and there was no need for them to do it. But that didn't mean they shouldn't. The government had ceased to own slaves during the time of the former emperor, and bureaucrats began hiring menservants and maidservants to do odd chores instead.

Maomao was now such a maidservant, serving directly under Jinshi.

In Maomao's experience, women who served in the rear palace were widely referred to as palace women, while those who worked in the outer court were frequently called court ladies. She might or might not have been exactly right about that, but it was a distinction Jinshi and others like him seemed to observe when they spoke.

All right, what's next? She turned toward Jinshi's office. The room was large but not luxurious; in fact, it was quite spare. Its chief occupant was a busy man; once he left his office, he rarely returned to it quickly. That made it easier for Maomao to do the cleaning, but there was one problem.

"Excuse me, but what precisely do you think you're doing?"

She registered that a number of unfamiliar ladies had surrounded her. They were all bigger than Maomao, and one among them stood a full head taller than her.

The better they eat, the bigger they get, Maomao thought, her glance unconsciously taking in both the girls' heights and their bustlines. The one who had spoken to her was noticeably tall, implying an excellent upbringing.

"Are you listening to me?" the woman demanded while Maomao entertained these somewhat untoward thoughts.

In a word, the ladies were upset that Maomao was serving Jinshi personally. They wanted to know why she had received such a privilege. Unfortunately, she wasn't privy to the inner workings of Jinshi's mind; she only knew that he had hired her. If Maomao had been a well-connected foreign gentlewoman like Gyokuyou, or if she had been as luscious as Lihua or as sexy as Pairin, no one would have objected, nor would they have had grounds to. But Maomao looked like nothing more than a scrawny, befreckled chicken. The girls couldn't stand it. It drove them mad to see Maomao by the side of the gorgeous eunuch. They would have given anything to trade places with her.

Hrm, Maomao thought, *what to do now?* She was hardly the world's fastest talker. Often, in fact, she would think hard but ultimately leave her mouth shut. But silence seemed likely to irritate these ladies as much as anything Maomao might actually say.

She decided to cut to the chase. "Do I understand correctly that what you're saying is that you're jealous of me?" It was more than enough to anger the ladies. It was only after she had been slapped across the cheek that Maomao started to reflect that maybe she'd chosen the wrong words.

13

There were five women around her, and Maomao hoped to avoid them killing her on the spot. But they herded her inexorably toward a dark corner of the hallway. She didn't have much to lose at this point, so Maomao decided to see if she could talk her way out of this. "You can't possibly think I'm getting special treatment somehow?"

The ladies' faces distorted further. Maomao kept talking before she suffered another blow. "That's absurd, and we all know it. What could a distasteful wench like myself have to do with one who could well be one of the heavenly nymphs incarnate?" She cast her eyes on the ground as she spoke, but the slight twitching of the ladies' cheeks didn't escape her notice. *This might just work*, she thought. "Is this noble man you so desire a person of such poor taste? When fine abalone and boar's meat are laid before them, who would deliberately wish to gnaw on a discarded chicken bone instead? One would have to possess very specific proclivities."

Those last words elicited another twitch from the women.

"I myself would not know, but do you believe that one of such beauty, with his ethereal smile, would possess such proclivities? I see, so his *proclivities* are—"

"N-nothing of the sort! That's ridiculous!"

"Yes, ridiculous!"

A general hubbub ensued among the women. Maomao thought she'd escaped by the skin of her teeth, but one of the ladies was watching her skeptically. "Yet none of that changes the fact that you *were* hired, isn't that true?" the comparatively calm woman said. She was the tallest of them, her face cool and composed. Now that Maomao thought about it, she realized this woman had remained detached throughout the preceding argument. Like the other women, she'd taken a half step back, but she continued to watch Maomao closely. She seemed like the type who might follow a mob just to see where it went, though not be a part of it herself.

Well, if that's not enough to put them off . . . Maomao thought, and then she said: "This is the reason." She held up her left arm and rolled down her sleeve. Then she began to unwrap the bandage that ran from her wrist to her elbow.

"Eek!" one of the women cried, and they all looked at her, speechless. Cruel scars covered Maomao's skin.

Those experiments with burns I did recently left some good, nasty ones too, Maomao thought. The aristocratic young women must have been disgusted.

"The heart of that most beautiful object of your affections is as celestial and pure as his smile. I can attest to it, for he has given even one such as me room and board." Maomao rewrapped the bandage as she spoke. She was careful to accent her remarks with a demure glance at the ground and a gentle tremble of her body.

"Let's get out of here," one of the women said. Thoroughly relieved of any interest in Maomao, they promptly left. The tall one glanced back at her, she but was soon gone as well.

There. Finally over, Maomao thought to herself. She cracked the joints in her neck and picked up her dusting rag again. Just as she was about to go find the next place that needed dusting, she discovered a gorgeous eunuch standing with his head pressed against the wall.

"Might I inquire as to what you're doing, Master Jinshi?"

"Nothing at all. And you, are they always after you? Those types? Say, were you holding up your left arm?"

"It's fine. Frankly, they're less trouble to deal with than the girls of

15

the rear palace. Incidentally, if I may ask, why are you standing like that?"

Maomao ignored the question about her arm. It seemed Jinshi had been unable to see everything from his vantage point. The position he had adopted wasn't particularly suited to nobility, Maomao thought. Judging by the way he was holding his head in his hands, Gaoshun, behind Jinshi, seemed to agree.

"If you don't mind, I'll be about my cleaning, sir." With Jinshi back again, it wouldn't be possible to clean the office. She would have to find somewhere else that needed dusting. Maomao went off with her rag and a pail, but from behind her she heard Jinshi mutter: "*Proclivities . . .*"

I don't think *I said anything wrong,* Maomao told herself. Even if Jinshi had witnessed the last moments of that confrontation, she saw no special reason for him to be upset. Instead, she focused on her cleaning.

*N*ot much around here in winter, is there?

Sitting cross-legged in her room, Maomao folded her arms over her chest and grunted to herself. She'd stolen a moment here and there in between jobs during the afternoon to collect some herbs, but pickings were slim, and she still didn't have nearly enough to properly work with. Left with scant choice, she simply cleaned them, patted away as much of the water as she could, and then hung them on the wall of her room to dry. She had been doing this ever since she came to the outer court, and Maomao's room had turned into quite a sight to see. Drying herbs hung everywhere.

She had been assigned a relatively nice room for the quarters of a live-in maid, but there was no getting around the fact that it was still a little cramped. Really no bigger than her quarters in the rear palace. The difference was that at the Jade Pavilion she had been able to ask for permission to use the kitchen, and combined with the abundance of available resources, producing her concoctions had been a simple matter—all of which had taken the sting out of the size of her accommodations.

What to do, what to do? Maomao regarded the paulownia chest she'd placed carefully on top of her wicker trunk. Tucked inside the chest, which was sealed with a silk cord, was the herb that grew from an insect. It was called dong chong xia cao—winter worm, summer weed—otherwise sometimes known as caterpillar fungus, and Jinshi had brought it with him along with the money when he came to the pleasure district. The mere sight of it had induced Maomao to sign the contract without a moment's further reflection, but now she wondered if she had let herself go too cheaply. She could never have overcome her desire for this uncanny herb, though.

She opened the lid and looked at the fungus within, and an unconscious smile spread over her face. It turned to a grin, and her cheeks veritably started to twitch.

No, no, must stop. The day before, she'd let the twitch turn into such a great yawp that her neighbors two rooms over had come pounding on her door to object. Apparently you weren't supposed to go shouting in the middle of the night. Allegedly, people were trying to sleep or something.

Maomao pressed her fingers into her cheeks to relax the smile, then lay down on her bed. A serving woman's work started early, even before the cock crowed. The person she served might have been miss-

17

ing something very important, but he was still gorgeous and still of high station. One ought not to displease him.

Maomao pulled up her thin sheet along with several layers of outer clothing that doubled as bedding and closed her eyes.

 s your current room not somewhat small?" the gorgeous eunuch inquired over breakfast.

Maomao blinked, then replied, "I dare say it's more than generous for a serving girl like me." Even she understood that she could hardly voice her true feelings. ("Yes, it damn well is small. If possible, I'd like to request a room with a generous fireplace, located next to a well.")

"You mean it?"

This time she simply didn't say anything.

The eunuch had just woken up and hadn't entirely made himself up for the day yet as he enjoyed his breakfast. His otherwise tousled hair was held back with a simple tie. It was a bit problematic, how lurid it looked.

Gaoshun was in the room along with Maomao, as was a lady-in-waiting in the first flush of old age. They were the only ones allowed here, and Maomao could understand why. A woman might be driven mad with lust by what Maomao was currently seeing, and even a man might forget the boundaries of gender. This esteemed personage, she concluded, could be downright sinful.

He's like a bug in heat. Some female insects produced exotic scents to attract mates. A single female could draw dozens or hundreds of males. Maomao herself had been known to take advantage of this characteristic to collect insects she needed as ingredients.

From that perspective, Jinshi's constitution might be considered extremely interesting. *If I could capture that subtle aroma and turn it into an incense, I bet it would sell.* Such was the mindset with which Maomao regarded her potential love-potion ingredient—ahem, that is to say, Jinshi. It was an unfortunate fact that when Maomao was focused on a particular thought, something not having to do with the situation at hand, her attention tended to wander from the present moment. It frequently prevented her from following conversations going on around her, a tendency that was compounded by her habit of nodding along whether or not she was actually listening.

"If you wish, I shall have a new room prepared for you."

Huh?

Jinshi, looking inordinately pleased with himself, was requesting more porridge from Suiren. She was one of just a few ladies-in-waiting ever to have served Jinshi. From her looks, Maomao guessed she was well past fifty. Suiren's face remained impassive as she doled out a new bowl of porridge, topping it with black vinegar.

Maomao hadn't exactly followed the conversation, but Jinshi seemed to be saying that he was willing to give her a nicer room—that much she understood. Then, though, her eyes met those of Gaoshun, who had his head in his hands again. Jinshi's ever-weary aide seemed to want to communicate something to Maomao, but she only cocked an eyebrow in response.

If he wants to tell me something, he has to say it, she thought. *I'm not a mind reader.* She refrained from saying this out loud, though, because she knew that she herself frequently failed to be articulate enough.

"Perhaps a stable near a well, then," she offered, and there it was: her true desire was out in the open.

"A stable," Jinshi repeated.

"Yes, sir. A stable."

To her, this represented the place she was least likely to be intruded upon as she cooked up her concoctions, but she couldn't help noticing that Gaoshun was shaking his head and forming an emphatic X with both hands. *So the guy has a playful side,* Maomao observed to herself.

"No stables," Jinshi said flatly.

Yeah, uh, I guess that makes sense, Maomao thought, but she said only, "Of course, sir."

A fter breakfast, Jinshi went out to work. He was frequently in his office during the morning, and cleaning his private residence often fell to Maomao.

"I am so very glad you came, my dear. I start to feel my age when I have to clean this whole place by myself," Suiren said, smiling openly. Before Maomao's arrival, she'd been responsible for the entire large building, but at fifty, a person's body started to get sore. "You're not the first new girl we've had here, I might add. But, well, you know. Things happen, and none of them have ever stayed. I think you're going to be fine on that point, Xiaomao." The cheerful lady-in-waiting seemed to have picked up Gaoshun's nickname for Maomao.

In addition to being quite a talker, Suiren's wealth of experience had made her a quick worker as well, and her hands never seemed to stop moving. She polished some silver eating vessels quick as a flash. Cleaning the bedroom came next. Maomao went to stop her—this was all obviously maid's work—but Suiren only said, "Well, but then we'd never have time for our afternoon tasks."

There you had it. It seemed Suiren had held herself solely responsible for the cleaning of the rooms ever since some blunders with those earlier maids and ladies-in-waiting.

Incidents of theft, maybe? Maomao thought. And probably not just of money, she surmised—she could easily imagine other targets of such activity.

According to Suiren, things didn't only disappear; sometimes she discovered they suddenly had *more* possessions than before. "Anyone would be upset to find underwear they didn't recognize in the dresser," she said. Made from human hair, at that! And with a name carefully embroidered on it. Maomao got goose bumps. This was not quite the explanation she had been expecting.

"That must have been very difficult, ma'am."

"I tell you, I was traumatized!"

As Maomao industriously polished another window frame, she reflected how life might be better if that eunuch were to wear a mask anytime he went out.

They finished cleaning Jinshi's private quarters and took a late meal. Next would be his office. This was, in principle, easier than cleaning his personal chambers because the room itself was less elaborate. But because they couldn't be seen wiping and polishing by anyone too important, it required a degree of discretion.

What shall I do today? Maomao wondered. When Jinshi had visitors at his office, Maomao had time to kill. At such moments, she often wandered the grounds of the outer court on the pretext of having some kind of business. *I've covered the western side pretty thoroughly by now.*

21

A map unfolded in Maomao's mind. She would have loved to check out the eastern side, but something held her back. That was where the military was based. They might not smile upon a serving girl sniffing around in the bushes near their camp. She could all too readily be mistaken for a spy and arrested. And then there was the fact that Gaoshun had specifically recommended she avoid the place.

Besides, she thought, *speaking of the military . . .* Involuntarily, every muscle of her face tensed into a scowl. It was a measure of exactly how strong a reason she had to stay away from the place, but at the same time, an area unexplored was an area that might yet hide new herbs.

Maomao was standing with her arms crossed, deep in thought, when she felt something hit the back of her head.

The hell? She turned, rubbing the back of her head and glaring, to find a tall, refined lady of the outer court. *I feel like I've seen her somewhere,* Maomao thought, and then she remembered the woman from the crowd that had accosted her a few days before. She was wearing only the most minimal makeup, but Maomao noticed that she had drawn on thick eyebrows. She had full, pouting lips, and yet she had only dabbed them with rouge. Her overall look was tidy, but oddly disappointing.

She could do so much better, Maomao thought. She had perfect bones and a beautiful face, but the makeup left her less remarkable than she was. If she would make the eyebrows thinner, use plenty of light rouge on her lips, and put up her hair in an ostentatious bun, then she could easily have been taken for one of the flowers of the rear palace. Then again, most people probably wouldn't have noticed the potential for such beauty in this woman. Maomao, who had spent her life

22

watching dirty street girls turn into captivating butterflies of the night, could see the possibilities.

"The likes of you aren't supposed to go any farther," the woman said, very blunt but sounding somehow tired. Maomao only wished she had started by talking instead of hitting.

Then the woman walked past, as if to communicate that as a certi-fied lady of the outer court, she had nothing more to say to a maid like Maomao. In her hands she carried a small, cloth-wrapped package, clutching it protectively.

Huh? Maomao sniffed the air. There was the aroma of sandalwood, accompanied by a distinct bitter odor. She cocked her head curiously, looking in the direction the woman had gone.

Maybe she serves one of the soldiers? she wondered. The woman had come from the direction of the military camp. And indeed, if she was spending time there, then modest makeup might be a wise move. The camp might not be as dangerous as the back streets of the pleasure district, but there were plenty of young (and not-so-young) men with their blood up there, and an attractive young woman would do well to avoid them.

What Maomao was really contemplating, though, was what that smell had been. Her reverie was broken by the ringing of a bell. *Guess I'll have to forget about it for today,* she thought. She did an about-face and headed back toward Jinshi's office, hoping the master of the place would be absent when she got there.

23

CHAPTER 2

The Pipe

The gorgeous noble—that is, Jinshi—was busier than Maomao had realized. As a eunuch, she'd assumed the rear palace represented his entire workload, but it seemed he had much business in the outer court as well.

At the moment, Jinshi was making a face at some paperwork. He'd indicated that he was going to be stuck in his office the entire day, so Maomao had no option but to work around him as she cleaned. She was collecting scrap paper in one corner of the room. The paper was of excellent quality but covered with awful suggestions, ideas that were in the trash because they were hardly worth looking at. No matter how worthless the suggested statutes scrawled on them, however, the paper they were written on couldn't be reused; it had to be burned.

Think of the tidy bit of pocket change it would bring if I could sell it, Maomao thought. (It wasn't a very nice thought.) Still, she reiterated to herself that this was her job. She knew she had to burn the stuff. There was a firepit for trash in one corner of the large palace complex surrounding Jinshi's office, over by the military training grounds and some storehouses.

Ah, the military . . . Maomao thought. Honestly, she wasn't eager to get anywhere near them, but she had no choice. She was just getting to her feet, resigned that this was her duty, when she felt something settle across her shoulders.

"It's chilly out. Please, wear this." Gaoshun, showing his thoughtful side, had placed a cotton jacket on her back. There was a dusting of snow on the ground, and the wind could be heard to rattle the desiccated branches of the trees. The warm room, heated by several braziers, made it easy to forget, but they were still hardly a month into the new year. It was the coldest season of all.

"Thank you very much," Maomao said. She really meant it. (It seemed such a waste to have made Gaoshun a eunuch!) That extra layer of insulation would make a lot of difference. As she ran her arms through the sleeves of unbleached cotton, she realized Jinshi was watching her intently. Practically glaring at her, in fact.

Did I do something wrong? Maomao tilted her head in curiosity, but then she realized it didn't seem to be her Jinshi was glaring at so much as it was Gaoshun. Gaoshun, noticing the gaze as well, flinched. "This is from Master Jinshi, I hasten to add. I'm only the messenger." For some reason, Gaoshun gesticulated broadly as he spoke. Suffice to say he didn't sound wholly convincing.

Is he being reprimanded for taking too much initiative? Maomao wondered, marveling that he should have to get permission for something so simple as giving a cotton jacket to a maid. It wasn't easy being Gaoshun either.

"Is that so?" was all Maomao said. She bowed in Jinshi's direction, then hefted the basket of paper scraps and made for the firepit.

I *wish you'd planted some here, too, Dad,* Maomao thought to herself with a sigh. The outer court was many times larger than the rear palace, yet boasted far fewer herbs that might make worthwhile ingredients. She'd succeeded in finding little more than dandelions and mugwort.

Then again, she'd discovered some red spider lilies as well. Maomao enjoyed eating red spider lily bulbs soaked in water. The only caveat was that the bulbs were poisonous, and if the poison wasn't successfully extracted first, it could produce the mother of all tummy aches. More than once the old madam had snapped at her not to eat things like that—but it was Maomao's nature, and that wasn't going to change.

Guess this is about the best I can hope for, she thought. The dearth of plant life in winter made it hard enough to find anything. Even with careful searching, she didn't expect to come up with much more than she had. Maomao started to consider planting some seeds on the sly.

As she walked back from the garbage pit, Maomao spotted someone she recognized. He was over by a row of plaster storehouses at some distance from Jinshi's office. He was a young military official with a strong, manly face that nonetheless showed an obvious decency, giving him something of the look of a big, friendly dog. Ah, yes: Lihaku. The color of his sash was different from before. Maomao discerned that he must have moved up in the world.

Lihaku was talking to what appeared to be some subordinates

standing beside him. *He's working hard,* Maomao thought. Every time he had a little break, it seemed, Lihaku could be found at the Verdigris House, chatting with the apprentices over tea. Of course, his real objective was Maomao's beloved sister Pairin, but to call her forth required almost as much silver as a commoner might make in half a year.

Oh, woe betide the man who had tasted the nectar of heaven. Now he sought even the barest, the most occluded glimpse of the countenance of that flower that grew on the high mountaintop.

Maybe Lihaku sensed Maomao's pitying gaze upon him, for he waved to her and came jogging over, bounding like the big dog he was. Instead of a tail, the kerchief holding his hair flapped behind him. "Hoh! How unusual to see you outside the rear palace. Accompanying your mistress on a day out?" He clearly didn't know that Maomao had been dismissed from service in her old workplace. She'd been back in the pleasure district only a very brief time, so she had never bumped into Lihaku there.

"No," she said. "I no longer serve in the rear palace, but in the personal quarters of one particular personage." It would be altogether too much trouble, Maomao thought, to tell the whole story of her dismissal and rehiring, thus she reduced it to this single sentence.

"Personal quarters? Whose? Somebody must have very strange tastes."

"Yes, strange indeed."

Lihaku didn't know how insolent he was being, but his reaction as such was an understandable one. Most people wouldn't specifically seek out a thoroughly freckled, spindly branch of a girl to be their personal attendant. In fact, Maomao hadn't necessarily intended to continue with her freckles, but Jinshi had ordered her to keep them

28

(though she didn't understand why), and if her master commanded, she had to obey.

I just don't know what he's after, that man. Maomao concluded that the thinking of nobles was simply beyond her.

"Say, I hear some important official just bought out a courtesan from your place."

"So it seems."

Guess I can't blame him for this one, Maomao thought. When the employment contract had been concluded and Maomao was to go with Jinshi, her overexcited sisters had prettied her up in every way they knew how, finding the most special clothes for her, doing her hair, and covering her in a mountain of makeup, until she looked like anything but an ordinary maid headed to an ordinary posting. She remembered her father, for some reason, watching her go as if watching a calf leave his barn.

To enter the palace looking like a tarted-up courtesan was bad enough, but Jinshi's presence attracted yet more attention, and Maomao found a very uncomfortable number of eyes on them. She'd changed as soon as she could, but no doubt quite a few people had seen her before then. Still, she was struck that Lihaku could be speaking *of* her *to* her and have no idea. But, she supposed, what more could you expect from a dumb mutt?

"If I may say so, you seem to be in the middle of something. Do you really have time to be talking to me?"

"Oh, ahem . . . Heh . . ."

One of Lihaku's subordinates was coming over to check on him. He looked happy at first to see a woman there; a man living on a salary as poor as his was apt to be suffering from a drought of the fairer sex.

But when he saw Maomao, his disappointment was palpable. She was used to this reaction, but it also showed some of what made the superior superior and the subordinate . . . not.

"There was a fire," Lihaku said, jerking his thumb in the direction of the storehouses. "Not a big one. They're not that unusual this time of year." Still, he had to investigate the cause, which was what he was currently doing.

Cause unknown, eh? Maomao thought. Now that she'd gotten a sniff of the story, she would have stuck her nose in even if someone had begged her not to. Maomao slipped between the two and headed toward the small building.

"Hey, better keep your distance!" Lihaku called.

"I understand," Maomao said, scrutinizing the building and everything around it. There was soot on one of the cracked plaster walls. It looked like they'd been lucky the fire hadn't spread to any of the other storehouses.

Hmm. If this was simply a small fire, then there were several unusual things about it. For one, why had Lihaku come to deal with it personally if it was so ordinary? Surely he could've ordered some lackey to do it. What was more, the building seemed substantially damaged. More like the effects of an explosion than a short-lived blaze. Maybe someone had even been injured. *They must suspect arson*, Maomao concluded. It would be one thing to burn down a random storehouse somewhere, but on the palace grounds themselves? That was something else.

Maomao's country was largely peaceful, but this wasn't to say no one had any grievances against the government. Barbarian tribes occasionally conducted raids, and droughts and famines did sometimes occur. Relations with other states were largely cordial, but there were no guarantees as to how long they would stay that way. And there must have been some inhabitants among the country's vassal states who were displeased with their status.

Most of all, the former emperor's practice of annual "hunts" for women had left the farming villages with a serious shortage of potential brides. It had been only five years since His Former Majesty had departed this world, and there must have been many who still remembered his rule all too well. As for more recent events, slavery had been abolished upon the accession of the current emperor, no doubt depriving more than a few merchants of their source of income.

"Hey, what do you think you're doing? I said stay back." Lihaku caught Maomao's shoulder, glowering.

"Oh, I was just curious about something . . ." Maomao peered into a broken window. Then she slipped neatly out of Lihaku's grip and scampered into the building. Scorched stores were everywhere. From the potatoes rolling around on the floor, she gathered that this warehouse had been used to store food. What a shame, she thought, that the potatoes had gone past the point of being well-cooked and were now hopelessly blackened.

Looking for anything else that might have fallen on the ground, Maomao discovered some kind of stick. The moment she touched it, though, it turned to ash, leaving only the carefully worked tip. *Is this ivory?* she wondered. *It looks like a smoking pipe.* She brushed off the decorative stummel and studied it.

"Listen, you can't just wander around in here," Lihaku said, finally (and understandably) starting to sound angry. But once Maomao was invested in a problem, she couldn't let it go. She crossed her arms, trying to put the pieces together in her head. An explosion, a warehouse full of food, and a pipe on the ground.

"Did you hear me?"

"I heard you."

Yes, she heard Lihaku; she just wasn't *listening* to him. Maomao was aware this was a bad habit of hers. She left the warehouse, heading toward the one directly opposite, where the goods that had been saved from the fire had been moved.

"Does this storehouse have the same sort of things in it as the one that burned?" Maomao asked the lower-ranking soldier.

"Yeah, I think so. Oldest stuff is farthest inside, apparently."

Maomao smacked a closely woven cloth sack, producing a cloud of white powder. Wheat flour, she presumed.

"Can I have this?" she asked, pointing to an unused wooden crate. It was well-built, with close fittings, probably intended for storing fruit or the like.

"Yeah, I guess. But what are you going to do with it?" Lihaku gave her a blank look.

"I'll explain later. Oh, and I'll take this too." Maomao grabbed a wooden board that looked suited to serve as a lid for the crate. Now she had everything she needed. "Have you got a hammer and saw anywhere? And nails, I'll need nails."

"What exactly are you planning to do?"

"Just a little experiment."

"Experiment?" Lihaku looked befuddled, but his curiosity got the better of him. He was apparently going to cooperate with her, though still somewhat grudgingly. His subordinate was looking at Maomao as if to say, *Who does this girl think she is?* But when he saw his superior was going along with her, he had no choice but to get what she asked for.

Supplies thus provided, Maomao began to diligently arrange her materials. With the saw she made a hole in the wooden board, then hammered it down on the empty crate.

"That's weird. It's like you've done this before." Lihaku, watching her, showed all the interest of a dog spotting a new toy.

"I grew up without much money, so I learned to make what I didn't have."

Her old man had likewise built a range of curious things. Her adoptive father, who had studied in the west in his youth, drew on those long-ago memories to create tools and gadgets no one had ever seen in this country.

"There, finished," Maomao said after a few moments. "All it needs is a bit of this." She took some of the flour from the stores and put it in the box. "You wouldn't happen to have a fire starter on hand, would you?"

One of Lihaku's subordinates volunteered to get one. While he was away, Maomao got a bucket of water from the well. Lihaku, still totally baffled as to what was going on, was sitting on the box, his chin in his hands.

"Thank you very much." Maomao nodded to the subordinate, who had returned with a length of smoldering rope.

The underling could grimace all he liked, but he was ultimately curious about what Maomao was going to do; he squatted at a distance and watched them. Maomao went and stood in front of the crate with her wick, but for some reason, Lihaku was standing right there beside her.

She leveled her gaze at him. "Master Lihaku. This is dangerous. Might I ask you to keep a safe distance?"

"Danger, hah! If a young lady like you can do it, surely a warrior like myself is at no real risk."

He was obviously set on acting as proud and manly as he could, so Maomao gave up the argument. Some people just had to learn through experience.

"Very well," she said. "But there *is* risk involved, so please take due caution. Be ready to run away immediately."

"Run away? From what?"

Maomao ignored Lihaku's incredulous look, tugging on the sleeve of the crouching underling and advising him to watch from behind the storehouse. When all was ready, Maomao pitched the burning rope into the crate. Then she covered her head and ran.

Lihaku only watched her in perplexity.

I told him! I told him . . .

A second later, fire burst from the crate, burning hungrily. "Ahh!" Lihaku dodged the pillar of flame by inches. Or most of him did, anyway; his hair managed to catch the edge of the conflagration. "Put it ouuut!" he cried, panicking. Maomao picked up the bucket of water she had prepared and doused him with it. The fire went out, leaving only some smoke and the smell of singed hair.

"I told you to run." Maomao looked at Lihaku as if to ask whether he understood the danger *now*. As Lihaku stood with snot dripping from his nose, his subordinate quickly tossed an animal pelt on him. The man seemed to want to make some sort of comment, but he couldn't bring himself to do it.

"Perhaps you would be so kind as to request the watchman of the

35

storehouse refrain from smoking tobacco on duty." Maomao's assessment of the cause of the fire was really speculation, but she felt safe treating it as fact.

"Right . . ." Lihaku replied, looking relieved. He was ghostly pale. However strong he might be, he would catch cold if he didn't warm up soon. He should have been hurrying back to his quarters to light a fire, but instead he was staring fixedly at Maomao. "But what in the world was that all about?" She could practically see the question mark above his head. His subordinates looked likewise flummoxed.

"Here's your culprit." Maomao took a handful of the wheat flour. A gust of wind came up and spirited the white powder away. "Wheat flour and buckwheat flour are both highly flammable. They can combust if there's enough in the air."

The flour had exploded: it was as simple as that. Anyone could understand it, once they knew what had happened. Lihaku simply hadn't been aware of the possibility.

There were few if any things in the world that were truly inexplicable. What a person deemed beyond explanation was only a reflection of the boundaries of their own knowledge.

"Pretty impressed you know about that," Lihaku said.

"Oh, I used to do it quite often."

"Used to do what?" Lihaku and his subordinate were looking at each other, confused once again. Fair enough: they'd never in their lives had to work in a cramped space full of flour. Maomao, meanwhile, had learned to be careful after she'd been blown backward out of the room she had been borrowing in the Verdigris House.

I thought the old lady would have my head that day. Just thinking about it was enough to give her the shivers. She'd thought she was going to wind up hung upside down from the highest floor of the brothel.

"Please take care you don't catch a cold, sir. But if you do, let me recommend the medicine of a man named Luomen in the pleasure district. It's quite effective."

Mustn't forget promotion. Lihaku might buy her father's medicine on one of his visits to Pairin. Maomao's old man was as terrible a salesman as he was brilliant an apothecary, so if she didn't do at least this much, he might not make enough to feed himself.

That took longer than I meant it to. Maomao picked up the basket of scrap paper and turned once more for the trash pit. It was just nearby; she would hustle the attendant and then get out of there. *Oops,* she thought, *looks like I unintentionally took a souvenir.*

She realized the item she'd picked up earlier was still at the collar of her robe. The pipe. This was the reason she'd said to warn the watchman about smoking. The stummel in her hand was a bit singed, but clearly of fine make, a rather finer piece than one would expect to be in the possession of a simple storehouse guard.

Might be important to him, she thought. A little polishing and a new shank, and it would be good as new. Word was that there had been injuries but no deaths in the explosion, meaning the pipe's owner was probably recuperating somewhere. He might not want it anymore—too many bad memories—but if nothing else, the stummel would sell for a decent price.

For the time being, Maomao tucked the soot-stained ivory piece into the top of her robe.

Going to have to work late tonight, she thought as she handed the waste to the trash-pit attendant.

CHAPTER 3

Teaching at the Rear Palace

"What in the world is going on in there?"

"No idea."

The question came from Gaoshun; the blunt answer, from Jinshi. They were standing before a lecture hall in the rear palace. Inside, the highest-ranking consorts were having some sort of lesson, supposedly in the interest of helping them fulfill their duties as concubines.

All around, eunuchs and lesser serving ladies who had been summarily driven out of the hall stood by, looking just as perplexed as Jinshi. A few even had their ears to the door; nothing makes a person more interested in something than being told it's a secret. But whatever could that secret be?

One special reason for the gripping curiosity was that the lecturer was a young, freckled maidservant. No one could say quite what she was doing there.

It had all started about ten days before . . .

Jinshi, still in his sleepwear, watched Maomao clean, just the prelude to another long day of hard work. "If you're looking for your breakfast, Lady Suiren is preparing it right now," she said. One person was more than enough to handle making the morning meal, so while Suiren did that, Maomao got a start on cleaning the room. Any wasted time meant she would never finish all the chores in this building before noon. The old lady-in-waiting certainly took full advantage of her new assistant.

I wonder if I did something to upset him, Maomao thought. If she had, it was probably that she'd quietly planted the seeds of some medicinal herbs in the garden—but she didn't think anyone knew about that yet. Her heart picked up speed all the same. Then Jinshi said: "As the new Pure Consort has arrived, the rear palace has requested education of the consorts."

The Pure Consort was one of the four highest-ranking ladies in the rear palace, and the title had been vacated at the tail end of the previous year.

"Is that so?" Maomao replied without interest as she continued to dust. She ran the rag along the floor as hard as if the timbers had killed her parents and she was taking revenge. It had been part of her daily routine since she'd been assigned to Jinshi's personal service. There were probably other jobs she could have been doing, but maid's work was all she'd known, and frankly, she couldn't think of what those other jobs might be. So instead she threw herself into cleaning as if her life depended on it. Jinshi occasionally gave her disapproving looks, but Maomao was of the opinion that if he didn't give her specific instructions, she was under no obligation to do anything in particular.

Now Jinshi crouched down so his gaze was on a level with Maomao's. He was holding some sort of scroll. "They want a teacher."

"Oh? They have someone in mind?"

"You."

Maomao reflexively glared at Jinshi. It was not ideal, perhaps, for a cleaning girl to give her direct employer a look as if she were regarding some dirt in a corner, but old habits die hard. It provoked an inscrutable expression from Jinshi.

"A fine joke, sir."

"Who's joking?" Jinshi showed her the scroll he was holding. Maomao's expression darkened as she read it, for what was written there was most inconvenient. Indeed, she would have liked to pretend the scroll didn't exist.

"You can't get out of this just by pretending not to look."

"Whatever do you mean?"

"I know you read it just now. I saw you."

"That was your imagination, I assure you."

Jinshi unrolled the scroll and pointed directly at the most inconvenient part of all. He pushed the missive toward Maomao. Most stubborn.

"Look here. A direct endorsement."

Maomao was silent. The words "Wise Consort, Lihua" hovered directly beside Jinshi's finger.

Now she's done it, Maomao thought. "Count me out" was all she said, and so, for the day, the matter was closed. But it couldn't last . . .

The next day, another scroll arrived with the same request. This time, the endorsement was provided by Consort Gyokuyou. With two of the great consorts having affixed their names to these letters, even Maomao couldn't ignore them anymore. She could easily picture the red-haired concubine laughing merrily to herself. This time the request further stipulated that an appropriate honorarium would be provided.

Maomao was resigned to it now, albeit with many a sigh and shudder, so she sent a letter home—a necessary first step in preparing for the job she had been asked to do. By "home," though, she meant not to Luomen, but to the courtesans who had been like parents to her.

Several days later the items she had requested arrived, along with an invoice from the madam. Maomao thought the old lady had seriously inflated the price, but nonetheless she discreetly added an extra zero to the number before passing the bill to Jinshi. He scrutinized it but seemed prepared to accept the cost, when Suiren appeared out of nowhere and said with a chuckle, "I think the ink of this number is just a slightly different shade from the rest." She plucked the invoice from Jinshi's hands and gave it back to Maomao.

Wily old lady, Maomao thought. So long as Suiren was there, it would be a tall order for anyone to make a mark of her sheltered young master. Maomao was left with no choice but to admit the original price. If they'd had a mind to, Jinshi and Suiren could have argued that

Maomao should cover the expense for herself, so she was just as happy when they complacently paid the sum.

When the goods from the courtesans were delivered, Maomao veritably shoved Gaoshun aside and took them herself. Jinshi was as interested as a nosy puppy, but Maomao steadfastly refused to break any of the seals, quickly requisitioning a cart and taking the items away.

"Shall I help you?" Gaoshun asked, but Maomao politely refused him, taking her acquisitions to her room. Jinshi demanded to see what she had received, but she opened her eyes as wide as she could and stared him down, and after a moment he quietly withdrew.

She could hardly show him her all-important teaching materials. Maomao had decided: if she was going to do this, she was going to do it right.

Finally, the day arrived. For the first time in a long while, Maomao set foot in the rear palace, in the inner court. She found the slight feminine fragrance that suffused the place to be oddly calming.

The lecture hall that had been prepared for her was in fact quite large, enough to seat several hundred people. It had been sleeping quarters for the maids under the previous emperor, when the population of the rear palace had ballooned and individual rooms couldn't be built rapidly enough to keep up. Now, though, it went largely unused. It was a complete waste to leave it standing empty, but it would have been an even greater waste to tear it down. Indeed, many such buildings dotted the rear palace.

I don't need all this space, Maomao thought. She wasn't teaching anything particularly important, so why was such a crowd gathering? Middle- and lower-ranked consorts and their entourages all but surrounded the lecture hall, while more than a few maids rubbernecked from a distance.

The subject of instruction on this occasion was of no small importance to the consorts and concubines. In some sense, it could even be said to bear on the future of the nation—but for Maomao, all it did was elicit a long sigh.

"All right, listen up," Jinshi said. "Only the high consorts are to receive instruction."

One might have expected disappointment among the lower-ranking consorts at this pronouncement, but quite to the contrary, many of them were seemingly satisfied at having gotten a glimpse of Jinshi. At least half had apparently come only to see or even hear him; they clung to pillars and railings all around. It looked awfully overdramatic to Maomao, but more than a few such ladies were doing it. She sometimes wondered if this eunuch wasn't in fact some fell spirit who bewitched those around him.

When the moment arrived, Maomao entered the lecture hall to find Jinshi trotting at her heels. She set her jaw and glared at him. "What?" he asked, but Maomao only pushed him back out of the room. His willowy figure belied how much work it took to shove him out the door.

"But why?" he said.

"Because what will transpire here is secret, confidential, and positively *not* for outsiders. I was asked to instruct our honored consorts, and last I checked, Master Jinshi, you were not one of them."

Then she shut and barred the door.

She let out a long breath, then took an appraising look around the lecture hall. Nine people were present: the four high consorts, with one attendant each, and Maomao.

There was an audible murmur from the other side of the door. Because she had ejected Jinshi, most likely. She had the distinct sense that someone, or several someones, were trying hard to listen.

Maomao pushed her little cart to the center of the hall, then slowly bowed her head. "My cordial greetings to you, honored ladies. I, Maomao, humbly present myself to you as your instructor."

Consort Gyokuyou, looking as lovely as ever, gave a friendly little wave. Her attendant, chief lady-in-waiting Hongniang, observed this dubiously.

Consort Lihua had finally gotten most of the meat back on her bones, and she was watching Maomao placidly. The same couldn't be said of the lady-in-waiting who attended her, whose face contorted when she saw Maomao. Maomao savored the moment.

As for Consort Lishu, she exuded the same slight air of nervousness as always. No doubt she was trying to take extra care with the three other high consorts around. The lady-in-waiting attending her didn't look any more comfortable than her mistress, but the way she was obviously set on protecting the consort brought a smile to Maomao's heart.

Finally, the last of the august ladies. A face Maomao hadn't seen before. The young woman who had replaced one of the former high consorts was about Maomao's age. She was Loulan, the new Pure Consort. She had her black hair tied up high on her head, and in place of a hair stick she used the feather of a bird from the southern reaches. Her dress suggested she might be a princess from the southern lands, but her physiognomy was more that of a northerner. Her lady-in-waiting looked the same way, and Maomao concluded that the style of dress must have been a personal preference.

Loulan was neither as alluring as Gyokuyou, nor as dazzling as Lihua. Unlike Lishu, she was of an appropriate age to share a bed with the emperor, but for the moment, it didn't appear she would threaten the delicate balance of the rear palace.

That costume, though: it made her by far the most conspicuous of the four high consorts. In particular, her makeup accented the corners of her eyes so emphatically that it was impossible to tell what they really looked like. Maomao could hardly picture how the consort must appear without cosmetics.

Not that it matters to me.

With her little introduction complete, Maomao pulled a stack of textbooks from among her supplies and began passing them out, one to each consort. Each had her own reaction as she took her copy: widening eyes, an amused chuckle, a furious flush of the cheeks, a furrowed brow. *About what I expected,* Maomao thought. Next she produced a collection of tools. About half of those present regarded them with confusion, while most of the others seemed to know what they were for. The handful in between didn't know exactly, but seemed to guess, and blushed.

"I wish to stress that what I'm about to teach you are trade secrets of the garden of women, and must not be divulged to outsiders," Maomao said, and then she instructed her pupils to open their textbooks to page three.

———◇———

A good two hours or so later, Maomao's lecture was finally finished. *Maybe I tried to tackle too much at once,* she thought; even Maomao was feeling a bit spent by it. She drifted over to the door of the lecture hall and undid the bar.

"That went on for a while." The gorgeous eunuch wandered in, looking quite at his leisure. He did seem ever so slightly annoyed, and for some reason, his left cheek and ear were red. Maomao was at least kind enough not to openly accuse him of eavesdropping.

Jinshi regarded the room he had entered with mute amazement.

"Is something the matter, sir?"

"You took the words right out of my mouth," he said, looking closely at Maomao.

"I'm afraid I don't know what you mean." She had only given the consorts of the rear palace instruction in the necessary knowledge, as she had been requested. As for the individual consorts, their responses to Maomao's lecture were as follows:

Gyokuyou was enthused. "Finally, some new tricks," she was saying. Hongniang attended her with her customary expression of fatigue. She might also have been occasionally casting glares in Maomao's direction, but the lecturer chose to ignore her.

Lihua's cheeks were slightly flushed, but her finger traced down the page as she reviewed the lesson. She seemed quite satisfied. The lady-in-waiting with her was red as a beet and looking firmly at the ground, trembling.

Lishu was in a corner of the room with her forehead pressed to the wall, mumbling, "I can't. I couldn't. It's impossible!" All the blood had drained from her face. Her attendant, only recently promoted to chief lady-in-waiting (Maomao believed she recognized the woman as Lishu's former food taster), patted her back consolingly.

As for Loulan, she was staring into space with a distant expression. Maomao couldn't guess what she might be thinking. Her attendant wasn't quite sure what to do with the textbook lying in front of them; with some embarrassment, she packed it in a carrying cloth.

I don't care what they do with it, Maomao thought as she packed up her things and accepted a cup of cool water. She let out a breath. She was tired, but the thought of the envelope full of money she would receive took the edge off her fatigue.

Each of the consorts was allowed to keep the instructional materials she'd received. Some clutched their books lovingly, while others touched them only with evident trepidation. In any event, Maomao urged them to wrap the items in traveling cloths so that they might not be seen, and further, reiterated that they should not be shown to anybody. Jinshi and the others who had been excluded from the lecture watched, mystified.

"What exactly did you teach them?" Jinshi inquired.

Maomao didn't quite look at him, but rather, somewhere just past him. "Next time you see the emperor, ask what he thought of my lesson," she said.

As to the content of her instruction, she would leave that to Jinshi's imagination.

CHAPTER 4

Raw Fish

"Xiaomao, may I have a moment?" Gaoshun asked as Maomao was about to head back to her room after finishing the day's work. Their shared master, Jinshi, evidently tired from his own exertions, had gone to take a bath directly after eating.

"What seems to be the matter?" Maomao asked, at which Gaoshun hesitated for a moment—stroking his chin to cover for himself—and finally let out a long breath. "There's something I'd like you to look at." Jinshi's aide seemed to have even more furrows in his brow than usual today.

What Gaoshun showed Maomao was something written on a bound collection of wood strips, which he unrolled on a table. Maomao looked closely at them. "A record of an old incident," she observed. The strips recounted the case of a merchant who had contracted food poisoning some ten years before. The victim had allegedly consumed blowfish.

Maomao swallowed in spite of herself. *Argh, I wish I could have some blowfish.*

Gaoshun was looking at her, noticeably vexed. Maomao shook her head and wiped the grin off her face.

"Next time we have a chance, I'll take you to eat something of the sort," Gaoshun said, though he added pointedly that blowfish liver would not be served.

Maomao was a bit put out by that (*Real gourmands know how to enjoy that unique tingle!*), but nonetheless, there was nothing like the prospect of a good meal to get her invested in a project. She started studying the materials closely. "Why are we looking at this, if I may ask?"

"Long ago, my work happened to involve me in the matter of this case. A former colleague of mine brought it up to me again, because a very similar incident occurred recently."

Was this former colleague, Maomao wondered, someone from before Gaoshun had become a eunuch? So he really had been a military official or some such.

"Very similar?" Maomao said. "How so?" She mentally set aside the question of her companion's history. She was, quite frankly, more interested in this case of poisoning than she was in talk of Gaoshun's past.

"A bureaucrat ate a dish of shredded raw blowfish and vegetables, and now he's comatose."

Comatose? Maomao didn't like the sound of that. Gaoshun had never been the type to mince words, and she doubted he had started just now. She took a discreet glance at Gaoshun's face. He had the same wrinkle in his brow, the same somewhat wrung-out expression as usual—but he also seemed to be studying Maomao in much the way she was studying him.

"My apologies, Master Gaoshun, but might I ask for further details?" Despite her directness, Gaoshun didn't flinch, but only nodded slowly, his hands still resting in his sleeves.

"Yes, of course. I'm quite happy to tell you, Xiaomao. I'm confident you know where you stand." She wasn't sure that was a compliment. The meaning was clear enough: *Keep your mouth shut.* "Besides," he went on, "could I really leave the story off there?"

What a tease. He knew perfectly well that Maomao's curiosity would be fired by now. "Please, by all means, continue," Maomao said, frowning at how amused Gaoshun seemed by his own sudden importance to her.

Gaoshun pointed at the strips of wood and said, "In the current case, the dish included blowfish skin and meat, almost raw, just given a quick scalding. The victim consumed the dish and fell into a coma."

"Meat? You mean, not the internal organs?"

"That's right."

Blowfish poison couldn't be removed by heating it, but the poison was concentrated in the fish's organs, principally the liver, and the flesh proper was substantially less dangerous. Maomao would have guessed that any case of coma on account of blowfish poison would almost have to have involved consumption of the liver. *Could that much toxin really have built up in the flesh?* she wondered. Depending on the exact variety of fish and the environment in which it was raised, the meat could, on occasion, be poisonous. She didn't have enough evidence to be certain one way or the other, so she couldn't rule out the possibility.

When Maomao had eaten blowfish, it had always been the less poisonous meat. Well, almost always—every once in a while she got it into her head to put a bit of liver in her mouth, but it was a dangerous game. She well remembered the madam forcing her to drink water until her stomach practically turned inside out.

"To be honest, I'm not hearing anything unusual so far," Maomao said.

"Well, there's one detail I haven't mentioned," Gaoshun said, shaking his head slowly and scratching the back of his neck as if embarrassed. "The chefs involved in preparing the dishes insist they didn't use blowfish. Not on this occasion, and not in the incident ten years ago."

Gaoshun was frowning openly now, but Maomao simply ran her tongue along her lips. This was getting more interesting by the minute.

There were several points of similarity between the two cases. For one thing, both the bureaucrat of the present case and the merchant of the older one had been epicures with a taste for unusual food. On these occasions, they'd been consuming dishes of shredded raw fish and vegetables in which the meat had been gently scalded by dipping it briefly into boiling water, but they had each been accustomed to eating fish completely raw as well. The fresh taste of raw fish could be wonderful, but the uncooked meat all too often hosted parasites. Most people didn't much like it, and in some areas eating raw fish was outright forbidden.

Adventurous eaters like the victims in question would have been accustomed to consuming blowfish. And although they would all deny it publicly, some such people on occasion deliberately had a little bit of toxin left in their fish, in order to enjoy the tingling sensation it produced.

And people would judge them for it! So uncultured! Maomao thought. She was of the opinion that people ought to be more or less tolerant of the preferences of others, at least when it came to food.

Neither of the chefs who had prepared the tainted food would admit to any wrongdoing; both were adamant that they hadn't used blowfish in the preparation of their dishes. And yet, the men who had eaten said dishes had nonetheless succumbed to food poisoning. Blowfish innards and skin had been discovered in the kitchen waste and submitted as evidence, but the fact that the internal organs were complete and accounted for was understood to show that no part of them had in fact been consumed.

They actually took this investigation really seriously, Maomao thought, finding herself oddly impressed. She knew there were far too many officials in the world who were happy to settle for pinning the crime on someone via circumstantial or, if necessary, doctored evidence.

Both chefs asserted that they had used blowfish in their cooking the day before the respective incidents, but not the day of. With the season as cold as it was now, it wasn't surprising that the trash might not be taken out for several days at a time—unlike, say, in summer, when it might have been disposed of more regularly. The dish in question had been prepared with a different fish, the remains of which were also discovered in the trash.

So this obviously isn't a setup by some official, Maomao mused, *but that doesn't necessarily mean the cooks are telling the truth.* Unfortunately, there were no eyewitnesses to the meals in question. Afraid of angering his wife with his outré culinary choices, the administrator frequently took his meals alone. The cook had brought in the dish, but the official's servant only saw him eat at a distance and couldn't identify exactly what fish had been used in the meal.

Moreover, the victim had succumbed only after he was well finished eating—the best part of half an hour after the meal was over. A servant bringing tea discovered the man twitching and barely breathing, his lips blue.

The symptoms are certainly in line with blowfish poisoning, Maomao thought. The information Gaoshun had given her, though, simply wasn't enough. She decided to give up trying to think the problem through for a while, until she could get more details from the eunuch. She was just mumbling to herself, "What in the world could have happened?" when an irreproachably handsome visage appeared beside her. Maomao felt the muscles of her face tighten reflexively.

"If you'll excuse me, perhaps you could not pull faces at yours truly? It wounds me." Jinshi's hair was still wet. Suiren was trying to wipe it with a towel, exclaiming, "Oh, goodness," as it dripped everywhere.

Maomao forced herself to resume a normal expression. It seemed she had been all but vibrating with distress.

"You were certainly hanging on every word Gaoshun said," Jinshi remarked. He didn't sound amused.

"I was only as engaged as anyone when a speaker has something interesting to say."

Jinshi looked scandalized. "Now, just a moment. When *I* talk, you never . . ." He couldn't even bring himself to finish the sentence, but for the moment, Maomao didn't care.

"It's gotten late," she said. "If you won't be needing me, sir, I'll be going back." She nodded politely to Suiren, still mopping at Jinshi's hair, then she pattered out of the room. Jinshi seemed to be trying to say something else, but Suiren snapped, "Don't move," and Maomao heard nothing more from him. She was somewhat exasperated with herself, acting so helplessly fascinated by the matter of a person's death. She wondered what her father would think of her as she headed back to her room.

The next day, Gaoshun brought her a cookbook. "These are copies of recipes the chef commonly prepared. The servants testified that most of the meals served to their master came from this collection. This is the recipe the chef claims to have been following." He set the notebook on the table and opened it to a page with instructions for raw fish lightly scalded and then shredded. Maomao looked at it, stroking her chin.

The recipe called for the fish to be accompanied with minced vegetables and lightly vinegared. A few scrawled notes indicated modifications to the vinegar, but overall there was nothing unusual. Several different vinegar dressings were listed, presumably to account for the season and available ingredients. Exactly which fish and vegetables were to be used weren't specified in detail.

Hmm. Maomao continued stroking her chin. "This doesn't answer the crucial question of what was actually used," she said.

"I'm afraid that's true."

Jinshi was watching Maomao with curiosity from a short distance away, although he didn't appear to be enjoying himself. He had longan fruit with him that he cracked open and ate listlessly. The dark, dry seeds emerged with each *crack*. Longan were like lychee, but smaller, and were normally a summer fruit. When dried, the fruit was much valued in traditional medicine.

"You haven't figured it out yet?" Jinshi said, settling his elbows restlessly on the table and looking across at Maomao. He clearly wanted to be part of the discussion. Gaoshun frowned but didn't go so far as to reprimand him. *Somebody ought to give him a piece of their mind*, Maomao thought, coolly regarding Jinshi as he leaned uncouthly on the table. At that moment, somebody plucked the longan from Jinshi's hand.

"Boys who can't comport themselves like gentlemen will go without snacks," Suiren said, chuckling openly from her place just behind Jinshi. Despite her laughter, Maomao felt the charge in the air. She couldn't shake the sense that she could see storm clouds rising up behind Suiren. Would it be strange to describe the lady-in-waiting as having the aura of a seasoned warrior?

"Yes, yes." Jinshi's eyebrows drooped, but he took his elbows off the table and resumed proper posture.

"Very good." Suiren nodded, placing the fruit back in his hand. Here Maomao had assumed Suiren was just a doting old lady, but apparently she could be a stickler for propriety.

But they were getting off track. It was time to bring things back to the subject at hand.

"This incident occurred just recently, didn't it?" Maomao said.

"About a week ago," Gaoshun replied. During the cold season. This dish typically used cucumber, but this time of year, they would have had to find something else.

"May I guess that it was prepared with daikon and carrots?" There were only so many vegetables that would be available in winter. To each ingredient there was a season, a window in which it could be best enjoyed.

"Ahem . . . The chef said he used seaweed," Gaoshun said.

"Huh!" said Maomao, her mouth opening in an expression of surprise. "Did you say seaweed?"

"Yes, seaweed," Gaoshun replied. Seaweed was a common ingredient in traditional medicine as well. And yes, it would make some sense appearing in this particular dish.

But a gourmand like that wouldn't want just any seaweed. He would want something different. Special. Maomao felt the corners of her mouth turn up. She suspected her front teeth were showing. Jinshi and the others looked at her with their own mouths agape.

Maomao, still grinning, turned to Gaoshun. "Perhaps I could inspect the kitchen of the house in question. If that's possible?" She wasn't sure he would go along with the idea, but it couldn't hurt to try.

G aoshun acted swiftly, and the very next day, Maomao had everything she needed to get into the kitchen where the trouble had started. She was given to understand that obtaining permission had been a simple matter, as the official inquest was already complete.

The estate was situated in the northwest of the capital. The north-

ern quadrant of the city was occupied primarily by high-ranking officials, and the area was packed with gorgeous houses. When they
arrived at the particular mansion they wanted, the victim's wife (allegedly wasting away with the stress) was asleep, so a manservant showed
them through the house. The wife had already given her approval,
they were told.

A *manservant*, Maomao mused as they entered the kitchen. Gaoshun had arranged another official to accompany Maomao, but he
spent most of his time looking at her doubtfully. He clearly didn't rel-
ish this assignment, but Gaoshun had told him to do it, and evidently
he would obey, so there was no problem as far as it went. Maomao
wasn't there to make friends with him, so it was all the same to her.

The man was with the military, but young. His body lacked the
bulk of a long-serving soldier, but his movements were brusque and
efficient. Under his furrowed brow was a face that was manly despite
its remaining traces of youth. He looked oddly familiar, Maomao
thought. She was just about to trot into the kitchen when a man came
running up to her in high dudgeon.

"What do you think you're doing? You can't just wander around
this house! Get out of here! Who let this riffraff in?!" He caught the
manservant by the collar.

Maomao was fixing him with a glare when the young man accompanying her stepped forward. "The mistress of the household gave us
her blessing. And this is official business." Maomao applauded the
calm but firm tone he took with the overheated newcomer.

"Is this true?" The man relaxed his grip on the servant's neck.
Through a coughing fit, the manservant managed to confirm that
it was.

58

"Now, may we proceed? Or is there some reason we shouldn't?" the young official asked, at which the man made a sound of disgust and spat, "Pfah! What do I care?"

The manservant later explained to them apologetically that the younger brother of the comatose official was overseeing his estate in lieu of the man's indisposed wife. He was the one who had accosted them.

So that's what's going on, Maomao thought, but recognizing that it would be improper to insert herself into someone else's family affairs, she left it at that. Instead, she looked around the kitchen. As she'd feared, the chef had already washed and cleaned his tools. However, aside from the fish, which had been disposed of lest it start to rot, the majority of the ingredients still remained.

She began to explore the room, and there, on a shelf near the back wall, she found it, sitting right out in the open. Maomao's discovery, salted and stored in a small pot, brought a grin to her face. "What is this?" she asked the servant. He squinted into the pot, his face suggesting he wasn't sure. So Maomao took a bit of it and dropped it into a jug of water. "Do you recognize it now?"

"Oh! This is that thing the master liked." The servant informed them that the master had eaten it all the time—it couldn't possibly be poisoned. The servant's mistress evidently trusted him, and he didn't appear to be lying.

"You heard the man. Hurry up and go home," the younger brother snapped. He'd been watching Maomao at work for some time now. In particular, he seemed to be fixated on the jar she was investigating.

"Yes, of course," Maomao said, putting the jar back where she'd found it—and grabbing a handful of the contents as she did so, secreting it in her sleeve. "Our apologies for disturbing you."

She left the kitchen, but she could feel the man's eyes boring into her from behind.

W hy did you just run away like that? You hardly even objected," the young military man said to Maomao as they rode home in their carriage. She was surprised he was willing to initiate the conversation.

"Oh, I hardly think I ran away." Maomao produced the bit of salted seaweed from her sleeve and placed it delicately in a handkerchief. It had left her sleeve disgustingly salty, but the young man would probably get upset if she tried to shake it out right there. "This is strange," she said instead. "It's a little too early in the year to harvest this particular kind of seaweed. But I don't think a salt-cured piece from last year would have lasted this long." No, this ingredient was well outside its season.

"That leads me to think it wasn't harvested around here," Maomao went on. "That maybe it was obtained from the south somewhere, through trade, for example. You wouldn't happen to know where such a thing might come from, would you?"

The young man's eyes widened. He seemed to understand what she was asking of him.

That just left Maomao's own task to attend to.

———◇———

The next day, at her request, Gaoshun arranged a kitchen for her to use. It was in one of the bureaucratic offices of the outer court, and included accommodations for someone to stay overnight. Maomao had prepared everything the night before. Now, she started to cook. Well, *cook* might be a strong word. She was only steeping the seaweed in some water to get the salt off. It was a simple enough process, but things being what they were, she'd figured it would be better not to use the kitchen in Jinshi's building, hence why she'd asked for a different one.

Two plates sat in front of her, bearing her preparation. She'd divided her pilfered seaweed into two portions and soaked them in water. By now they were a rich, deep green.

Also before her were Gaoshun and the official who had consulted him about this case, along with the young soldier from the day before, and, for some reason, Jinshi. Maomao thought Suiren was likely to rake him over the coals again for being a rubberneck.

"I discovered you were right," the soldier said. The seaweed had been imported from the south. "I tried asking the manservant we met about it. He says that indeed, that seaweed was never eaten in winter. I inquired with the other servants as well, but the answers were all about the same."

The stranger in the room, the man who had consulted Gaoshun about the incident, shook his head. "I already spoke to the cook about it. He says it's the same kind of seaweed he always uses. He swears it can't be poisonous."

In fact, Maomao agreed: it was the same kind of seaweed. But there was a difference. "One of them may yet be poisonous," she said. With a pair of chopsticks, she picked up one of the pieces of seaweed from its plate. "Tell me, do people in the south normally eat this kind of seaweed? Or could it be that a gourmand official imported dried samples from the plant's native land, thinking there might be money to be made?"

"And what would be the problem if he had?" Jinshi asked. Today he had none of the loose, almost informal quality he'd sometimes demonstrated recently. Perhaps it was because there were other people present. Gaoshun looked as serene as ever, but the other two officials seemed somewhat uncomfortable in the presence of the radiant eunuch.

Maomao twiddled the chopsticks playfully as she replied, "There are ways to make a poison not poisonous."

Several, in fact. Eels, for instance, were normally poisonous, but if one drained the blood and heated them enough, they became edible. To take another example, this particular kind of seaweed, Maomao recalled, had to be cured with quicklime. One of the two pieces before them was treated with quicklime; the other was not. At the moment, Maomao was holding in her chopsticks the piece she had been steeping in a quicklime solution overnight. She took a big bite of it, distressing the onlookers. They crowded around and fussed over her.

"I'll be fine . . . I think," Maomao said. In truth, she only knew the theory. She wasn't actually sure if a single night's steeping would be enough to neutralize the poison. This was another important test for her.

"You *think*?" Jinshi demanded.

"Oh, calm down. I have an emetic right here." She showed them the pouch of herbal medicine hanging around her neck.

"Aren't we a little overconfident?!" Jinshi snapped. A moment later, Gaoshun had Maomao in a bear hug from behind while his master forced the medicine down her throat. Thus she ended her demonstration by vomiting in front of four important men. Lovely. What a thing to do to a young woman who had yet even to be married.

Worse, the emetic induced vomiting through its awful flavor, so it was a poor chaser for the seaweed.

And here I was trying to prove that seaweed was safe, Maomao thought. She wiped away the stomach juices, composed herself, and then said, "Here's the question as I see it: who suggested the idea to the tradesman to import this salted seaweed?" The merchant had gone to a foreign land, one where there was no custom of consuming this plant, simply in order to obtain it. Presumably he was at least aware of the potential danger. "The man who fell into a coma from it could be said to have reaped what he sowed."

But what if something else was going on? What if the possibility of poison had been well accounted for?

Here I go, speculating again.

There had been a similar case ten years before. What if it had given someone a hint—inspiration? Maomao had no way of saying whether the two were really connected. But as far as the current case, she trusted her intuition. Everyone here in this room with her was intelligent. She doubted she needed to say anything more, and she didn't intend to. Maomao was a person of such minor consequence. She had no desire to ponder anyone's particular guilt.

"I see." Gaoshun nodded slowly, evidently comprehending what Maomao was driving at.

She let out a relieved breath, then grabbed the seaweed in front of her and ate it—this time, from the other plate.

And thus, for the second time that day, Maomao was induced to retch by a pale-faced Jinshi and his companions.

The culprit turned out to be the younger brother of the comatose bureaucrat. Once they found out where he'd purchased the sea-weed, he could hardly confess fast enough. So Maomao had been right to be suspicious of the way he'd been watching her in the kitchen. He might as well have told them outright there was something he didn't want them to see in there.

His story was a common one: with the elder son alive and well, the younger went forgotten. Maomao and the others were almost disappointed to discover such a comically prosaic motive at work.

However, a problem remained. Apparently the man had been willing to commit murder over this simple grievance, but how had he learned about the poisonous seaweed in the first place? He claimed a fellow patron at his favorite bar had happened to mention it in the course of a conversation. And neither Maomao nor anyone knew at the time whether this was simple chance, or if it went deeper.

Maomao was cleaning up, muttering over the fact that she never did get to eat the toxic seaweed. But it was no use crying over spilled milk—or regurgitated seaweed—so she determined to think about something else.

Ahh, I wonder what I'll use my precious new ingredient for. The bizarre herb sprouting from a bug danced in her head. Just as it threatened to take over her every thought, she shook her head. She had to stay focused. She was on the job. But she couldn't keep herself from grinning at the thought of that disgusting dried insect with the grayish mushroom popping out of it. She was overjoyed just thinking about the possibilities: maybe she would make a medicinal wine out of it or turn it into pills.

The overweening happiness caused her, to her chagrin, to greet the master of the room with a giant smile on her face. The moment she registered Jinshi—and the shocked look he was giving her—Maomao dropped her eyes to the ground.

I'll bet that *wasn't very appealing.* Slowly, uncomfortably, she looked up, to discover Jinshi was suddenly beating his head against a pillar. It made a clacking sound like a woodpecker. The noise brought Gaoshun and Suiren running.

Gaoshun seemed to be fixing Maomao with a glare. *It wasn't my fault!* Maomao protested wordlessly. *Your master is wrong in the head.* Silently she was pouting, but all she actually said to them was, "Welcome back." She could at least act polite.

Jinshi had been spending especially long days at work of late. He claimed it was because there were so many things that needed taking care of. In which case, perhaps he should have been working the other day rather than standing around gawping at Maomao's experiment.

Jinshi's assessment of the person he'd recently had to entertain to get his work done was less than flattering: "You could say we don't get along. Or at the very least, that there's a stark difference of opinion." Now he sighed as he accepted some fruit wine from Suiren. Everyone in the room had a well-developed tolerance for Jinshi, so it didn't affect them, but if some girl had happened to see him like this, she might have fainted on the spot. A most troublesome eunuch indeed.

So there was someone out there who could successfully *have* a different opinion from Jinshi. That was impressive in its own right.

"There are some people even I can't deal with easily," Jinshi said.

The person in question was evidently a high-ranking military official, a man of sharp intellect but unorthodox character. He would nitpick, bring visitors to people's offices, barge in, challenge them to a game of shogi, distract them with simple banter, and otherwise prevent paperwork from getting stamped for as long as possible.

And on this occasion, Jinshi was his target. Jinshi had found himself obliged to entertain the man for a good two hours each day, which meant he had to make up the time later.

Maomao's face contorted. "What old hermit would waste his time like that?"

"Old hermit? He's only just past forty. The worst part is, *he* gets *his* work done before he comes to bother me."

A forty-something, eccentric, highly ranked military officer? These particular characteristics rang a bell with Maomao, but she had the distinct feeling that recalling exactly why would bring nothing good, so she decided to forget about it instead. Unfortunately, forgetting wasn't likely to make her bad feeling any less accurate.

"I believe the matter you were concerned with has already been approved," Jinshi said, bringing his nymphlike smile to bear on his uninvited guest. It took a genuine effort not to scowl.

"Hell, sure it has, but flower viewing is just so *hard* in the winter. Thought this would be the next best thing."

Jinshi was confronted by a middle-aged man with an unshaven face and a monocle. A loiterer if ever there was one. He wore a military uniform, but his build was more that of a civil official, and his squinted, fox-like eyes carried equal parts intelligence and madness.

The man's name was Lakan, and he was a military commander. In some other era, he might have been considered a sleeping dragon, a great military mind waiting to be discovered, but in this day and age he was just another oddball. He came from a good family background, but he was still unmarried at more than forty years old. He had adopted a nephew of his to oversee his household.

Lakan was interested in three things: go, shogi, and gossip. He would engage anybody in one of these, even if they weren't interested. As for why he had made himself such a nuisance to Jinshi recently, it was because Jinshi had taken on as a maid a young woman with a connection to the Verdigris House.

The situation was simply what it was, yet it couldn't look good to society at large to take a girl from a brothel. Yes, she was nominally just his maid, but what were people supposed to think? This rumor-loving official had run with the story of Jinshi's youthful new acquaintance, until the military was thoroughly convinced that the eunuch had purchased her out of prostitution. And it was hard to say they were wrong, exactly.

Jinshi let the old fart's jabbering (where did he get all these stories?) go in one ear and out the other as he stamped away at the papers Gaoshun had brought him.

Until the moment Lakan said something rather unexpected. "I used to have a friend at the Verdigris House myself, you know. Someone I was very close to." Jinshi had never known him to show any interest in things carnal.

"A courtesan? What was she like?" he asked, his interest aroused (much to his annoyance).

Lakan grinned and poured a bit of the fruit juice he'd brought with him into a glass. Reclining on a couch, he could have been relaxing in his very own room. "Oh, she was a fine lady. Excellent go and shogi player. In shogi I could hold my own against her, but in go, oh, I was always losing."

To defeat a military commander at a game of strategy was no mean feat, Jinshi reflected.

"I thought about buying out her contract. Figured I would never meet a woman so interesting again. But life doesn't always give you what you want, boyo. A couple of interested parties showed up, both very rich, and started a bidding war. Drove up the price."

"Goodness."

Sometimes buying out a courtesan's contract could cost as much as building a small palace. In other words, the bidding war had put the woman out of Lakan's reach.

But why was he telling Jinshi this?

"She was one odd duck, that lady. Sold her arts but never her body. Hell, she didn't seem to think of her customers as customers. When you had tea with her, she never would act like she was serving her master or anyone important. No, no. Instead she'd look at you, imperious, like royalty granting an audience to the basest peasant. Now, there are those that like that kind of treatment, and they went mad for her. I mean, listen to me—takes one to know 'em, eh? Ah, the very thought sends a shiver down my spine!"

Jinshi, growing more and more uncomfortable with the conversation, tried to look away from Lakan. Gaoshun was stationed quietly in the background. His mouth was pulled into a single, straight line, and he was biting his lip hard.

There were a great many people in this world who shared Lakan's predilections.

Jinshi wasn't sure if Lakan realized the effect he was having. In any event, the arch-eccentric went on: "Ah, what I wouldn't have given to take her to bed!" His leering grin betrayed no small hint of madness. "I admit, in the end I just couldn't let her go. I resorted to a bit of an underhanded scheme. Suffice it to say that if she was too expensive for me to afford, all I had to do was make her cheaper, mm?" Shave off the premium, as it were.

Behind his monocle, Lakan's fox-like eye was sparkling. "Aren't you curious what I did?"

Jinshi found himself inexorably drawn into Lakan's story. This was what made the man so fearsome. "We've come this far. I suppose it would be a waste not to at least hear the end of your tale." Jinshi suddenly realized his tone had become chilly. Lakan smirked at him.

"Don't be in such a hurry, boyo. I have a little favor to ask first." He laced his fingers together and stretched mightily.

"And what might that be?"

"The serving girl you got in recently—I hear she's quite an interesting specimen."

Jinshi was on the cusp of letting out a sigh of exasperation: *This again?* But what Lakan said next caught him by surprise.

"They say she has a knack for solving mysteries." Lakan didn't miss the flinch this provoked from Jinshi. "I have a friend," he went on. "A metalworker who used to produce pieces for the palace. But he kicked the bucket a bit back, see? He had three pupils, but funny enough, he didn't designate a successor."

"Oh?" Jinshi said politely, while thinking how unusual it was for Lakan to have a craftsperson among his acquaintances.

"It's a sad thing, a master craftsman who doesn't pass on his secrets before he passes on himself. I keep thinking he must have left some hint, something to make sure his art didn't die out, but I'm not finding it."

"What are you getting at?" Jinshi asked curtly. Lakan removed his monocle and said, "Oh, it's nothing. Nothing to speak of. Just wondered if there might be some way to find out what secrets that old man took with him to his grave. Such as by having a particularly clever young maid look into the matter."

Jinshi didn't say anything.

"Our dead friend was a funny guy. Left a will, *very* portentous stuff. Makes a man think there must be more to it."

Jinshi still didn't say anything. He closed his eyes and let out a breath. It was all he could do to muster: "I'm not making any promises. Tell me about the will."

CHAPTER 5

Lead

Around evening, Jinshi came to her with an extraordinary story. "I'm sorry to trouble you," he began, which was striking enough in itself. Normally, he didn't seem to care how much trouble he was causing Maomao at any given time. The preface, though, had the effect of piquing Maomao's interest.

At issue, it seemed, was a dispute having to do with an acquaintance of an acquaintance of Jinshi's. Something that was almost, though not quite, a family squabble. A craftsman had died without conveying his most important secrets to his disciples—who also happened to be his sons. Among those secrets was a technique never divulged to any outsiders.

"So all we have to do is figure out this metalworker's most secret art. Yes?" Maomao said.

"Gee, when you put it that way, it sounds so simple! I must say, though, you seem uncommonly eager."

"Do I?" Maomao asked, averting her eyes.

Here's what Jinshi had told her: The metalworker had three disciples, all of whom were his blood sons, and all of whom were respectable craftsmen in their own right. Their father had held a special commission from the palace, and with him gone, there was talk that one of his boys might succeed him. The father had left a will providing an inheritance for each of his children. His eldest son received a small workshop, the second eldest a piece of furniture his father had decorated, and the third, a goldfish bowl.

The will also contained one cryptic suggestion: *"Would that you boys would sit down and share tea together like you used to."*

"What a very intriguing final testament," Maomao commented. She had no idea whether it was intended literally, or if there was something else at work.

"It is. And evidently it's just as opaque to the young men as it is to us."

Maomao nodded thoughtfully. "I must say, the division of the inheritance doesn't seem very fair."

The family's main house was still occupied by the boys' mother, so it wasn't included in the will, but when one child got a workshop, another got furniture, and the third received a goldfish bowl, well, it was hard not to think the last child got a raw deal.

"Do you know anything about this goldfish bowl?"

"I'm afraid I don't. But if you're curious, you could pay them a visit. I have the address." What fine preparation on Jinshi's part. He must have assumed it would come to this.

"Then perhaps if I could be spared for a while tomorrow?" Maomao said with a discreet glance at Suiren. The old lady-in-waiting waved a hand as if to say *Have fun,* but Maomao suspected she would find her workload increased more than ever in the days to come.

The craftsmen's house was past the far end of the main thoroughfare that ran through the capital. Situated in an area full of shops, it was an impressive place, with a great chestnut tree standing in the yard.

Jinshi and Gaoshun were not with Maomao; instead, the same young man who had accompanied her when she was investigating the case of the poisonous fish was there. His name was Basen.

Doesn't seem like he thinks much of me, Maomao thought, observing how he only spoke the absolute minimum necessary to her. It came across less as reticence than as active disdain. But Maomao was perfectly happy with that, so long as it didn't interfere with her work. It wasn't their job to make friends with each other.

"I've spoken to the family, and they're willing to accommodate us," Basen said. "Outwardly, however, I'm the one who's here to ask the questions. You're my attendant."

"Very well." Better, even, Maomao thought. This was ideal. They arrived at the house, Maomao pattering obediently behind Basen, and when they knocked on the door a member of the family appeared, a grim-looking man of some twenty years old or so.

"I heard you were coming," the man said, ushering Maomao and Basen into the house politely despite his dark demeanor. Within, the home gave much the same impression as it did from outside, tidy and well-maintained. Small arrangements of flowers were placed here and there. In a recess in one wall was an unusual object: what appeared to be a chunk of rock ornamented with metal that seemed to shine with a faint bluish hue.

Maomao studied the object intently. "Oh, that thing," the sullen man said, coming over to her. "Father bought that when he was getting some materials. He always did have a soft spot for . . . strange things." For the first time, a hint of joy entered the man's face.

They left the main house and proceeded down a covered walkway. Near a building Maomao took to be a small workshop, they found two more men. One was tall, one was a bit round, and both looked as morose as the first.

"Here they are, dear elder brothers," their host said. From his respectful tone, Maomao guessed that their guide was the youngest brother. He at least had the decency to act polite. His two siblings looked downright hostile. When Maomao and Basen approached, they quickly concluded a muttered conversation and showed the visitors into the workshop.

The interior of the workshop was pleasant, tools all neatly in their places. The men told Maomao and Basen that the real workshop was in the main house. They hadn't used this place in quite some time. Now it was a repository of old tools where the craftsmen sometimes took tea.

"What an odd arrangement," Basen said, looking around the room. Maomao silently agreed. Smack in the middle of the space was a chest of drawers. It looked like it could only be in the way sitting there, but closer inspection revealed delicate decorations. The overall shape was not quite like anything Maomao had ever seen, either, making it seem rather at the forefront of furnishing fashion. It almost made the chest look good, sitting there in the middle of everything. Tables were set up around it, the whole arrangement surprisingly unified.

The corners of the chest were nicely rounded, with worked metal adornments on them. The topmost of the three rows of drawers had keyholes, as did the center drawer, each one accented with a different metal. The plump brother came over to Maomao, who was studying the chest intently, and said in a quiet voice, "You're welcome to look, but keep your hands off."

She dipped her head in acknowledgment and took a step back. She recalled that the dead craftsman's will had included a bequest of furniture to the second-oldest son. Was this the piece in question? Presumably that would make her interlocutor the second son himself.

Her supposition was soon bolstered: the youngest son came over holding something clear and round.

"Do you really think you can make heads or tails of these odds and ends our father left us?" the tall man, most likely the eldest son, asked Basen.

Basen took a peek at Maomao, who nodded and jerked her head in the direction of the three brothers. She couldn't be sure whether he took her meaning, but he looked at the young men and replied as calmly as anything, "I'm afraid I won't be able to say until I've heard a little more."

Then he sat down in a chair. Maomao stood behind him, taking the opportunity for a fresh look around the room. *The architecture really is strange*, she thought. For one thing, the window was in an unusual place. It was uncommonly tall (perhaps it was supposed to be in the western style?), which would allow more than ample sunlight into the room. There was just one problem: the giant chestnut tree outside blocked all the light. Only what could filter past its leaves made it into the room, except in one particular spot. She could tell as much by the faded color of the shelf hanging from the wall, although there was a square space still in the original color betraying that something must have sat there for a very long time, until just recently.

While Maomao scanned the room, the lanky elder brother entertained Basen. "We've already told you everything there is to know," he said. "Our father departed this world never having told us his deepest secret. And then he left me with this workshop."

"And me with these drawers," the second son said, slapping the chest demonstratively.

"And me, I only have this." The youngest son held out the clear, round thing. Now they could see that it was made of thin glass, with a flat bottom. Jinshi had said the youngest son had received a goldfish bowl, but Maomao hadn't pictured something made of glass. She'd imagined something primarily of wood, or at least ceramic. Now she could see that at least each of the sons had received something of some value. Yet even so there seemed an unmistakable disparity, a chilling distance, between the bequests of the first two sons and that of the third.

What's going on here? Maomao looked from one man to the next. Each had calluses on his hands bespeaking a craftsperson, but the hands of the youngest son particularly caught her attention. They had a succession of unusual red welts on them. Burns just starting to heal?

The second son heaved a sigh and ran his hand along the chest of drawers. "Don't know what the old man was thinking. He leaves me this whole chest, but there's only one key . . . and it doesn't fit any of the locks!"

Maomao followed the man's gaze to several metal fasteners on the bottom of the chest. Evidently it was secured to the floor. The key appeared to go to the centermost drawer, but the man insisted it wouldn't fit. The remaining three drawers all opened with the same key—one they evidently didn't have.

"Look at this," the second son said irritably, indicating the fastenings. "I can't take this thing anywhere. So what am I supposed to do with it stuck in my brother's workshop?"

The oldest brother nodded as if to say he felt the same way. Only the youngest sibling looked unsure. "But Father said to have tea like we used to, didn't he?"

The other two looked at him like they'd had this conversation before. "Easy for you to say. You're the lucky one. Your bequest is like money in your pocket."

"Yeah, just your luck. Pawn that thing off, and it'll keep you eating fancy for a good long time."

The two older brothers sounded like they were trying to chase off a mangy dog. Maomao considered things. She gave Basen a gentle tap to urge him to ask another question. He frowned but did what he was supposed to do. "If I may," he said, turning toward the brothers, "could you tell me again about your father's last message to you?"

"Just like the kid said," one of the older brothers replied.

"Yeah, have a tea party, just like we used to. Whatever the hell that's supposed to mean."

Maybe it was an exhortation for the three of them to get along. It would be very fatherly advice to leave behind. But Maomao had no way to be sure what he meant, nor did she think they were going to get anywhere simply contemplating the three bequests. She was just pondering what to do when the young men's mother appeared with a tray. She set cups of tea for each of them on the long table in the center of the room.

"Here you are," was all she said before leaving again. Three cups were lined up on one side of the long table, with two more across from them, leaving the space in front of the chest of drawers open. The two cups were presumably for Maomao and Basen. The brothers sat, but not wherever was closest; they each moved to a particular spot, suggesting they had occupied those seats for some long time.

Hmm, Maomao thought. Light streamed in through the tall window, stretching out toward the chest. The seat in front of it was vacant—considering the time of day, the sun would have been too bright for anyone to sit there for tea. Just a little farther, and the sunlight would brush the chest, but there was no sign of fading on the wood. Evidently the sun never reached that far.

Signs of fading? Maomao stood up from her seat and looked at the window. With the big tree outside, the light wouldn't actually fall into the room for very long. She stood in front of the window and peered at the chest of drawers. The position of the lock nagged at her. Not the keyholes on the three uppermost drawers, but the middle row, where only one drawer was locked.

She advanced toward the chest with curiosity, drawing perplexed looks from the siblings. Basen pressed a hand to his forehead and looked down. The gesture was distinctly familiar. Maomao realized with a start that he looked much like Gaoshun.

Basen sighed and looked at Maomao with undisguised displeasure. "You've found a clue?"

"That drawer with the keyhole won't open, is that right?"

"It used to, but Father fiddled around with it enough that now it won't," the second son responded.

"And there's only one key?"

"This is it. And our old man told us—I guess you know by now how he loved to say things that don't make sense—he said that if we break the lock, whatever's inside will break too. So we can't just go smashing it."

Maomao positioned herself in front of the chest and examined the keyhole. She had the impression that something was packed inside.

Maybe there's a reason the chest is stuck to the floor too, she thought, turning over what she knew in her mind. The bequests to the three brothers: the workshop, the chest, the bowl. The drawer that wouldn't open. And . . .

Maomao looked at the youngest brother's goldfish bowl. "Pardon my asking, but did that bowl used to sit on that shelf there?" she said.

"Er, y-yes, yes, it did." The younger brother walked over to the window, still holding his bowl. He folded a handkerchief and placed it on the faded spot, then set the bowl on top of it. "We used to keep a goldfish here. But the cold would kill it, so in the winter, we only put it here at noon, when it was warmest. We haven't had a goldfish in years, though. This bowl has been nothing but a decoration." He smiled, a bit sadly.

Hmmm. Maomao gave the arrangement a calculating look, then left the workshop.

"H-hey, where are you going?" Basen demanded.

"Just to get some water," Maomao said. She returned shortly thereafter and poured the water into the goldfish bowl. "I presume it once had water in it, like this."

"Yes, that's right. And the design on the side was always pointed toward us, like this."

Thought so, Maomao said to herself, looking again at the bowl. Light entered through the window and struck the goldfish bowl. From there, it was focused on a single point: the chest of drawers. Specifically, the center lock, which glittered in the beam of sunlight.

"May I further presume this is the exact time of day at which you customarily took tea?"

"H-hey! What's going on here?" the second-oldest brother said, stepping between the bowl and the chest.

"Stay back!" Maomao shouted, more vehemently than she'd meant to. It was effective, though: the big man suddenly seemed to become smaller.

"Pardon me," Maomao said. "If the beam gets in your eyes, you might go blind. And I need this space to be clear, so please, keep your distance. Otherwise the lock won't open." She watched them both closely, lock and light, and waited.

No one knew exactly how long it took; no one was counting. The light reflected from the goldfish bowl moved bit by bit, working its way around the lock. At length, the light disappeared, blocked by the chestnut tree, Maomao supposed. Now she inspected the lock critically. The metal was warm to the touch, and she detected a strange odor.

"What's the meaning of this?" someone asked, but Maomao replied only, "By any chance, did the deceased suffer from anemia and stomachaches?"

"Yes, he did . . ."

"And perhaps you observed vomiting and fits of lethargy?"

The way the three brothers looked at each other in response to this question convinced Maomao she was on the mark. Then she remembered the strange objet d'art, the crystal.

"I'm not very knowledgeable about metalwork, but was soldering done here as well?"

"Yes . . ."

"All right. Please open the drawer with the key."

"I told you, it doesn't fit," the second son grumbled, but he nonetheless slid the key into the lock. It fit as naturally as anything. The man, startled, turned the key and was rewarded with a clicking sound.

"Wh-what happened?" the eldest son said, while his brothers looked on in amazement. Even Basen appeared suitably impressed.

"Nothing special," Maomao said. "We simply followed your father's last request. You all had tea together, just as you used to." Then she removed the drawer from the chest and set it on the table where everyone could see it. It contained a key-shaped mold, which was giving off a dull glow. Strikingly, it contained metal that was still warm. Maomao tapped the metal with her finger, checking the hardness. "May I remove this?" she asked.

"Y-yeah, sure . . ."

With the brothers' consent, she took the key out of the mold, feeling the last of the radiant warmth against her hand. When she tried it in the chest, it fit neatly in the locks in all three drawers. She opened each of them in turn, provoking more perplexed looks and expressions of surprise.

"Wh-what's this stuff?"

The first two of the drawers, all of which varied in size, contained metal and something that looked like crystal. In the largest drawer was a bluish gem like the one that decorated the entryway of the house.

"I'm afraid I don't know. I've only done as we were told." Maomao shook her head and placed the three lumps on the table. There was nothing more for her to say.

"Dammit. Be friendly to each other, he says! Like hell! Father just couldn't resist pulling one last prank on us!" the elder son exclaimed.

"He must have been laughing all the way to his grave!" said the second.

The third man, though, the youngest, was silent as he looked at the three lumps. Then he studied the drawers from the chest. Maomao saw his hands again, with their half-healed burns. His older brothers had no marks on their fingers.

Apprentice see, apprentice do, perhaps? she wondered. She remembered the words: they'd been spoken by someone who had visited her father, someone who'd had the unmistakable air of a craftsman about him. She also remembered taking the advice to heart, trying to mix the herbs her father had brought by imitating what she thought she'd seen him do—and ultimately poisoning herself. In the future, her father insisted, she should ask him first.

Maomao suspected this youngest child was the only one who saw what the old craftsman had been after. Soldering involved mixing several different types of metal together so that they would melt at a lower temperature than normal. Maomao knew of one such possible combination: lead and tin. Why in the world did she know this? Because lead was poisonous, of course. She'd once seen a metalworker who had poisoned himself melting lead. Then there was the face-whitening powder that had been popular in the rear palace: her father had told her that it was lead-based.

What if two of the three lumps of metal were lead and tin, and by mixing them with the third lump, a new metal entirely could be created? The goldfish bowl had focused the light, true enough, but not for very long. The metal's melting point was evidently very low. And finally, perhaps most importantly, the old craftsman had made the drawers different sizes, it seemed quite deliberately.

Maomao was sure she didn't have to say anything further, but there was one thing she wanted to add. She walked over and addressed the youngest brother. "At an establishment called the Verdigris House in the pleasure district, there's an apothecary named Luomen. A healer of substantial accomplishment. If you ever feel unwell, please let me recommend that you visit him."

"Uh—y-yes, thank you," the young man said, surprised by the unsolicited advice. Maomao bowed her head slowly. The youngest brother politely said farewell while the other two continued to bicker. Maomao left them all behind.

She noticed the look on Basen's face; he seemed no more pleased now than ever. She realized perhaps she'd overstepped herself and took up walking behind him. Whatever happened after this had nothing to do with Maomao. Whether the clever third son chose to show generosity, or else to keep the hard-won secret to himself, was all the same to her.

CHAPTER 6

Makeup

Maomao was preparing for the evening meal when Jinshi said, "Do you know much about makeup?"

The question came completely out of the blue. *What in the world is he asking about that for?* Maomao thought, making no effort to hide her confusion. For the first time in a while, she found herself looking at him as if she were studying a caterpillar—not that she really meant to.

Jinshi had just come back from work. Suiren was helping him change clothes. And this was what he wanted to know?

It was true that, growing up in the pleasure district, one learned the basics of doing makeup by osmosis, and sometimes Maomao concocted cosmetics as well as medicine. She couldn't deny she had a fair amount of knowledge about the subject.

"Do you wish to give some to someone as a gift?"

"You misunderstand. It's for me."

That struck Maomao dumb. Her eyes became bottomless black pits, vacant and empty. She no longer even looked like she was gazing at a dead bug or a puddle of mud.

"What are you imagining?" Jinshi snapped. Well, what else would she be imagining? Jinshi in makeup. He was the one who'd brought it up.

He doesn't need any damn makeup! Maomao thought. He already had the beauty of some denizen of the heavenly realm. A touch of crimson around the eyes, a dab of rouge on the lips, and a flower mark upon his brow would be enough to bring the nation to its knees. History was full of pointless wars, and more than a few of them had been caused by a beautiful woman too close to the seat of power.

And this man, he had the potential to transcend gender entirely.

"Do you want to destroy this country?" Maomao asked flatly.

"What in the world gave you that idea?!" Jinshi exclaimed, pulling his outer jacket on and sitting in a chair. Maomao served him congee from a clay pot. It was made with good, salty abalone, and the bite she took to test it for poison was delicious. She knew that when Jinshi was finished, Suiren would split the leftovers with her, so she wished he would hurry up and eat before it all went cold.

"How do you make that stuff you use?" Jinshi asked, indicating her nose.

Oh . . . My freckles, Maomao thought, and then it came to her. His beauty was already so overwhelming that he needed nothing to enhance it. But perhaps something to blunt it. "I dissolve dry clay in oil, sir. If I want the product to be especially dark, I mix in charcoal or red lip pigment."

"Hmm. And can you do that on short notice?"

Maomao produced a clamshell from the folds of her robe. Inside was tight-packed clay. "This is all I have on me right now, but give me a night's time, and I can easily make more."

Jinshi took the clamshell, scooped up some of the contents with his finger, and rubbed it on the back of his hand. It was a bit too dark, Maomao thought, for his almost porcelain skin. She would have to thin the mixture out.

"Will you yourself be using it, sir?"

Jinshi chuckled softly. It wasn't a real answer, but Maomao figured she could take it as a yes.

"If you know of any medicine that can change a man's face, I would love to hear about it," he said lightly.

He was joking, but Maomao replied: "Such things exist, but you would never be able to change back." Lacquer, for instance, would do the job in a hurry.

"I suppose so," Jinshi said with a strained smile. He wouldn't want that—and neither would anyone else around here. Maomao could easily picture herself torn to pieces and fed to the beasts if she dared to do such a thing.

"There are certain techniques, sir, which might achieve the same effect," she said.

"If you please, then." Jinshi smiled as if this was what he had been waiting for, and finally set about eating his congee. He was enjoying some perfectly cooked chicken meat so much that Maomao despaired of getting any leftovers. When Suiren took the tray away, there was only a single bite left on it.

"I want you to make me someone else entirely," Jinshi said.

I wonder what he's planning, Maomao thought, but she valued her life more than to ask. Besides, she had nothing to gain by knowing. She need only do as she was told. "Very well," she said, and then she watched Jinshi continue his dinner, silently urging him to hurry up. That abalone congee looked so good.

The next day, Maomao set out a cloth with everything she needed: a batch of her makeup, thinned down, and a few other items she thought would help. She arrived earlier than usual to find the lights already lit in Jinshi's personal rooms. The master of the place had finished his bath and was reclining on a couch while Suiren dried his hair. Only a noble could know or expect such luxury. His outfit was plainer than usual, but his every movement betrayed his aristocratic background.

"Good morning," Maomao said, looking as if she didn't think it was very good at all.

"Morning," Jinshi replied, for his part sounding entirely pleased; he seemed like he might start humming at any moment. "Something the matter? It seems early for such stormy looks."

"Not at all, sir. I was merely contemplating the fact that you'll spend yet another day being perfectly beautiful."

"What's this? Some new way to snipe at me?"

Perhaps it sounded like it, but it was only the truth. Jinshi's hair caught the light as it fell. The way it glittered, Maomao thought, it could have been turned into quite a fine textile.

"Don't feel like doing your job today?" he said.

"I do, sir. But are you quite certain you wish to become someone else *entirely*?"

"Yes. I said so last night."

"Then, if you'll pardon me . . ." Maomao strode up beside Jinshi, grabbed the sleeves of his outfit, and shoved them against her face.

"Goodness gracious," Suiren said. She left off combing Jinshi's hair and hustled out of the room, taking Gaoshun with her as he tried to come in. (They didn't go far, though: certainly not so far that they couldn't quietly watch what was happening.)

"Wh-what do you think you're doing?" Jinshi's voice threatened to crack.

When she had been given a task, Maomao only felt right when she had performed it to the utmost. She had assembled a panoply of tools to help her make Jinshi unrecognizable.

He has no idea, does he? Maomao thought. "No commoner would wear such fine perfume," she said. The outfit Jinshi had chosen was that of a townsman, or perhaps a lesser government official. Not the kind of person who would have any contact or connection with ships bringing exotic, expensive fragrant woods from beyond the sea. Maomao's sense of smell was especially sharp, honed in the service of distinguishing medicinal from poisonous herbs. She had detected Jinshi's perfume the moment she entered the room, and that was what had caused her ill humor. Suiren had probably perfumed the outfit, trying to be helpful, but quite frankly she'd only made things worse.

"Do you know how to discern the various types of customers at a brothel?"

"I don't. Perhaps by their body type, or their clothing?"

"Those are possibilities, but there's another way. The smell."

Overweight patrons who gave off a sweet odor were sick but most likely rich. Those who wore several perfumes at once, creating a noxious miasma, frequented the common prostitutes and most likely had a sexual disease. A young person who reeked like an animal indicated an unsanitary failure to take baths.

The Verdigris House was not in the habit of accepting first-time customers without introductions, but every once in a while one would prevail upon the old madam and gain entrance. That such people almost always became excellent regulars showed that the old woman knew how to judge her clientele.

"Anyway, the first thing we need is a different outfit. And something else." Maomao went over to the bathtub and got a bucket of still-warm water, which she brought over to Jinshi. Suiren and Gaoshun watched her anxiously. Since he was there, Maomao sent Gaoshun on an errand. They were going to need clothing other than what had been prepared.

Now she took a small leather pouch from her cloth bag. She dipped her fingers in it, and they emerged dripping with viscous oil, which she dissolved in the bucket of water.

"One thing commoners do *not* do is take baths every day," she informed him. She wet her hand in the bucket, then ran it through Jinshi's hair. With a few passes of Maomao's hand, his lustrous locks began to lose their shine. She thought she was being careful, but she wasn't as experienced at this as Suiren was, which must have been why Jinshi seemed so antsy.

Have to be careful not to pull his hair, Maomao thought, growing a little nervous herself. It was all too easy to forget, but this august personage could cause a permanent rift between her head and her shoulders if he were too much displeased.

When the shining silk strands that had once adorned Jinshi's head had become dull hemp, Maomao tied his hair back. She didn't use a proper hair tie so much as a scrap of cloth. For his new persona, anything would do so long as it served its purpose.

By the time Maomao had put the bucket away and washed her hands, Gaoshun was back with exactly what she'd requested. Now *that* was good help.

"Are you quite sure about this?" Gaoshun asked, looking distinctly uneasy. Beside him, Suiren was making no attempt to hide her repugnance. No doubt it was hard for such a long-serving lady-in-waiting to believe what she was seeing.

Gaoshun had procured a largish and very well-used commoner's outfit. It had at least been washed, but the cloth was thinning in places, and the original owner's musk still clung to it.

Maomao put the outfit to her nose and said, "I might have preferred something a little stinkier." Now Suiren truly looked astonished, her hands on her cheeks. She seemed about to speak up, but Gaoshun silenced her with a motion of his hand. Still, he couldn't conceal the furrow in his own brow.

Maomao felt bad for Suiren, but she still had plenty to do that would test the woman's spirits. "Master Jinshi, please undress."

"Er . . . Yes. Certainly," Jinshi said, though he didn't sound very certain. Maomao paid his reluctance no mind, but bustled around the room looking for something that would serve her purpose. She found several handkerchiefs, then produced some binding cloths from her bag.

"Might I ask the two of you to help me?" she inquired of the nervous spectators. She pulled them both in, giving Gaoshun a handkerchief to wrap around Jinshi's skin. He might have been a man of near-celestial beauty, and he might have been lacking an important part that most men possessed, but nonetheless, Jinshi's torso was reasonably well-muscled. He must have thought he would be cold wearing only his undergarments, for he had left his trousers on. Maomao, who had thought the room quite warm enough, realized maybe she hadn't been very generous with him, and added some coals to the brazier.

Gaoshun wrapped the handkerchiefs around Jinshi, Suiren held them down, and Maomao secured them in place with the cloths. When they were finished, Jinshi had acquired a rather portly silhouette. The slightly oversized clothes fit just right now. Maomao had given Jinshi a not-quite-average body type, and the last traces of his perfume would soon be overcome by the odor on the clothes. Jinshi's face, the only thing that was obviously and unmistakably still his own, looked very strange floating there above his new body.

"All right, let's move on to the next thing, then." Maomao got out the batch of makeup she'd prepared the night before. It was slightly darker than Jinshi's skin tone. She began applying it delicately with her fingers. *Yeesh*, she thought, *I am literally close enough to touch him, and he's still outrageously beautiful.* Not only did he have no facial hair, but he seemed to have no body hair of any kind.

Once she'd done a thorough application of foundation, a mischievous thought came to her. For after all, when would she ever have such a chance again? When would there ever come another opportunity to indulge her curiosity about exactly how lovely Jinshi would be if he were made up like a girl?

Maomao took a shell containing red pigment from among her implements. She dipped her pinky in and brushed some carefully onto Jinshi's lips.

Then Maomao was silent. Gaoshun and Suiren, looking on, were likewise speechless. Each of them looked first uncomfortable, then deeply conflicted, then they all looked at each other and nodded.

"What's going on?" Jinshi asked, but no one answered. Their minds were too full of something much bigger. They were clearly all thinking the same thing: it was a blessing that only the three of them were present at this moment. If there had been anyone else around, be they male or female, it would have been a tragedy. There were some things which, no matter how transcendent, the world was not meant to see. It was fearsome to realize that with just a dash of lip color, Jinshi might possess the power to bring low at least a couple of small villages.

"It's nothing, sir," Maomao said, taking the handkerchief Suiren offered her and rubbing it along Jinshi's lips hard enough to make sure she got everything off.

"Ow, that's uncomfortable. What in the world was that about?"

"As I said, sir, it's nothing."

"Nothing at all, I assure you," Suiren added.

"Not a thing, sir," Gaoshun said.

Jinshi was skeptical about this sudden show of concord between the three of them, but he asked no further questions. Maomao put the momentary distraction out of her mind and got back to work.

The next step called for slightly darker coloring. She smeared some of the pigment on his face, creating bags under his eyes. While she was at it, she went ahead and tried a mole on each cheek. His gracefully arching eyebrows she thickened bit by bit, working carefully on one side and then the other.

There were ways to alter the contours of the face, but at close proximity it would be obvious that it was makeup, so Maomao decided to forgo that step. On a woman, a bit of makeup might go unquestioned, but on a man's face it would arouse suspicion. Instead, she stuffed cotton into Jinshi's cheeks to change his profile. Gaoshun and Suiren looked on, surprised she would go that far, but she wasn't done yet. She daubed the remaining pigment here and there to complete the effect. For example, a bit of the stuff under his nails made him look positively filthy.

Can't have his hands looking too pretty, she thought. Jinshi's hands, like his torso, were noticeably masculine. Maomao had always taken him for someone who had never lifted anything heavier than a pair of chopsticks or a writing brush, but his palms had detectable calluses on them. He implied he had been trained with the sword, or perhaps a fighting staff, although she'd never seen him practicing. They weren't skills a eunuch would normally need. She couldn't muster the curiosity, though, to wonder about something so trivial as why Jinshi might have been trained in the fighting arts. Instead, she continued to systematically dirty his hands, turning them into those of an ordinary townsperson.

"Are you quite finished?" Jinshi asked when Maomao started packing up her cosmetics and tools, wiping some sweat from her brow. The gorgeous eunuch had vanished, replaced by an ungainly urban dweller who looked none too healthy. His face retained its appealing symmetry, but his protruding belly, the spots on his hands, and the dark bags under his eyes bespoke a less than sanitary lifestyle. The fact that he *still* looked like someone who could have got himself cast as a ladies' man in some stage play showed how much trouble his natural beauty was apt to cause.

"Gracious, is that really my young master?" Suiren said.

"Don't call me that."

Suiren had seen the entire process from start to finish, and even she was surprised by the transformation. Now, Jinshi could have moved unrecognized almost anywhere in the palace. Unrecognized by his looks, at least.

Maomao removed a bamboo cylinder from her pouch. She pulled the stopper, poured some of the contents into a cup, and handed it to Jinshi. He eyed it dubiously and frowned. The characteristic, nose-prickling odor, Maomao suspected. It was a combination of a number of different stimulants, and honestly speaking, the flavor could hardly be called appetizing.

"What exactly is this?"

"A special draught of my own devising. Drink slowly, so it gets on your lips, and then swallow. It should cause swelling of the lips and throat, thereby changing your voice. Oh, you may want to take the cotton out of your mouth first."

Jinshi could look and even smell different, but certain people would know him instantly if they heard that honeyed voice. If Maomao was going to do something, she was going to do it right.

"It's quite bitter," Maomao added, "but don't worry. It isn't poisonous."

A collective stunned silence greeted her. Maomao ignored it and resumed industriously cleaning up her workspace. She'd gotten permission to take the rest of the day off. For the first time in a while, she would be able to go back to the pleasure quarter, and above all, to do a little of the mixing and concocting she loved so much. The thought made her unusually cheery, but her parade was swiftly rained on.

"Xiaomao, you said you'd be going home today, yes?"

"Indeed, sir. I intend to leave presently," she said. Gaoshun greeted this with a smile, as if to say that that was perfect. It was an unusual expression from the reticent aide.

"In that case, you'll be going the same way as Master Jinshi," he said.

Ugh! Blargh! Maomao thought immediately. Her saving grace was that she didn't give voice to her disgust, but it was probably written all over her face.

Gaoshun snuck a glance at Jinshi, who looked just as shocked as Maomao. His mouth hung slightly agape. Gaoshun continued, "You went to all the trouble of changing your appearance, sir. It would undermine the effect if you traveled with the same attendant you always do."

"Goodness, I hadn't thought of that," Suiren said with an exaggerated nod that suggested the two of them had very much thought of it—ahead of time.

"Do you see what I mean, Master?" Gaoshun said. He looked uncommonly eager about this. Pleased to be foisting Jinshi off on someone else for once, most likely.

"I do. Yes, that would be helpful." Suddenly Jinshi was on board too.

Now, this won't do, Maomao thought. "I'm exceedingly sorry," she said, "but I'm afraid that even in my company, Master Jinshi would have quite the same problem."

It was true that with his new, less remarkable appearance, it would be suitable for Jinshi to have a plain attendant such as Maomao, but it was already well-known in some quarters that she was his personal maid. It would be best if they didn't travel together, against the slightest chance of them being recognized.

Ah, but that crafty old lady-in-waiting, Suiren: she greeted—and dismissed—this idea with a smile. She came over holding a lacquered box, from which she produced a pair of eyebrow tweezers and an ornamental hair stick. "Then I believe a disguise of your own is called for, Xiaomao," she said, and her smiling eyes contained a sharp edge that prevented Maomao from objecting further.

That nagging premonition, though, got worse and worse.

CHAPTER 7

A Jaunt Around Town

They would take a carriage from Jinshi's rooms to the gate of the outer court. Maomao's dramatic and successful transformation of her master was a double-edged sword: if a man who looked like Jinshi now did bumbled around the palace, it would attract suspicion. Even the lowliest of maids and manservants were supplied with halfway decent clothing here.

It might have seemed obvious to simply put on more-refined clothing for the journey out, but considering Jinshi's stomach was artificially stuffed, a change of clothes later would have been tricky. This was a source of irritation to Maomao, who wanted everything to be perfect and was rather incensed at Jinshi's failure to understand his own beauty.

They disembarked the carriage in a quiet spot, and almost immediately, Maomao began lobbing critiques at Jinshi.

"Master Jinshi, your posture is much too good. Slouch a little!" At the moment, Jinshi stood as straight as if there were a string attaching his head to the heavens.

"Well, speak for yourself," he grumbled. "A little heavy on the formalities, aren't we? And don't use my name—it defeats the point!" His tone was rough, just like the man he now ostensibly was.

Maomao privately admitted that he was right. But in that case, what should she call him? She narrowed her eyes and stared closely at Jinshi. Though she hadn't meant to, it made her look as though she were studying a moth that had fluttered up to a lantern. Jinshi's expression shifted to something difficult to describe.

"What shall I call you then, sir?" Maomao finally asked.

"Good question," Jinshi said, stroking his chin. He *hmm*ed for a moment, then said, "Call me Jinka."

Jinka? Maomao thought. It wasn't particularly odd, and she was happy to use it, but the deliberate choice of the character *ka*, which meant "flower," was somewhat surprising in a man's name. But then again, "Jinshi" wasn't the most masculine name in the world either. Maomao briefly regretted that she hadn't simply disguised Jinshi as a woman, but then she remembered that dab of rouge and thought better of it. She shook her head: Jinshi must never appear in women's clothing, lest the very world tear itself apart.

"Very well then, Master Jinka—" Maomao started, but she caught Jinshi glaring at her. Ah, yes. The formality. "Jinka, then. No honorifics, no deference." Maomao found the ornate mode of polite speech employed at the palace tricky to navigate, but in her mind, completely casual language was even harder. And what was that gleam in Jinshi's eyes? She'd worked so hard to make him appear sickly. He would bring the illusion crashing down if he looked too pleased.

"Excellent, milady," he said, his tone somewhat facetious.

"Huh?" Maomao gaped at him, and Jinshi grinned broadly.

"I should think this manner of speech the most suited, considering our respective appearances," he said, looking Maomao up and down.

Maomao's own disguise had been arranged by Suiren, who had dressed her in hand-me-downs from her own daughter. There was a whiff of camphor about them, but the make and material were excellent and the design thoughtful, so they didn't look out of vogue. Her hair had been carefully gathered up and secured with a hair stick. She did indeed present the image of an affluent young lady.

Now Maomao pursed her lips and trotted off. "Let's get this over with."

"Yes, ma'am."

Maomao was profoundly uncomfortable with this reversal of their accustomed roles, but Jinshi looked like he was having the time of his life.

Jinshi's destination was a restaurant just outside the pleasure district. Apparently he had a meeting with some sort of acquaintance there, but Maomao didn't press for details. Not asking too many questions, she felt, was frequently a wise way to get by in the world.

Still, she couldn't help feeling somewhat used by Jinshi and Gaoshun. *Maybe I should act a little more oblivious,* she thought as she walked down the street. This road was home to a market bustling with merchants hawking their wares. Leafy green vegetables were still few and far between at this time of year, but there were plenty of fat daikon. Maomao had been given a bit of pocket change. She was just thinking that maybe she would have someone wring a chicken's neck for her and boil it with some daikon when someone grabbed her by the collar.

"What is it?" she asked. Jinshi was looking down at her with a most distressing grin on his face.

"You're going to go shopping?" he said.

"I saw something I want. I was just going to go get it."

"Looking like that?"

She took his point. A woman who was well-off enough to have an attendant with her would never dirty her hands purchasing her own produce—let alone having a chicken slaughtered. Maomao gazed longingly at the vegetables. *But I wanted to make it for my old man . . .* she thought. Pops was both a doctor and an apothecary par excellence, but he had one glaring flaw: a total inability to weigh profit and loss. Thus, though apothecary's work should have kept him eating luxury foods for the rest of his life, he instead lived in a shack that looked like it could fall down in a stiff breeze. Of course, if he ever seemed like he was really going to starve for want of food, the old madam would probably have funneled it into him.

Maomao resumed walking, pouting now. Jinshi was still trying to pretend to be her manservant, but he had a long stride, and before she knew it, he was in front of her. Maomao had to pick up her pace to keep up with him. *Hrm*, she thought, *he's got a long way to go.*

Jinshi's eyes were still sparkling. He at least managed not to gawk, but he was obviously enjoying where he was and what he was doing. To a pampered aristocrat like him, a common market must have been a novel sight. Maomao overtook Jinshi and glared at him. He seemed to realize he'd been careless and looked chastened for a moment, but then he set off walking again as if nothing had happened. At least he stayed behind Maomao this time.

Maomao said nothing out loud, but she thought to herself, *When I get home, I've got to see how the field is doing.* She crooked her fingers, counting as she imagined what herbs she might find there. *I wonder if the mugwort has come in yet. And how terrific would it be if the butterbur were ready to pick?* Still she said nothing aloud. She was just imagining herself frying the butterbur with some meat and miso when she realized Jinshi was looming just beside her.

"What is it, sir?" Maomao said, glaring at Jinshi and inadvertently reverting to her usual deference. Jinshi was clearly itching to say something.

"Why so quiet?" he asked, likewise adopting the directness to which he was usually entitled.

Why wasn't she saying anything? Well, there could really be just one reason, couldn't there? "Because I don't have anything to say?"

She had only spoken the truth, but apparently that was a mistake. Jinshi bit his lip, and an inscrutable expression crossed his face. Maomao wasn't worried that he might burst into tears—he wasn't a little boy—but he still managed to look thoroughly pathetic.

He was the one who said I should act more brusque with him! Maomao thought. She wasn't normally the type to initiate a conversation anyway. So when she didn't have anything in particular to talk about, and when no one was asking her any specific questions, she tended to keep her peace. Why this was such a shock to this man mystified her.

She was just scratching the back of her neck nervously, wondering what to do, when a meat-skewer stall came into view. She broke into a brisk trot and ordered two skewers from the man behind the counter.

105

Just looking at the perfectly crisped chicken meat made her mouth water.

"Try it," she said, passing one of the skewers to Jinshi. He slowly took it, looking at it as if he'd never seen one before. "Quick, before it gets cold." Maomao guided them to a small side street just off the main road. She brushed some dust off a wooden crate and sat down on top of it. When she bit into the grilled meat, the juices exploded in her mouth, and the fragrant chicken skin gave an audible snap.

God, that's good. Maomao leaned forward to keep the juices from running onto her clothes. Jinshi wasn't eating, but he watched her.

"Not going to have yours? As you can see, it isn't poisoned."

"No, that's, uh, not what I'm worried about," Jinshi said, tapping his cheek.

"Ah." Now she remembered—she had stuffed cotton into his mouth to help give him a different profile. Maomao took out a square of paper and passed it to him; he spat out the cotton balls and tossed them into a nearby wastebasket. A versatile paper square like that one was very valuable—just another of Suiren's thoughtful touches, along with the clothes.

I didn't think to bring any replacement cotton, Maomao thought. This rubbed her perfectionist streak the wrong way, but she doubted it was something most people would actually notice. Still inspecting the skewer with a certain amount of wonder, Jinshi brought it to his mouth. It must have been a little warm for him because he blew on it forcefully before chewing and swallowing.

"What do you think, sir?"

"Damn sight better than what they served at the bivouac. Good and salty," Jinshi said, wiping the juice off his lips with his fingers.

Maomao took a handkerchief out of her pouch and handed it to him, but she was thinking, *Bivouac?* Eunuchs, as far as she knew, didn't normally serve in the military, so she wasn't sure what to make of this. Maybe a person like Jinshi would be roughing it out in the wilderness if a war started or something, but under normal circumstances? What would lead to a eunuch spending his nights in the field?

As she entertained the question, Maomao studied Jinshi's face. A bit of the makeup had come off around his mouth, but it wasn't enough to worry about; she looked away. *All right, whatever our business is here, let's get it over with,* she thought. She finished the last of the meat on her skewer and stood up from the crate. She was determined to go back and buy that daikon and chicken once she'd ditched Jinshi.

Despite her haste, Jinshi insisted on doing everything with slow, elegant movements, much to Maomao's annoyance. "Are you quite sure you're going to be in time for your meeting, *Jinka*?" she asked pointedly, using his fake name.

"I think we've got a few minutes yet."

"Wouldn't it be best to arrive early? It's bad manners to make someone wait for you."

Now it was Jinshi who looked annoyed. "If I didn't know better, I'd think you were trying to get rid of me."

"Would you?" Maomao said innocently, but of course Jinshi had hit the nail on the head. He looked a bit sullen but didn't complain further. Instead, he changed the subject.

"I can't imagine life in the palace is *that* bad. Surely it must be better than here in the pleasure district."

Maomao had to admit, it wasn't terrible, particularly now that she was serving there of her own volition. She had a small but clean room, and an offer to move to other quarters. She had been quite lucky, she felt. But the lifestyle wasn't the only reason she might have to want to go back to the pleasure district. "I'm worried whether my old man is taking proper care of himself," she said. Jinshi's mouth practically hung open. "What?" Maomao asked.

"It's nothing. I just . . . never knew you were interested in anything besides drugs and poisons."

Maomao replied with a glare. Rude bastard. "My adoptive father is my teacher in matters of medicine, so I certainly *hope* he'll continue to live a good long time." Then she turned her back decisively on Jinshi and started walking. Yes, she knew for sure now: she wanted to get this over with.

Jinshi, looking slightly frazzled, came up alongside her. "This father of yours. I gather he's indeed a talented apothecary."

After a moment Maomao answered hesitantly, "He is." She didn't think it was fair of Jinshi, leveraging talk of her father like this. "Apparently he studied in the west when he was a young man." Thus he was familiar not only with her own region's traditional medicine, but with western medical techniques as well. She occasionally saw him taking notes in a foreign language, and once in a while he would use words that sounded quite unusual to her. It made her think he must have been quite some time in that foreign land.

"Really? He did that?" Jinshi asked. "He must have been something special, then. I believe people are only sent on those studies by endorsement from the government." His transparent amazement only confirmed for Maomao that her father was an exceptional person.

"Yes, he is rather incredible. The old proverb holds that 'Heaven doesn't give two gifts to one man,' but I guess there are exceptions to the rule." The excitement was creeping into her voice now, and she was growing more voluble than usual.

"He must have been quite a man, indeed . . ." Jinshi, in contrast, looked more subdued than before. Perhaps she'd said too much and something in her flood of words had upset him.

He was the one who insisted I talk, she thought. She wished he would make up his blasted mind.

Jinshi, desperate to look at anything but Maomao, let his gaze wander among the shops that lined the street. The restaurants and food stalls had given way to places selling textiles and accessories. Men flitted from one to the next, picking presents to please their nighttime butterflies.

"And what is such a distinguished person doing running a druggist's shop in a nameless corner of the pleasure district?" There was a thorn hidden in Jinshi's words.

"Heaven gave him many gifts, but luck was not one of them. And as much as he was given, something was also *taken* from him. Something important."

Ill fortune: that was Luomen's one great flaw, if he had one. His study in the west had proven sufficient pretext for the former emperor's mother—that is to say, the former empress dowager—to have him made a eunuch.

Jinshi watched Maomao silently. Just as she was starting to fear that another of her red-light-district jokes had fallen flat, he said, "You're telling me that the father who adopted you is a eunuch?"

"Yes, sir," Maomao said, wondering if she hadn't mentioned it before.

Jinshi started mumbling: "Eunuch . . . Apothecary . . . Doctor . . ."

Amid this talking and mumbling, they reached their destination. Maomao looked at the note Gaoshun had given her. "I believe that's it, sir," she said, pointing to a place just at the border of the pleasure district. The upper floor was an inn and the lower a restaurant, a fairly standard arrangement.

"Yes, I think you're right. But we still have a few minutes," Jinshi said, looking around.

Ah, now I get it, Maomao thought, narrowing her eyes. She understood why Jinshi had gone to all the trouble of disguising himself and marching around the town market. Yes, she saw it all now.

Maomao let out a long breath. "I fear that traipsing around too much will cause your makeup to come off. Besides, the person you're meeting might be inside already. Better to go have a look than to risk making them wait, isn't it?" Jinshi finally seemed to take the hint. "I shall part ways with you here then, sir."

"What, here?"

"Yes. You took the trouble of disguising yourself. It would spoil everything if I walked in with you." Maomao gave a polite nod of the head and started back toward the market. As she went, she glanced over her shoulder to see Jinshi entering the restaurant. *I guess even eunuchs need a day off now and then,* she thought. She crossed her arms and nodded. And then she started thinking again. If he was going to come all the way out here, he might as well just go into the pleasure district proper. For she knew what kind of restaurant it was that Jinshi had just gone into. They served the waitresses along with the food.

Well, I hope he has a good night, she thought a touch caustically, staring at the restaurant with a freezing look in her eye.

CHAPTER 8

The Plum Poison

M aomao awoke to the twittering of sparrows. She sat up in her meager bed, the characteristic odor of brewing medicine prickling her nose.

"Good morning," said a calm, grandmotherly voice. It belonged to her father.

That's right . . . I'm back home, she thought. This was her first trip back since she had begun working in the outer court. Typically, maids in her position had no vacations to speak of. Of course not: even if their master were to take a day off work, it wasn't as if he stopped living his life. Most such people had more than just one or two servants, leaving a little leeway for one of them to take time off. But matters were different with Jinshi; he had so few attendants.

I can't believe she made it this long by herself . . . Maomao could only tip her proverbial hat to Jinshi's attendant Suiren, whose indulgence was the only reason she had been able to take this break. Although Maomao paid for it: the rest of the time, Suiren worked her relentlessly.

Maomao got out of bed and sat in a crude chair. Her father brought her some warm congee in a chipped bowl. She sipped at it: it needed salt, but her father had at least given it a good, hearty flavor by mixing in some fragrant herbs. Maomao added a few drops of vinegar and stirred.

"Make sure you wash your face," her father said.

"Yeah, once I eat."

Maomao continued stirring the porridge with her spoon while her father prepared the ingredients for the medicine he was mixing up. "What do you plan to do today?" he asked.

Maomao looked at him, almost a bit confused. "Nothing special," she said.

"In that case, perhaps you could go to the Verdigris House for me."

There was a beat before Maomao said, "Sure. All right." She added another liberal dash of vinegar to her congee.

Her father's apothecary was situated inside the Verdigris House, but when he asked her to "go" there, he had something else in mind. When Maomao arrived, she greeted the manservant outside with a familiar hello and went in. She passed through the elegant atrium of the entry hall, then she proceeded down a covered walkway to one side. The central courtyard was as fine as that in any aristocrat's mansion, and at night it was lit with burning lanterns. It was kept in good enough order to impress those who occasionally came by for tea during the day.

Maomao didn't stop in the courtyard, though, but continued to a lonely little outbuilding. This was no place for customers. Once within, the reek of illness filled her nostrils.

"Morning."

A woman slept inside, her hair disheveled. She looked like a particularly unpleasant skeleton.

"I brought your medicine," Maomao continued. The woman, though, didn't speak. One might almost suspect she had long ago forgotten how. She used to chase Maomao out, seemingly from sheer hatred, but in the past few years she'd lost the energy to do even that.

Maomao went to where the woman lay indolently on her back and helped her swallow the powder she'd brought. It was what her father used in place of quicksilver or arsenic. Less poisonous, he said, and more effective, but at the moment it wasn't even serving to help sedate the woman. Yet they had no other way to treat her except to give her this powder.

The noseless woman was nearly forty now, but once she had been celebrated as a butterfly, feted as a flower. The Verdigris House was a prestigious enough establishment to pick and choose its customers now, but it hadn't always been so. In the years after Maomao's birth, there had been a time when the place had little more than a mud-spattered sign to its name. It was during that time that this woman had been a courtesan taking customers, and to her misfortune, she'd contracted syphilis, known in Maomao's language as "the Plum Poison."

If this medicine had been available to her in the early stages of her illness, perhaps she might have been cured, but by now the state of her body barely bore looking at. The illness had ravaged not only her appearance, but her mind as well, leaving her memory in tatters.

Time—time was a cruel thing.

When Luomen had first seen the woman, her illness had been in a dormant phase. If she'd only told him about it then, instead of holding back, things might not have taken such a brutal turn. But then, not everyone was willing to immediately trust a eunuch who showed up seemingly out of nowhere, a pariah from the rear palace. The simple reality of a courtesan's life was that she took customers, or she didn't eat.

When the lesions began again several years later, the tumors spread with startling speed. So the woman was confined to this room where customers wouldn't see her. Yes, she was being swept under the rug, but this was still, by one standard, remarkably compassionate treatment. A courtesan who could no longer work was typically chased out of the establishment. The woman was lucky not to be simply daubed with some whitening cream and eyebrow ink and left in a ditch.

Maomao took a rag from a washbasin and began wiping the woman's body as she lay there. *Maybe I'll burn some incense too,* she thought. The perpetually closed door penned the stench in the room.

There was some incense on hand that the woman had received from a certain noble. Fancy stuff, and an aroma the man himself was said to enjoy—but it was rarely used. It could be a problem when mixing medicines, many of which suffered from absorbing unusual odors. The only times the stuff was regularly burned was when the man himself appeared, at which point a token amount would be lit. Maomao helped herself to a bit of the stuff now.

The incense had an ever so slightly sweet scent, and when it wafted over to her, the barest of smiles passed over the woman's face. She began to hum a children's song in a broken voice. It seemed she had regressed to her childhood. Hopefully she was at least reliving a pleasant memory.

Maomao set the incense burner in a corner of the room so the courtesan wouldn't accidentally knock it over. Just then, she heard pounding footsteps from outside.

"Good lord. What is it?"

One of the apprentices appeared. Maomao seemed to remember she served Meimei. The girl was reluctant to come into the sickroom but hovered in the doorway. She was probably scared of the woman with no nose.

"Um, Sis said to bring you a message," the girl told Maomao. "She said if I found you here, to tell you you'd better stay here for a while. She said there's a weird guy with a monocle out there."

"Ah," Maomao said. She understood who the girl meant. The weird man with a monocle was a long-standing customer of the Verdigris House, but he was not someone with whom Maomao wished to cross paths. As long as she stayed in this room, however, she would be safe. The madam would never do something so stupid as to show a customer something she had worked so hard to hide.

"Okay," Maomao said. "I've got it. You can go back."

Then she let out a breath. The woman with no nose stopped her song and pulled out a set of marbles made from colored pebbles. She began lining them up one next to the other, as if trying to organize the tattered bits of her memories.

Fool woman, Maomao thought. She went over to a corner of the room and crouched down.

———◇———

It was Meimei who came shortly thereafter to let Maomao know that the coast was clear. Unlike her apprentice, the courtesan entered the room without hesitation, as though she knew it well. "Thanks for taking care of her today."

Maomao set out a round pillow. Meimei sat and smiled down at the sick woman. The patient didn't react; she had fallen asleep at some point.

"Maomao," Meimei said. "They talked about you-know-what again."

Maomao did indeed "know what." The very thought was enough to give her goose bumps. "Persistent old bastard, isn't he? I'm amazed you can stand him, Sis."

"He's a good customer, if you can accept him as he is. And given what he pays, the old lady's not about to object."

"Yeah. And I'm sure that's why she's so keen for me to become a courtesan." The customer in question was the reason the madam had been so intent on bringing Maomao into her employ these past years. If Maomao hadn't been hired by Jinshi, there was a distinct chance she would have been sold off to this customer by now. "I don't even want to think about it," she said, her face contorting.

Meimei exhaled pointedly when she saw this expression. "From an outside perspective, it might look like an excellent opportunity."

"You've got to be kidding."

"Don't make that face at me." (Courtesans had a somewhat different idea from most people of what constituted a good match.) "Do you know how few of us get to end up with someone we truly desire?"

"I know. Because for the madam, personal attraction weighs nothing, but silver is very, very heavy."

"That's the cost of a ticket on the boat to heaven," Meimei said with a jovial laugh. She ran her fingers through the sick woman's hair, then whispered to Maomao: "I think the old lady's of a mind to sell one of us off one of these days. We're getting to be about that age."

Meimei wasn't quite thirty yet, but for a courtesan, it was entirely natural to start thinking about retirement at that age. Sell high, as it were; or rather, sell before your looks started to go.

Maomao silently studied Meimei's profile. Her face, still beautiful, appeared awash in a bevy of emotions, but Maomao didn't want to think about them too hard. Those were feelings she still didn't understand. If there was such a thing as love, Maomao thought she had left it in the womb of the woman who bore her when she came out into the world.

"What if you started up a place of your own?"

"Hah! The *last* thing I want is to be a competitor to that old hag."

Meimei must have enough money to free herself, Maomao thought. If she chose not to leave the courtesan's life, it must be because she wasn't ready.

"Just a little longer," Meimei said with a smile. "I won't be in this line of work forever."

Jinshi pressed his chop to some paperwork, his face long. The outing the day before had tired him.

He sighed: never had he imagined that the establishment at which the meeting took place would be a virtual extension of the pleasure district. He hadn't gone there for that! What's more, the whole point of his disguise had been that it was difficult for him to go out in public quietly. Yet he had ended up accompanied by Maomao practically to the very doorstep of his meeting. Something else he hadn't envisioned. The idea had come instead from the aide quietly organizing the papers beside him.

This man had served him for many years, but perhaps it made him too willing to take matters into his own hands. No doubt he thought that what he had done was for Jinshi's benefit, but Jinshi could have raised a number of objections.

"Gaoshun . . . What are you plotting?" Jinshi asked.

Gaoshun shook his head as if to say the idea of plotting anything had never occurred to him. "Allow me to answer a question with a question, sir: how was your little jaunt into town?"

"Ah, yes . . ." Jinshi wasn't quite sure what to say about it. He took a sip of tea in hopes of stalling. He was sure now: Gaoshun thought he was helping, howsoever that was. Jinshi searched his mind for some way to change the subject. "Ahem. I discovered something interesting. The girl—her adoptive father is a eunuch and was a doctor here once."

" 'The girl'—you mean Xiaomao? If she was taught by a palace doctor, that would explain a great deal about her medical knowledge. A eunuch, though . . ."

"You heard me."

The simple fact was, no doctor of the rear palace was likely to be a man of renown. Someone who had the wherewithal to become a qualified medical practitioner had no need to become a eunuch in order to find work. The only physicians who found their way to the rear palace were the ones with problems.

"Could such a talented practitioner really have been among the eunuchs?" Gaoshun asked.

"That *is* the question, isn't it?" Jinshi said.

Gaoshun mulled that over, stroking his chin. Jinshi felt he had said enough. His aide was a sharp enough man to take the investigation from here.

They heard the clear ringing of a bell, a little device set up so Jinshi would be immediately aware of any visitors to his office. Gaoshun put down his work and stood by the entrance, waiting for the new arrival.

A nother day, another visit from the weirdo with the monocle. He didn't have any particular business; he simply lounged around on a couch, sipping juice. "Thanks for taking care of that little thing the other day. Whew, it did turn out to be quite a story, didn't it?" Lakan stroked his chin and squinted at Jinshi, making his already narrow eyes even narrower.

"It seems the youngest of those brothers was the most capable after all," Jinshi said as he flipped through some papers. He suspected the commander had known all along. After the incident with their father's inheritance, the three men had appeared to reconcile with each other, but it was no more than that—an appearance. The youngest brother had suddenly revealed a heretofore undisclosed ability, and there was even talk that he could soon be doing work for the palace. Jinshi had seen some of his products, and the delicacy of the workmanship impressed even him. He didn't know exactly what had happened, but he strongly suspected the apothecary's daughter did—and wasn't saying anything about it.

"I think if we got that young man to handle the furnishings for the ritual, it would redound to the glory of our ruler."

"Yes, of course." Jinshi hated the way Lakan could make virtually anything sound important. A man of Jinshi's stature would normally hardly even hear of ritual preparations.

"Then there's the last work the father left behind. Just simple metal fittings, but so fine they could be fit for ritual use themselves."

"I find I keep wondering, Master Strategist, why it is you feel you must speak with *me* about these craftsmen."

"Why not? It's a waste to leave buried talent buried."

Lakan could be obnoxious, but when he was right, he was right. Even if there was an ulterior motive for whatever he happened to be saying. If nothing else, Lakan was an excellent judge of talent. It wouldn't be an exaggeration to say it was that ability that had seen him rise to the position he now occupied. He might look as if he was slacking off at the moment, but in fact his work was being done, and industriously at that, by the various people he had discovered and employed. Jinshi could almost be jealous of him.

"What does it matter whether he's the elder brother or the younger? The cream should rise to the top!"

He made it sound so simple. That penchant for simplicity made him useful in his way, but he took careful handling.

Jinshi straightened his papers and passed them to an official who took them away.

"Incidentally, I wanted to ask you about something. The thing we talked about before," Jinshi said.

He meant the courtesan he had heard about previously. Did Lakan intend to play dumb again?

The commander put his hands on his cheeks and grinned. "If you want to know about that world, better to ask someone who comes from it." Then he got to his feet. The official attending him let out a sigh, relieved to finally be going home. "Hah, I see it's that time. My lackeys won't let me hear the end of it if I keep them too long."

He finished the last of his juice, then set the other bottle he'd brought with him on Jinshi's desk. "Let your little serving girls have it or something. It's easy on the throat—not too sweet." The middle-aged soldier waved a hand in Jinshi's general direction. "See you tomorrow."

Then he was gone.

CHAPTER 9

Lakan

The night before, Maomao had had a strange dream. She had dreamed of long ago—or rather, of something that must have happened long ago, for there was no way she should have been able to remember it. She wasn't sure if what she dreamed of had even really occurred.

It must have been visiting that woman, she thought. *Brought back old memories.*

In the dream, a grown woman looked down on Maomao from above. Her disheveled hair tumbled around a drawn face, and her eyes glinted hungrily as she stared. Her makeup was flaking off, the rouge on her lips starting to smear.

The woman reached out and grasped Maomao's hand in hers. Her skin was stippled with minuscule welts, like a leaf in autumn.

In her other hand the woman grasped a knife. The hand that held Maomao's was wrapped in bleached cotton cloths, layer after layer, all of them seeping red. The fluttering cotton smelled rusty.

Something like the mewl of a kitten escaped Maomao's vocal cords. She realized she was crying.

Maomao's hand was pressed against the bed. The woman raised the knife high. Her lips were contorted and trembling, her red, swollen eyes still running with tears.

Fool woman.

The woman brought the knife down.

Goodness, are you tired? I'm afraid bedtime won't be for a little while yet," Suiren said as Maomao yawned. She sounded polite about it, but the old lady could be a real disciplinarian, so Maomao straightened up and focused on polishing the silver eating vessel. She would be practically begging for trouble if she appeared to be slacking the very day after she'd taken time off. The fact that it was evening was no excuse.

"I'm quite fine, ma'am," Maomao said. It was just a dream, strange or no. She'd assumed that if she threw herself into the routine of her work, she'd soon forget it, but it had refused to go away all day. *This isn't like me,* Maomao thought, a rueful smile flitting across her face.

Just as she was stacking the dishes back on the shelf (*clatter clatter*), she heard rapid footsteps. The honey candles were burning in the room. It was time for their master to return. Suiren took a dish Maomao had polished to perfection and began preparing a snack.

Jinshi trooped clear through the living area and appeared in the kitchen. "A gift, from a weirdo. Share it with Suiren." He set some sort of bottle down on the table. The "weirdo" was a particularly unpleasant official who had been making himself something of a nuisance to Jinshi lately.

Maomao undid the stopper and was greeted by a sour, citrusy smell. Some kind of juice, she figured. "We're accepting gifts from *weirdos* now, are we?" she asked, her voice completely flat. Jinshi had already retreated to the living area and was resting on the couch. Maomao added some coals to the brazier.

Gaoshun observed that they were scraping the bottom of their coal supply and left the room. Going to get more, Maomao figured. Now there was a man you could rely on.

Jinshi gave a great scratch of his head (most uncouth) and looked at Maomao. "Are you familiar with the regulars at the Verdigris House?" he asked.

Maomao cocked her head, surprised by the question. "If they're conspicuous enough about it, yes."

"What kind of people go there?"

"That's confidential."

Jinshi knitted his brow at the terse response. Then he seemed to realize he was coming at it the wrong way and tried something else. "Let me ask you this, then. How would one go about reducing the price of a courtesan?" He sounded uncommonly careful as he picked his words.

"What a distressing topic." Maomao huffed. "But there are any number of ways. Especially when it comes to the top-ranked women."

The most renowned courtesans, the most sought-after, weren't working constantly. In fact, they might work only a few times a month. Accepting customers every single day was for the "nightwalkers," the women who had to take work to survive. The more highly ranked a courtesan was, the less she liked to be seen. Hiding herself away induced would-be customers to inflate their estimation of her value all on their own.

Such women attracted patrons by virtue of their singing and dancing, their musical accomplishments, or other facets of their education. At the Verdigris House, apprentices were given basic instruction, then divided into those with looks and prospects, and those without. The latter began taking customers as soon as they made their debut. They weren't selling their arts, but their bodies.

As for those who showed potential, they started by sharing tea with the customers. Those adept at entrancing patrons with their conversation or ravishing them with their intelligence rose in value. Then, by deliberately keeping a popular courtesan from seeing too many people, you could produce a woman who commanded a year's wages in silver just to share a drink. By this system, there were even women who went their entire careers, until the day their contracts were bought out, without a customer ever laying hands on them. This in itself played to men's fantasies; everyone wanted to be the first to pick such a blossom.

"A flower is valuable because it's untouched," Maomao said, lighting some soothing incense. She was doing it for Jinshi, who had looked tired lately, but this evening it seemed it might help her as well. "When someone picks it, its value immediately drops by at least half. But there's more . . ." She gave a small sigh, then took a deep sniff of the incense. "If such a woman were to become with child, her value would be practically nothing." That same emotionless tone.

It was all because of that stupid dream.

Jinshi let out a deep breath as he pressed his chop to some paperwork. He wondered what was going on. It nagged at him, what the apothecary's daughter had said the night before. She'd sounded so solemn.

And then, conveniently, the man most likely to know the answer to Jinshi's private question appeared.

"Hello, hello." The grinning fox knocked on the door and entered without waiting to be invited in. He'd come, just as he had promised he would yesterday. He'd even made a subordinate haul along a couch with a nice, soft cushion. Jinshi tried to resist pulling a face as he wondered how long the man would be here today.

"Shall we pick up where we left off yesterday?" Lakan asked, pouring some juice from a bottle he'd brought with him. He'd even brought treats of some kind: he placed on the paper-riddled desk a baked snack that smelled richly of butter. The occupants of the office wished he would stop putting food directly on the table. Gaoshun could only hold his head in his hands when he saw the oil stains left on the papers.

"It seems, sir, that you did something quite reprehensible," Jinshi said as he pressed his chop to another piece of paper. He hardly registered what it said, but Gaoshun, standing behind him, didn't speak up, so it was probably fine.

Based on what Maomao had told him, he had a fairly good idea what this wily madman must have done. And after that thought came another, equally unwelcome one. Namely, that his actions weren't incomprehensible. That they had a consistency. Even a certain logic. Jinshi thought he understood why Lakan had started with the talk of buying out a contract at the Verdigris House. Why he'd spoken of his old "friend." But Jinshi didn't want to admit the implications. To do so would only invite yet more trouble.

"Reprehensible? How rude. And the last thing I want to hear from a thieving little magpie." Lakan's eye narrowed behind his monocle, and then he laughed. "I had finally brought the old lady around, do you know that? It took me ten years of work. And then you swoop in and snatch her away from me—just imagine how that feels." Lakan gestured emphatically with his cup. Ice floated in the juice.

"Are you saying I should give back your shiny trinket?" By this, Jinshi meant the reticent young woman.

"No, keep it. I don't want to get stuck in the same rut as before."

"And if I don't want it?"

"Then what could I possibly do? I could count on one hand the number of people who could go against your will, *milord*."

Lakan was resolute about never saying quite what he really meant. It drove Jinshi to distraction. Lakan knew who and what Jinshi was. Otherwise he never would have said what he did. But the logic was there, in his words.

Lakan took off his monocle, wiped it with a handkerchief, then replaced it—in front of the other eye. So it was just an affectation. Jinshi had always known Lakan was a strange one.

"But I do wonder what my, ahem, *little girl* will think."

The way he emphasized the words *little girl*—ugh. So it must be true. Much as Jinshi resisted admitting it.

Lakan was Maomao's birth father.

Jinshi finally stopped stamping paperwork.

"Could you let her know I'll be popping by for a visit one of these days?" Lakan said. Then he left the office, licking the butter off his fingers. He'd left the couch where it was, though, implying he would be back.

Almost in unison, Jinshi and Gaoshun hung their heads and let out great sighs.

———◇———

I met an official who said he'd like to see you," Jinshi told Maomao as soon as he got back to his room. Realizing it would do no good not to say anything to her, he had resolved to get it out of the way.

"And who is this official?" she asked. Jinshi thought he detected a flicker of unease behind her studiously indifferent expression, but she was hiding it well, her voice just as toneless as ever.

"Ahem. His name is Lakan . . ."

No sooner were the words out of his mouth than Maomao's expression shifted. Her eyes widened, and she took a step away from Jinshi, almost, it seemed, involuntarily. To date she had looked at him like a beetle, like a dried-out earthworm, like mud, like dust, like a slug, and even like a flattened frog—that is to say, in many demeaning and belittling ways—but he realized that all of these were kind and gentle compared to the look she leveled at him now.

It was, frankly, hard to describe, but even Jinshi felt he could barely survive it. Maomao looked as if she might smash open his heart and pour in molten metal so that not even ashes remained.

This one look communicated to Jinshi clearly how Lakan's daughter felt about her father.

"I'll turn him down. Somehow," Jinshi managed, still a little dazed. It was a wonder his heart didn't stop.

"Thank you, sir." Maomao, for her part, regained her customary expressionless affect, and then resumed her work.

CHAPTER 10

Suirei

So he knows. She'd had a feeling about the person Jinshi had been talking about the other day. He was, after all, part of the reason Maomao diligently avoided going anywhere near the military encampment.

She heaved a sigh. The way her breath fogged in the air was proof enough that the cold was still present and accounted for, the footfalls of spring still far off.

There was nobody else in the room. Jinshi and Gaoshun had gone out first thing in the morning. In the two months Maomao had been serving him, she'd begun to get to know Jinshi's routine. One particular task seemed to come up about every two weeks. The day before, he would take a long, slow bath, and burn incense before he went out. Maomao took advantage of those days to give the floor a thorough polishing, and that's what she was doing today, wiping a cloth industriously across the ground. Her hands were going numb with the cold, but with Suiren watching her, mild but implacable, Maomao couldn't even think of slacking off.

When Maomao had dusted about half the building, Suiren finally seemed satisfied and suggested they stop for tea. They pulled two chairs up to a round table in the kitchen and sat with warm cups of tea in their hands. The leaves were leftovers, not new, but were of such high quality that the brew still smelled wonderful. Maomao savored the sweet aroma as she ate a sesame ball.

Wish we could have something more savory, Maomao thought, but it would sound churlish to say aloud. She suspected Suiren had prepared the snack assuming that a young woman would enjoy a sweet treat. So Maomao felt compelled to look appreciative, but then she noticed that Suiren herself was munching away noisily on some grilled rice crackers.

Maomao said nothing for a moment.

"Ah, that salty tang is like an addiction," Suiren said. She and Jinshi were certainly of a piece, Maomao thought. She reached out toward the dish of crackers, but Suiren snatched up the last one before she could get to it. Now Maomao was sure she was doing this on purpose. Very disagreeable, this attendant.

Maomao always ended up the listener when she took a snack with other women, and so it proved at tea with Suiren. Unlike the ladies of the pleasure district or the rear palace, Suiren didn't favor idle gossip, but was given to discoursing on the master of the house.

"The meal tonight is vegetarian, so make sure you're not snitching any meat or fish on the sly," Suiren said.

"Yes, ma'am." Maomao knew better than to ask why they were eating as though they were undergoing some kind of ritual purification, but Suiren implied just enough with her tone that Maomao could guess. *Can eunuchs perform ritual offices?* she wondered. Purification was typically performed by those who would be participating in religious rituals. Those of aristocratic or noble birth could expect to preside at such functions from time to time.

There were a number of things about Jinshi that Maomao didn't understand. For one, why a man of birth such as his should have become a eunuch at all. Then again, when she considered the time of his life at which it had happened, it made a certain kind of sense. The former empress dowager, who had been viewed as all but an empress in her own right in her time, had been a woman of considerable abilities. It was said to be her influence, and no thanks to her incompetent son, that had prevented the country from falling into chaos during the former emperor's reign. But the natural corollary of that fact was that she had leaned on her own authority for many of the actions she took. Such as forcibly making a eunuch of a very capable physician she happened to favor—Maomao's father. It would be reasonable to suppose that Jinshi had become a eunuch under similar circumstances.

"Oh, and I need you to run a little errand for me this afternoon. You'll have to go to the doctor and get some medicine—"

"Yes, ma'am!" Maomao blurted out before Suiren was finished speaking.

"I could wish you were always so enthusiastic," she said, and stuffed the last of the rice cracker into her mouth.

The medical office was located on the eastern side of the outer palace, near the military headquarters. Perhaps it was convenient for all the injuries the military produced. Maomao remembered what Jin-shi had said about this physician, but she was interested in him for other reasons as well. She'd once had firsthand experience with one of his medicines, and it was more than enough to convince her that he was an accomplished practitioner. The rear palace had an absolute quack running its medical office, a real waste, but Maomao was acutely curious as to how things were done in the outer court.

"I've come to pick up some medicine," she said, presenting the tag Suiren had given her. The doctor, a man with high cheekbones, looked at it, then asked Maomao to sit down and disappeared into a back room.

Maomao sat, then took a deep breath in. A profusion of acrid smells and bitter flavors filled her nose and mouth. Over at the desk where the doctor had been until her arrival, Maomao could see a mortar and pestle with some half-crushed herbs in it.

With a supreme effort of will, she managed to control her urge to turn the place upside down. She would have given anything to have a good, close look through the cabinet full of medicines in the next room.

No! she implored herself. *Got to stay strong . . .* She could feel her body edging its way toward the other room in spite of herself.

"May I ask what you're doing?" a woman's cold voice said. Maomao snapped to reality, discovering behind her a very exasperated-looking court lady. Maomao remembered her: it was the tall woman. Maomao realized she must look profoundly suspicious slinking toward the other room as she was, and promptly returned to her chair.

"Just waiting for some medicine," she said innocently. The other woman looked like she wanted to say something to that, but at that moment the doctor reemerged with the prescription. "Oh, Suirei. When did you get here?" he said lightly.

The woman he called Suirei frowned as if she didn't appreciate his tone. "I've come to restock the medicine they keep on hand at the guardhouse," she said. She must have been referring to someplace in the military camp. Now that Maomao thought about it, she realized the last time she'd run into Suirei, it had also been in the vicinity of the military area. At the time, she'd felt strangely as if Suirei had it out for her, and the attitude she saw from the woman now only confirmed her suspicions. Suirei was looking at Maomao as if she wished the young serving woman were *anywhere* else.

If nothing else, Maomao now understood why Suirei had smelled of medicinal herbs when they'd met.

"I've got everything right here. Anything else you need?" the doctor asked.

"Not to speak of. I bid you good day." Suirei met the doctor's downright ingratiating tone with near indifference. The doctor looked almost a little sad as he watched her go.

So that's how it is, Maomao thought, studying the disappointed doctor and reflecting on how easy he was to read. When he realized she was watching him, he frowned and thrust out her medicine at her.

"Does that woman work with the military?" Maomao asked. She didn't really mean anything by it. It was just a passing thought.

"Yes. Though there's no need for a qualified woman of the outer court to handle that sort of thing . . ." Maomao looked at him expectantly, but the doctor didn't elaborate. He only shook his head and said, "It's nothing. Anyway, here's your medicine!" He shoved the packet at her, then gave a dismissive wave of his hand: *Go on, get out.* Apparently Maomao had said something she shouldn't have, but exactly what it was eluded her.

Something a court lady wouldn't normally handle? she repeated to herself. She concluded, though, that there was no special need to tie herself in knots wondering about the portentous pronouncement. Instead, she took the packet and peeked inside. There was some kind of powder in it. Wondering what it was, she put a fingertip's worth on her tongue. (Her bad habit.)

"Is this . . . potato dust?"

She left the doctor's office perplexed.

D o you need anything from the doctor's office today?" Maomao asked with a glance at Suiren, but the lady-in-waiting was not to be outfoxed.

"I won't have you slacking off," she said firmly.

I don't think of it as slacking, Maomao mentally replied. She was just so eager for even a sniff of that rich aroma of medicine.

"On that note," Suiren said, drying her hands, "I gather you've quietly been using our storage room to keep some unusual herbs. I don't want that to continue."

She never did forget to twist the knife. Maomao's face contorted into a scowl as she squeezed a rag and wiped the floor. Suiren was a far more fearsome force than the head lady-in-waiting of the Jade Pavilion. Maybe age really did bring wiles.

"If you feel you haven't enough space in your room, maybe you could speak to Master Jinshi. We have more than enough rooms here. If you only ask, you might be surprised how accommodating he may turn out to be." Suiren sounded unusually cheerful.

Maomao wondered if that was true. After all, Jinshi had turned her request for a stable down flat.

"No, ma'am," she said now. "I could never turn a noble's residence into medicinal storage."

Suiren put a surprised hand to her mouth as she took a seat in a chair. "You don't look like the kind who would care, Xiaomao, but you always turn out to be so circumspect."

"I *am* only a lowborn young woman. No one is more surprised than I am to find me here."

"I can understand that. But . . ." Suiren got a distant look in her eyes. She was gazing out the window. Brief flurries of snow occasionally drifted down. "I urge you not to imagine that those who are highborn are fundamentally different creatures from you. None of us, however princely or however poor, know what will happen in our lives. That by itself unites us across every divide."

"You think so, ma'am?"

"I very much do," Suiren said with a smile, standing up from her chair. Then she came over hauling a large basket stuffed to the brim with trash. "And now it's time to work, Xiaomao. Do you think you could go throw this away for me?" Suiren wore a placid smile on her face, but the basket came up almost to Maomao's chest and looked very heavy.

Not just any random maid or manservant could be trusted to dispose of the trash in Jinshi's building. There were any number of people out there who would all too eagerly rifle through it to find anything that might afford a strategic advantage.

"The way to the trash pit goes past the doctor's office," Suiren said. "If all you do is go past it, I certainly don't mind."

That's not a favor, that's torture, Maomao thought with a frown, but nonetheless she hefted the basket onto her back, wobbling under the weight.

Maomao studied the stark indentations the straps of the basket had left on her shoulders, wondering just how much had been in there. Well! At least no one would be able to root through this particular noble's garbage now. It had all turned to ash. As for Maomao, all she could do was sigh at this important personage's ignorance of how much trouble he caused for those around him.

She was just about to go back when something caught her eye. *Is that what I think it is?!* Not far from the trash pit was some kind of building—from the neighing of horses, she suspected it was a stable. Grass, natural and untended, grew nearby. Except clearly, not everything there was forage . . .

Maomao gave a furtive glance in one direction, then the other, then dashed over and fell upon her target. To the untrained eye, it looked like simple withered grass. It smelled like a plant wasted by winter. Pull it out of the ground, and it showed long roots, along with a small but unmistakable tuber-like growth.

It was a wild plant frequently used to flavor medicine; in and of itself, it wasn't that unusual. What *was* unusual was to find it growing seemingly at random among a patch of other grasses.

Lots of fertilizer out here behind the stables, maybe? Maomao thought. But it just didn't seem like the sort of thing that would normally grow in a place like this.

Maomao looked around again. There was a modest hill nearby, on which was growing a profusion of herbs that looked distinctly medicinal. She put down her basket and ran for the mound.

She found a field of soft, rich soil brimming with flowers and odd-smelling herbs—these were no ordinary kitchen produce. They were still a bit colorless, on account of the season, but it was more than enough to make Maomao's eyes shine. Elated, she started to inspect each plant, trying to determine what it was—when the sound of footsteps, muffled by the soft earth, approached her.

"And what are you doing?" asked a most irritated voice. Maomao, still crouching on the ground, looked back to discover the tall woman standing behind her. In one hand she held a small basket; in the other, a sickle. Suirei, that was what the doctor had called her.

Shit. Maomao knew she had to look suspicious here. She decided to try to explain herself, keenly aware that the sickle could come down on her at any moment. "Please, ma'am, there's no cause for alarm. I haven't picked anything yet."

"Meaning you were about to, may I take it?" Suirei remained impressively calm. The sickle wasn't swung at Maomao, but instead was set gently on the ground along with the basket.

"Any farmer would want to inspect such a fine field," Maomao said.

"And what palace is peopled with farmers?"

She had Maomao there—but Maomao had thought it was a clever line. Where there were fields, there had to be farmers, right? Unfortunately, Suirei didn't find this logic as coherent or compelling as Maomao did.

Instead, the woman sighed. "I'm not here to hang you by your thumbs or something. This garden isn't technically allowed, anyway. A word of warning, though—the doctor shows up here periodically, so I wouldn't recommend making too many visits." She started pulling weeds as she spoke.

"So he let you be in charge of this place?"

"Sort of. He lets me plant what I like, anyway."

To Maomao's ears, Suirei sounded notably disinterested. Maomao didn't exactly overflow with enthusiasm herself. It looked like she'd found a kindred spirit. Suirei, though, seemed to have enough social sense to join the other court ladies when they picked on Maomao.

"And what *do* you like to plant?"

Suirei looked at Maomao without saying anything—but only for a second. Then she returned her gaze to the ground. "A medicine to revive the dead."

That was enough to get Maomao's heart pounding. She nearly grabbed Suirei and demanded to know what she was talking about, but rationality got hold of her at the last moment.

Suirei eyed Maomao and then said the cruelest thing imaginable: "I'm kidding." Maomao didn't reply, but the devastation must have been clear on her face, for the other woman gave a humorless laugh. "Word has it you're an apothecary."

Maomao wondered where she'd heard that but nodded. Suirei was once again expressionless as she plucked dead leaves. She left any thick roots, trimming the leaves with the sickle. "I wonder just how good an apothecary," she said, and Maomao, if she wasn't mistaken, heard a barb in Suirei's voice.

She looked at Suirei and replied only: "Good question."

"Mm," Suirei said, and stood. "I plant morning glories here every year. It's not quite the season yet, though." Then she collected her herbs and went back down the hill.

A medicine to revive the dead . . .

If such a thing existed, Maomao would do anything to get her hands on it. Humanity had sought a means of immortality virtually throughout its history. Could such a thing exist? Maomao believed, in fact, that the possibility couldn't be ruled out—but she shook her head at the idea that it would just happen to be a *drug* that brought people back to life.

She looked longingly at the field for a moment as the part of her that wanted to help herself to a little something and the part that knew she shouldn't argued back and forth. In the end, the mental dispute only made her late getting back.

Suiren's discipline was unassuming but severe: Maomao found herself cleaning and polishing right up to the ceiling beams.

CHAPTER 11

Chance or Something More

Maomao was cleaning a hallway somewhere in the outer court, as she so often did, when she heard a very strange tale.

A large figure came up to her in a mild panic. On closer inspection, it turned out to be the big dog, Lihaku.

"What's going on?" Maomao asked, setting down her cloth. The burly military officer wouldn't have a reason to come to Jinshi's office—unless he needed something from Maomao.

"No time for chitchat! There's trouble!"

"And what might that be?" If he'd come all this way, it must be serious. Despite the way he sometimes acted, Lihaku hardly had time to kill.

"You remember the fire at that storehouse? Later we found out that on the exact same day, there was a burglary at another one." He scratched his head as he spoke. "The only thing I can think is that someone was using the fire as a diversion."

Maomao crossed her arms: so that was the story. "What was stolen, if I may ask?"

At that, Lihaku fell into an uncomfortable silence. He tapped her on the shoulder and gestured, apparently wanting to go somewhere they wouldn't be overheard. Maomao let him lead her out of the gallery and toward the garden. Lihaku squatted in the shade of some trees, tapped his finger against the side of his nose conspiratorially, and said, "Some ritual implements disappeared."

"Ritual implements?" A very strange thing to steal, Maomao thought.

"Yeah. Several seem to have vanished, but I'm afraid we don't know exactly what." Lihaku gave a helpless shake of his head.

"You don't know what was in there? Was the keeper of the storehouse that careless?"

"No, it's not like that . . . There's no one in charge of the place right now. An important official who'd been closely involved with it died last year, and that turned everything on its head."

A matter of new superiors shuffling things around, perhaps.

"Perhaps you could ask whoever oversaw it before him, then?"

"There's a wrinkle in that too. See, he's in no shape to come back to work. He came down with food poisoning not long ago, and . . . well, he's still unconscious." Lihaku heaved a sigh as if to emphasize what dire straits he was in.

But the words *food poisoning* set Maomao's memory working. Hadn't there been a case of that just after the fire? In fact, almost simultaneously with it . . .

"That wouldn't happen to be the clerk-gourmand, would it?" she asked.

Lihaku's eyes went wide. "How do you know about that?"

"It's a long story."

The fire, the theft, and the indisposition of the clerk: could they all be one giant coincidence? On some level, it was always possible—but it seemed deeply unlikely. Something else Lihaku had said got her attention too.

"You mentioned an important official who passed away last year. What kind of person was he?"

Lihaku put a finger to his forehead and grunted. "I remember he was some old fart who always had a stick up his—er, I mean, always stood on principle. What *was* his name? Blast, it's on the tip of my tongue! I know he was real big into sweets . . ."

"Perhaps you're thinking of Master Kounen," Maomao said, remembering the person Jinshi had told her about the year before. A strait-laced, sweet-toothed official who had died from an overdose of salt.

"Yes! That was it! Wait . . . you know about him too?"

"It's a *long* story."

Lihaku's surprise was understandable. Maomao was by no means enough of an optimist to assume all these coincidences could be, well, mere coincidence. Each looked like an accident in isolation. But there were no guarantees that what appeared to be an accident was in fact accidental, as the case of the blowfish had proven. Was it possible that all of these incidents were deliberate, aimed at some larger goal?

Maomao looked at Lihaku. "I'm sorry, Master Lihaku, but what does this have to do with me?"

"Right! That's what I came here to talk to you about!" He rifled through a bag and pulled out something that turned out to be the ivory pipe Maomao had discovered in the burned storehouse. She'd delivered it to him not long ago, after cleaning it up and rebuilding it. He'd said he would see that it made its way back to the storehouse watchman, but he still had it.

"It's not my fault," Lihaku said now. "The watchman told me to keep it. Said he didn't want it anymore."

The guard had been dismissed after blame for the storehouse fire had fallen on him. Maomao had taken the pipe to be a potentially expensive purchase, but evidently it had been a gift. Someone was very generous, she thought.

"He said one of the ladies of the outer court gave it to him. Doesn't that strike you as strange? Why would one of them give something like this to a random watchman?"

"It might make sense, depending on the person." When courtesans received a gift from a particularly despised customer, they would promptly sell it for cash, or otherwise give it to someone else. But Maomao could think of another possibility too. "Maybe she knew that he would want to put such a rich gift to use right away."

Not everyone would have that impulse, but many would. And if that was the mystery woman's objective . . . she must have guessed the course of events: The fire would break out. People would come running. Security would be lighter elsewhere—the perfect time for sneaking.

Lihaku, anticipating what Maomao was about to ask, said, "Unfortunately, he said he couldn't see the face of the woman who gave him the pipe. It was too dark."

A woman walking around in the dark? That was strange too. Even the palace wasn't a place where a woman should be walking alone at night. The storehouse watchman had found the woman doing just that, and he had been so kind as to accompany her for her safety. She'd thanked him by giving him the pipe. It had been cold, and the woman's face had been hidden by a tall collar.

"He did say that she seemed unusually tall for a lady, though, and that she smelled faintly of medicine."

"Medicine?"

"Don't worry, I know it wasn't you. He said *tall*. But I just wondered. Sound like anyone you know?"

Although he might look like a lummox, Lihaku could be pretty sharp. *Can't exactly claim I've got no idea,* Maomao thought. Maybe she should simply tell him exactly what she suspected. But then her father's mantra ran through her mind: *don't draw conclusions based on assumptions.* Maomao thought the matter over and decided on a compromise.

"Has anything else unusual happened besides the accidents and incidents you mentioned?"

"That sounds like a portentous question and all, but I wouldn't even have connected this many dots without your hints," Lihaku said, crossing his arms. "Are you saying there's something else I should be investigating?"

"Possibly. Or possibly not."

"Which is it?" Lihaku said, exasperated.

Maomao crouched down and grabbed a stick off the ground, with which she proceeded to draw a circle in the dirt. "Two things often happen coincidentally." She drew another circle, partially overlapping the first. "Three things may happen and still be chance." She added another circle. "But don't you agree that at some point, it stops being coincidence and becomes deliberate?"

She filled in the segment at the center of her three overlapping circles. "Suppose this lady of the outer court—if that's what she is— stands at the nexus of these deliberate coincidences."

"I get it!" Lihaku clapped his hands. As for Maomao, an image of Suirei flashed through her mind, but she felt that was neither here nor there. "You're smarter than you look," Lihaku said, slapping her on the shoulder with a huge grin.

"But you're just as wildly strong as you look, Master Lihaku, so please do be careful."

Lihaku must have felt a chill as Maomao glared at him. He turned around to discover she wasn't the only one giving him the stink eye.

"I'm glad to see you're having fun." The voice was gorgeous, but thick with sarcasm. Lihaku took an intimidated step back when he saw who it belonged to.

"I'm not particularly having fun at all," Maomao said.

Jinshi stood watching them closely, half-hidden by the shade of the tree. Gaoshun stood behind him, his brow wrinkled in his customary, perpetual expression of chagrin.

The big mutt promptly went home, leaving Maomao to deal with Jinshi, who was acting put out for some reason.

"You seem quite friendly with that man."

"Do I?" She poured tea from a small teapot she had put on to boil. A ceramic cup might have made for a better-tasting drink, but most of the dishware Jinshi used was silver. Maomao still wasn't entirely clear on Jinshi's place in the political hierarchy. He was more than a eunuch who flitted around the inner palace. He had real business here in the outer court as well.

"What is he, some kind of military officer?"

"Indeed, sir, as you could see. He came to talk to me about something that was bothering him."

Maomao placed snacks to go with the tea on the desk. She couldn't be completely sure whether Jinshi might have a stake in what Lihaku had told her. After all, Kounen was somehow connected. So Maomao offered: "Shall I tell you exactly what he was asking about?"

Jinshi only sipped his tea in silence.

When Maomao had finished a detailed explanation, Jinshi closed his eyes and frowned, looking faintly distressed. "A tangled web indeed."

"Yes, sir."

Jinshi hadn't touched the snacks. Gaoshun was standing by the entrance of the office, looking as disturbed as his master.

"And how do you think it's all related?" Jinshi asked.

"That I don't know," she said honestly. She had no idea what any of this had been intended to accomplish. Any of the cases might have been accidental. The one thing that was certain was that as long as they looked like they *could* be accidents, it was unlikely that anyone would put the pieces together. "Personally, I think they look less like a single grand scheme and more like a series of traps, the success of any one of which would serve the purposes of the one who set them."

Jinshi took another sip of tea in response. The mouthful emptied his cup, so Maomao went to boil more.

"I must agree," Jinshi said. "And that means there's a possibility that there are other traps."

"We can't be certain." Even Maomao had only her speculation to go on. If somebody told her definitively that it had all been a series of coincidences, she could only have nodded and accepted it.

"Hmph. Not feeling too eager about this one?"

"Eager, sir?" she said. *And? It's not like I stick my nose into these things out of personal interest.* She just took note of what was going on around her. There were too many people all too prepared to involve her in their own risky business, that was the problem. Maomao would have been perfectly happy to live a quiet life as an apothecary: sitting on her veranda sipping tea and doing her medicinal experiments. "I'm only a maid," she said. "I simply do the work I'm given."

"Hmph," Jinshi said again, apparently finding this answer lackluster. He played half-consciously with a brush in his hand. He had pushed the snacks to one side of his desk. Maybe he wasn't interested in them. Maomao thought he looked uncommonly youthful. "How about this, then?" he said. He called Gaoshun over with a grin and whispered in his ear. Whatever he said, Gaoshun was clearly not enthusiastic about it.

"Master Jinshi . . ." he said.

"You heard me. Get everything ready, please."

Gaoshun nodded without conviction, and meanwhile Jinshi dunked the brush he was playing with in some ink, then began writing on a piece of paper in fluid, flowing motions. "When I was making the rounds of the trading merchants the other day, I heard tell of a very interesting item. I believe this was the name."

He pulled up the paper with a flourish and displayed it to Maomao. Her eyes immediately began to sparkle.

Written on the paper were two characters, *niu huang: calculus bovis.* Ox bezoar.

"Would you like it?"

"I would!"

Almost before she knew what she was doing, Maomao rushed up to—and then *onto*—Jinshi's desk.

Calculus bovis was a medicine, a gallstone from a cow or ox. Supposedly, only one in a thousand cattle produced one; it was considered among the rarest and most valuable medicinal supplements. A poor apothecary from the pleasure district would be lucky ever to see one in her lifetime. It was a mouthwatering prospect.

And this eunuch was saying—what? Would he actually give her one? Really and truly?

Jinshi drew back slightly from Maomao, who had begun to lean closer and closer to him. She didn't realize what she was doing until Gaoshun tugged on her sleeve, bringing her back to reality. She slowly climbed down off the desk and straightened her skirt.

"*There's* that motivation."

"Can I really have it?" Maomao gave Jinshi a cautious look, but he now appeared somewhat more adult than before. Maomao recognized this as the alluring gaze he frequently turned on maidservants in the rear palace.

"That depends on how hard you work. Let me start by giving you all the details." Jinshi began wadding up the paper and threw it into the trash basket, the familiar honeyed smile on his face. Maomao couldn't have cared less about the smile, but he was offering to reward her with something she desperately wanted if she did good work, and that was all she needed to know.

"Understood. You need only tell me what you wish, Master Jinshi." And then Maomao cleared away the teacup and the untouched snacks.

CHAPTER 12

The Ritual

As instructed, Maomao shut herself up in the archives the very next afternoon. The building contained reams of public records and had a distinctly musty smell. A pale-faced official brought Maomao armloads of scrolls. He was the only other person she saw there; the posting seemed to be something of a sinecure.

It wouldn't hurt him to get out in the sun every once in a while, though, she thought.

She unrolled one scroll after another, each made of excellent paper. They listed in brief both accidents and crimes that had occurred in the palace complex over the past several years. This wasn't confidential information. The scrolls were quite public, and could be viewed by anyone who requested them.

She looked through them with interest. Most of the cases were mundane accidents, but a few piqued her curiosity. Cases of food poisoning, say . . .

She'd expected such cases to spike during the summer, but there were a surprising number in winter as well. Autumn could bring its own troubles, with people eating unidentified or inappropriate mushrooms.

Maomao asked the official for another bundle of scrolls. She'd expected him to treat her as a nuisance, but he seemed quite pleased to finally have an opportunity to do some work. It looked like he wasn't here just because he liked to kill time. He was clearly curious about what Maomao was researching, occasionally stealing little glances as she worked.

Maomao ignored him, flipping through the sheets until she found what she wanted: a description of the recent food-poisoning incident. Maomao stopped when she saw the government organ with which the victim had been associated.

The Board of Rites?

That, at least, was what his official title suggested to her. Maomao's recollection, such as it was, was that the Board of Rites was responsible for education and diplomacy. Maybe, she thought, she would be more sure if she had studied harder for the court ladies' exam.

"Having trouble with anything?" the pallid official asked her. Anything to pass the time, perhaps.

Maomao decided that now was not the time to be embarrassed by her ignorance. "Yes," she said. "I'm not quite sure what this title signifies." She suspected the admission made her sound absolutely brainless.

"Ah. This person oversees the observance of ritual," the man said, sounding rather pleased to be providing this knowledge.

"Did you say ritual?"

Right, the food-poisoning victim had been in charge of ritual implements, hadn't he?

"Indeed. I'd be happy to fetch a more detailed book on the subject for you, if you'd like," the official said, not unkindly. Maomao, though, hardly heard him; the gears were spinning in her brain. Suddenly, she smacked the long table in front of her. The man just about jumped out of his skin.

"Do you have anything to write on?" Maomao demanded.

"Er, y-yes . . ."

Maomao went rapidly through the register of incidents she'd been examining. She took down exact positions and terms of office.

When coincidence piled upon coincidence, it suggested something deliberate. And if she laid out all these seeming coincidences, the place where they overlapped would tell her where to look.

"Observance of ritual . . . Ritual implements . . ."

Rituals as such weren't uncommon. All manner of rites were observed throughout the year. The keeping of minor observances could be done by a village chief, but the most important ceremonies were performed by the Imperial family. The implements that had been stolen would have been for at least a mid-level ceremony, if not something even more important.

A mid-level ceremony, Maomao thought to herself. She remembered Jinshi performing a purification rite. If she had a question about something related to rituals, it might be quickest to ask the eunuch.

"Are you interested in ritual matters?" The official, who was turning out to be not only bored but in fact quite friendly, came over with some kind of large drawing.

"Huh . . ." Maomao said. It was a fairly detailed illustration of the ritual grounds. An altar stood in the center, with a banner fluttering above it. A large pot was placed at the foot of the altar, perhaps to hold a fire.

"Rather unusual place, isn't it?" the official said.

"So it is . . ."

It certainly looked elegant and imposing. The banner appeared to have some kind of writing on it—did they change it each time there was an observance?

Seems like a lot of trouble to take it up and down every time, thought Maomao, ever practical. The banner was up high enough that even getting a ladder up to it would be a headache.

"They've got a special contraption there," the official said. "A large beam hung from the ceiling. It can be raised and lowered so they can write the appropriate ritual inscription on the banner."

"You seem to know quite a bit about this," Maomao said, studying the pale man.

"I daresay I do. I used to do more dignified work than marking time in the archives. But, I'm ashamed to admit, I must have slipped up at the wrong moment or offended the wrong person, because I earned myself exile to the stacks."

He had, he added, formerly been assigned to the Board of Rites himself, which, Maomao realized, explained why he'd been so interested in what she was doing. And then the official said something that really got her attention: "I was concerned whether it would be strong enough at first. I'm so glad there haven't been any problems."

"You were concerned whether *what* would be strong enough?"

"The beam. The system that holds it up. That's a huge thing. I hardly dare imagine the tragedy that would result if it fell. But no sooner had I raised the issue than I found myself banished to these archives."

Maomao stared at the picture in silence. If the beam did come loose from the ceiling, the one in greatest danger would be the person directly below it: the officiant of the ceremony. Potentially a very important person indeed.

And he's worried about how strong the system is, Maomao thought. In order to raise and lower the beam, it would have to be attached to something. And if the fasteners were to break . . .

How strong it is . . .

There was a fire pot in the immediate vicinity. Maomao was suddenly seized by the question of what ritual implements had been stolen. She slapped the table again, producing another startled reaction from the official. She turned to him where he stood stiff as a board and said, "I'm sorry, but when is the next ritual observance?! And where's the place shown in this picture?!"

"It's a structure called the Altar of the Sapphire Sky, on the western edge of the outer court. And as for when it will be used . . ." The official flipped through a calendar, scratching his ear. "Why, there's an observance today."

Before the man had finished speaking, Maomao was dashing out of the building, without even straightening up the scrolls.

The Altar of the Sapphire Sky, to the west, she thought, trying to organize her thoughts as she ran. This plan, she suspected, had been brewing for a long time. Prepared with the understanding that some individual parts of it might be foiled, but if just a few could be made to overlap, it would provide the opening the plotter wanted. *I'm still just guessing.* Nothing more than that. But it was dizzying to imagine the consequences if her guess was right.

Soon, she spied a round pagoda. Similar buildings flanked it to either side, and there was a row of officials in front of it. From their clothing, she guessed a ritual was going on even now.

"Hey, you!" one of them called. "What do you think you're doing?"

That was only to be expected when a filthy maid tried to race past them. Maomao gave a cluck of her tongue. She didn't have time for this. If she could have gone for Jinshi or Gaoshun, they might have solved the problem for her, but they were going to be out all day.

"Let me through, please," she said.

"Absolutely not. A ritual is being celebrated," said a warrior holding a nasty-looking war club. He glowered at Maomao, but she could hardly blame him for simply wanting to do his job. Instead, she cursed herself for not being a smooth talker.

"It's an emergency. You have to let me inside."

"A maid like you would dare impose herself on the holy rites?"

He had her there. Maomao was nothing but a maid. She had no authority. If this man let a girl like her into the ceremonial venue just because she asked him to, he might as well kiss his head goodbye.

Unfortunately, Maomao couldn't back down either.

Maybe nothing will happen, she thought. But if it did, it would be too late for I-told-you-sos. By the time we realize something irrevocable has happened, it's always already too late.

The soldier stood head and shoulders taller than her, but she looked him full in the face. The officials nearby were starting to murmur and look at them.

"I'm not here simply to besmirch the ritual," Maomao said. "Someone's life is in danger. You have to stop the ceremony!"

One of the nearby officials spoke up. "That's not for you to decide. If you have an opinion you'd like to share, we have a suggestion box." He was openly mocking Maomao, lowly servant that she was.

"You would never see it in time. Let me through!"

"No!"

They were never going to get anywhere arguing like children. Perhaps it would have been the mature thing for Maomao to acknowledge that she was never going to get through and simply back down. But she didn't have it in her. Instead, a sarcastic smile worked its way over her face. "There's a fatal flaw in the construction of that altar. And I believe someone may have taken advantage of it. If you don't let me through this minute, believe me, you'll regret it. Dear me, but I tremble to think what will happen to you when they find out I warned you and you didn't listen!" She put her hand to her cheek in an exaggerated expression of surprise. Then she said: "Wait . . . I see. Is *that* what's going on here?" She smacked her fist into her open palm as if it all made sense now. Her smile turned mean. "You *want* whatever it is to happen. You're delaying me here because you're in league with whoever booby-trapped the—"

She was interrupted by a dull *thud* from her own head. Almost before she knew what had happened, she was lying on the ground, her vision blurring.

Got to stay conscious, she thought, but wishing wasn't going to make it so. She heard the voice of the soldier who had struck her, but he sounded as if he were a great distance away, and she couldn't make out what he was saying. Well, at least she knew she had their attention.

Any soldier would be angry about abuse like that from a little girl like her. Angry enough to raise a hand without thinking, perhaps.

She couldn't complain; she'd brought it on herself. But if she passed out now, it would all be over.

Slowly, Maomao pulled herself to a sitting position. Her ear burned, and her vision was still blurry. As color filtered back into her world, she perceived the soldier, his arm still raised, his companions restraining him.

Thought starting a fight might help, but . . . no good . . .

There hadn't been enough of a commotion to interrupt the ceremony. She could still hear music from the direction of the altar. The show was going on.

At last she dragged her body onto its feet. A few red specks stippled the ground in front of her. *Nosebleed,* she thought. Not something to worry about. The blow seemed to have caught her on the ear, but it only burned—there was no pain. Maomao pressed a thumb to one side of her nose and blew the blood out. A murmur ran through the assembled officials. Maomao realized maybe it was inappropriate to shed blood at the site of a ritual, but she hardly had time to apologize.

"Are you quite satisfied?" she said. With her still-fuzzy vision, she couldn't see exactly what response she got. She only heard the general buzz of voices around her. There was no time for these games. There was something Maomao had to do.

Her voice went up an octave: "Let me through!"

I have to get in there!

It would be too late, once everything was over. Too late. If she didn't get in there right now . . .

I'll never get my ox bezoar!

Her head was spinning and her vision was still hazy, but that thought gave her the motivation to stay standing.

Maomao looked hard at those around her. "I'm not asking you to stop the ceremony. Only to let me by. Say a rat snuck in when you weren't looking." The current emperor was a compassionate man. She didn't think anyone's head would roll for this. Except possibly hers. She could only beg Jinshi to intercede on her behalf. Or at the very least, to let her die by poison. "What will you do if something *does* happen, and you detained me here? I know that has to be someone important inside celebrating the ritual. Then you *will* pay with your lives!"

She didn't know who was officiating, only that everything about the situation implied it was someone highly ranked indeed.

A few of the guards looked at each other as if shaken by her words, but it was clear they weren't all about to step aside.

"Why should we listen to a nobody little girl like you?" the soldier asked.

That was the real question, wasn't it? Maomao had no answer, but only stood staring daggers at the man.

It was then that they heard a swift *clack-clack* of shoes. "Perhaps you would listen to *me*, then?" someone said, almost jokingly. Maomao could practically hear the smile in the voice. And she knew who it belonged to.

The soldier blocking Maomao's way took a half step back. The assembled officials had gone pale, as if confronted with something they'd hoped never to see.

Maomao didn't look behind her. It was all she could do to keep her scowl from getting any deeper. Her temples were already starting to twitch.

"Anyhow, nobody little girl or no, I'm not sure I can condone hitting a young woman. Look—she's injured. Who did it? Fess up!" A cold edge entered the voice. Everyone looked unconsciously at the man with the war club. His face had gone tight.

"For a start," the voice resumed, "why don't you do as the girl says? I'll take full responsibility for whatever happens."

Whoever was behind her, he couldn't have had better timing if he'd tried. Maomao gritted her teeth. *Can't think about that now,* she thought. She still didn't look back. Instead, she cast one final glance at the people around her, and then she ran for the altar.

She decided she didn't care who the voice belonged to.

The aromas of smoke and incense drifted through the arena. The plinking of musical instruments was accompanied by the flapping of the banner that hung from the beam on the ceiling. The prayer of the celebrants was written on it in flowing, beautiful letters, displayed aloft in the hopes that it might reach heaven.

The appearance of a grimy young girl in this sacred space set the crowd mumbling. *I must look awful,* Maomao thought. She'd dirtied her uniform running, and now her face was streaked with dried blood from her nose. She was determined to have a nice, long bath when this was all over. She wouldn't be caught dead using the bath in Jinshi's residence, though. Maybe she could wheedle Gaoshun into letting her use his.

That was, of course, provided her head was still attached to her body by the time she got to that point.

At the far end of a scarlet carpet stood a man in black. On his head was a distinctive cap of office hung with pendants of beads. He was intoning something in a loud, clear voice.

The huge fire pot stood in front of him, burning brightly. And there, over his head, was the beam with the flapping banner. And securing the beam to the ceiling was . . .

Maomao thought she heard a distinct creaking sound. It had to be her imagination; there was no way she could have heard it at this distance. Nonetheless, she kept moving. She could feel the soft material of the carpet under her feet as she drove toward him as fast as she could.

The officiant noticed Maomao and turned. She paid that no mind, but flung herself against him, wrapping her arms around his stomach and pulling him to the ground.

At almost the same instant, there was an earsplitting crash. A hot, sharp sensation shot up her leg. She looked back to discover a large metal beam pinning her leg. It had managed to cut the skin.

That'll need stitches, she thought. She reached for the folds of her robe, where she always carried some medicine and simple medical supplies—but a large hand caught hers and held it. She looked up, and her vision was filled with the beads dangling from the hat. Somewhere beyond them floated a pair of eyes as dark as obsidian.

"And how do we find ourselves like this?" The voice sounded almost celestial.

The beam that had fallen from the ceiling lay on the ground. Had the owner of the voice been standing directly under it when it came down, he would certainly have been killed instantly.

"Master Jinshi . . . Can I . . . Can I have my bezoar now?" Maomao asked of the gorgeous eunuch who, she now discovered, was also the officiant at this ceremony. But why, she wondered, was he here at all?

"A fine thing to think of at a moment like this," Jinshi said, his face puckering as if he'd bitten into something sour. His large hand brushed Maomao's face. The pad of his thumb traced its way along her cheek. "Look at your face." He winced. Why would he do that?

Maomao was more interested in fixing the problem at hand. Or foot. "Would you let me stitch my leg up?" It didn't hurt so much as it burned. She twisted to try to get a look at the wound, but instead her body shuddered.

"H-hey, now—!"

Jinshi's voice sounded far away. *Uh-oh,* she thought. It was that whack on the head.

Her strength abruptly left her. Her vision grayed out again, and then Jinshi was shaking her, shouting something, and she couldn't tell what, but oh, how she wished he would be quiet.

CHAPTER 13

Thornapple

It felt pleasant, as if her body was rocking gently. A faint smell of fine incense tickled her nose. The swaying made her feel like a child in a cradle, but after a moment it ceased, and she felt she was being laid down on something soft.

Then time passed, but she didn't know how much.

Where am I? Maomao thought upon waking. As her eyes fluttered open, she found a glorious canopy above her head. She recognized it—because she'd had to dust it every day.

She smelled the incense again, the finest sandalwood. This was Jinshi's bedroom, and that would make what Maomao was sleeping in his bed.

"Ah, you're awake," said a calm, gentle voice. It came from an attendant in the first flush of old age, reclining on a couch nearby. She stood and took a carafe of water from a round table, pouring liberally into a cup. "Master Jinshi brought you here, did you know? He couldn't stand to leave you to rest in the medical office." Suiren chuckled and passed the cup to Maomao.

Maomao brought it to her lips. She was in sleeping clothes. (When had that happened?) A sharp pain shot through her head, and meanwhile her leg felt like it might cramp.

"Now, don't strain yourself. You needed fifteen stitches."

Maomao rolled back the covers to find a bandage wrapped around her left leg. The dull quality of the pain suggested she'd been given some kind of analgesic. She touched her head: more bandages.

"I'm sorry to ask this when you've just woken up, but may I bring the others to see you now? We can give you a few minutes if you'd like to change clothes."

Maomao saw that her regular outfit was folded neatly beside the bed. She nodded her understanding.

Suiren led in Jinshi and Gaoshun, accompanied by Basen. Maomao had successfully changed into her day clothes. She welcomed them but remained seated. A breach of etiquette, she knew, but Suiren had given her approval and Maomao decided, in this case, to take it.

Basen was the first to open his mouth: "What in the world is going on here?" He was staring straight at Maomao, looking unusually angry.

"Basen," Gaoshun said sternly. The soldier only clucked his tongue and took a seat. Jinshi positioned himself on the couch, his expression carefully neutral.

His master was in considerable danger, after all, Maomao thought. But she had done nothing to warrant being yelled at, so she simply sipped her tepid water, her expression as cool as her drink.

Jinshi looked at Maomao, his hands stashed in his sleeves. "I'd like you to explain a few things for me. What brought you to that place at that time? How did you know that beam was going to fall? Tell me."

"Very well, sir." Maomao set down the water and took a breath. "First of all, these events lie at the confluence of a series of coincidences. When enough such coincidences occur at once, one might suspect that they aren't happenstance at all. Thus perhaps this was not accident, but incident."

Maomao already knew of a number of related cases. There was Kounen's death the year before. Then that fire had broken out in the storehouse, while at the same time, ritual implements had been stolen. Finally, the very official who oversaw those implements swiftly came down with food poisoning.

"So you believe somebody caused all of these things deliberately?"

"Yes, sir, I do. And I believe there's one further connection, which I had previously overlooked."

Maomao didn't know exactly what had been stolen, but it would have been something appropriate to the celebration of an important ritual. Something no doubt produced by a master craftsman. And she happened to have heard of one of those recently . . .

"You're not saying . . . the metalworker's family?" Jinshi said, startled. Maomao knew he was quick.

"That's right," she said.

She had a fairly good idea of what had killed the old craftsman. Lead poisoning, she suspected. It would be easy enough to dismiss it as an occupational hazard, but there was always the possibility that it was something more. It was conceivable that this, too, was deliberate. Give him some wine and a lead drinking cup as a gift, then wait for him to waste away. That would be one way to do it, anyway. There were others.

"The old man didn't personally teach his apprentices—his sons—about his most secret discovery. It's possible the art would have gone with him to his grave, a riddle no one else ever solved. Someone might have found that very convenient."

This would imply that whoever it was already understood the technique in question. They wouldn't have to know exactly how it worked, just what it did.

"So you believe the stolen implements were produced by the dead craftsman?" Jinshi asked, but Maomao shook her head.

"No, sir. In fact, I believe the opposite: that the stolen implements were *replaced* with something produced by that craftsman."

Maomao got paper and a brush, and quickly sketched out a picture. In the center was a large altar accompanied by an iron fire pot, while a beam dangled from the ceiling above. Ropes were looped around either end of the beam. They passed through pulleys on the ceiling and were secured to the floor with metal fasteners.

"If several ritual implements disappeared, perhaps we can presume that various other parts went with them. Elaborate pieces, I would suspect."

"That seems like a likely possibility," Gaoshun said, but he didn't sound completely sure. He probably didn't have all the information on the subject—this was outside of Jinshi's jurisdiction, after all.

"As I recall, the wires that held the beam up ran directly past the fire pot. Suppose the fasteners that held them in place were made to give way when heated . . ."

"Ridiculous," Basen said, snorting. "We would have known about that long ago. They would never use anything that might catch fire near the altar."

"And yet the beam did fall," Maomao replied. "Precisely because the fasteners broke."

Jinshi agreed with Basen: "They shouldn't break, no matter how hot they get. They're made to stand up to a little heat!"

"They broke," Maomao reiterated. "Or more specifically, they melted."

Everyone looked at her.

Maomao decided to divulge what she had discovered about the deceased craftsman's most secret art. "Many metals by themselves melt only at a high temperature. But by mixing them together, believe it or not, it's possible to create a substance that melts at a lower heat."

The technique had been around for a very long time, but such substances still demanded substantial heat to melt. That was the crux of the old craftsman's discovery: the ratio he had perfected melted the metal at a considerably lower temperature than usual. It would be enough, for example, if the metal were to be near a burning fire pot . . .

Silence descended on the room. The only sound was Suiren, blithely preparing tea.

The builders of the altar must have sworn up and down that the beam on the ceiling would never, ever fall. Otherwise such a construct would never have been approved. Important people stood under that beam to perform ceremonies, after all. If Maomao hadn't connected the dots, there was a very real chance that Jinshi would be dead right now. Not that she had ever expected it to be him she found standing there.

Just who is this guy? she asked herself. But she felt her station was nowhere near high enough to actually ask the question aloud, so she stayed quiet. Besides, she suspected that knowing the answer would only lead to more trouble.

She thought it seemed most reasonable to assume there was some connection, however remote, among all these things. Whether directly or indirectly, somebody was pulling the strings.

"I've said all I can say," she told them. Now that they had the information, she presumed Jinshi and the others would flush out whoever was involved. There was a chance Lihaku was already working on it.

The image of the tall lady flitted through Maomao's mind.

Nothing to do with me, she thought, slowly shaking her head and casting her eyes at the ground. Still, she couldn't shake the memory of the woman's detached expression: it was as if she no longer cared what happened, as long as *something* did. Maomao was still bothered, too, by what the woman had said to her when they were at that small patch of a garden.

A medicine to revive the dead . . .

They heard from Lihaku not long after. As Maomao had expected, his message concerned the lady, Suirei.

Suirei, it turned out, had taken poison and died.
Maomao was brought up short by this abrupt end to the wom-

an's life. Somehow, it didn't compute for her. When the Board of Justice—the officials responsible for keeping the law—had gathered their evidence and come bursting into Suirei's bedroom, they had discovered her collapsed on her bed. An overturned wine cup had been confirmed to contain poison. The doctor had been requested to perform the inquest and had duly certified the death.

As a criminal, Suirei was to be punished in her coffin as she could not be in life. After one day and one night, she was to be burned—that is to say, cremated. At the moment, she was awaiting her punishment in the same place as those who had died in jail.

Maomao didn't know if the Board of Justice had been able to move so quickly because Lihaku had done such a thorough job of gathering evidence, or if they had been pursuing this case for some time already. But ultimately, Suirei was the only conspirator named. Maomao wondered at this: *Did she really implement such an elaborate plot all by herself?* The idea lacked a certain persuasiveness.

Perhaps she was a scapegoat, then? Perhaps. But something more basic bothered Maomao. *Would Suirei really accept that?* They hadn't known each other very well. Maomao was not such a good reader of people that she could understand who a person really was in the span of such a short acquaintance. It was always possible that Suirei's apathetic manner sprang from a lack of will to live.

But still, something nagged at Maomao. It was the tone Suirei had taken when she spoke, as if she was testing Maomao. *No, I can't just go on intuition. I have to be sure.* But Maomao had no way to *be* sure; all she could do was go silently back to her daily chores. Such was a maid's lot in life.

Supposedly, anyway . . .

———◇———

B ut her curiosity got the better of her.
"Master Jinshi, I have a favor to ask of you." This was her open-ing gambit. "I'd like to speak with the doctor who performed the in-quest." At the mortuary, ideally.

Much to Jinshi's mystification, Maomao's face as she said this threatened to break into a grin.

T he mortuary was dim, pervaded by the stench of death. Accord-ing to the law of the land, no one who died in jail was permitted to be buried, but had to be cremated. Several coffins sat in a stack in one corner, housing criminals waiting to meet their fate. Suirei's cof-fin was slightly apart from the others, and a black-and-white tag hung on it.

Jinshi and Gaoshun were both present. Gaoshun didn't seem to like Jinshi being at the morgue, but if he wished to be there, Gaoshun couldn't stop him.

The doctor, when summoned, wore an expression as grim as the morgue itself. Maomao didn't blame him: a lady with whom he had been on good terms was dead, to be treated as a criminal, no less. *But is that all there is to it?* she wondered. If he was the one who had done the inquest, then he might know something no one else did. And Mao-mao had an inkling what it might be.

She got straight to the point: "The poison that woman drank. Did the ingredients by any chance include thornapple?" She studied the doctor from the chair where she sat. Gaoshun had made it ready for her on account of her injured leg. A hoe leaned against the wall beside the physician. This, too, Gaoshun had prepared at Maomao's request. Jinshi kept peeking at it as if he wondered what it was for, but it would have been time-consuming to explain, so she ignored him.

The doctor went pale almost before he could say anything. Still, he refused to be explicit, shaking his head instead. "The poison contained a number of ingredients, and it's hard to determine what any given one was. From the condition of the body, I would say the possibility is distinct, but I can't be certain." The answer was surprisingly confident and collected considering the way he had blanched at the suggestion. And he was telling the truth as far as it went, Maomao thought. She hadn't known what ingredients had been involved in the concoction either when she had evaluated it.

"There's a field on a small hill behind the stables, as I think you may know. Isn't there thornapple planted there? It may not be in season right now, but I can't imagine your pharmacy doesn't stock some of it."

Thornapple was highly poisonous, but in a measured dose it could act as an anesthetic. Suppose Suirei had taken some from the doctor's office.

The medical officer himself remained silent. This man was an excellent physician, Maomao had concluded. But not a gifted liar.

Thornapple had another name: the Uncanny Morning Glory. Maomao thought of Suirei's flat affect as she told Maomao she planted morning glories in that field.

"Let us find out for certain whether that particular toxin was involved, then," Maomao said. Then she picked up the hoe and advanced on the coffin with the black-and-white tag.

"What do you think you're doing?"

"*This!*"

She shoved the hoe under the coffin lid and pushed down on the shaft. One of the nails securing the lid popped up. The others watched in astonishment as Maomao worked. When all of the nails had been freed, they lifted the lid to discover a woman's corpse. It appeared to be some unfortunate nightwalker who had died under a bridge.

"It's . . . not Suirei?" the doctor said, peering into the coffin. He was clearly shaken; his hand trembled as he touched the box.

If he's pretending to be surprised, then he's a damn fine actor, Maomao thought.

"This woman, Suirei—you're quite certain she was dead?"

"Yes. The most untutored amateur could have seen it. She was still as lovely as she was when she was alive. But the heart behind that beauty was no longer beating." The doctor's face was still white. He had treated Suirei's corpse with care, Maomao suspected. She also suspected Suirei had counted on it. She'd known he wouldn't feel the need to chop her up to figure out exactly which poison she had taken.

"In other words, sir, she used you."

The medical officer went from pale to visibly seething. Just as it seemed he might lose control of himself and lunge at Maomao, Gaoshun grabbed him from behind.

Suirei had used thornapple in her poison. And she would have had access to a wide range of other medicaments as well, had she wished for them. If they checked the medical office's stores, it was likely they would find discrepancies with the listed inventory. The worst thing the

176

doctor could be accused of was a failure to keep close track of his supplies, Maomao supposed.

"Explain this," Jinshi said, narrowing his eyes. "Why isn't it the body of the condemned in there?"

"Because people would be suspicious if there wasn't *something* in the coffin, even if it is to be burned," Maomao said.

There were a number of coffins in the mortuary. Some of them were no doubt bodies destined to be burned, just like Suirei was supposed to have been. New coffins would presumably come with them, as well. Enough activity that a substitute corpse might be prepared and the two switched.

"Then what happened to Suirei's body? It can't have been carried away. Somebody would have noticed."

"It didn't have to be. She walked out on her own two feet."

Shock silenced Maomao's audience.

"Would you be so kind as to help me check those coffins over there?" she said to Gaoshun. She wanted to do it herself, but her leg was throbbing. Gaoshun didn't so much as flinch as he regarded the empty boxes. Alert as he was, he could tell something was off about one of the coffins; he pulled off the one above it to free the suspicious casket. The thing would normally have taken at least two men to move, but Gaoshun was strong enough to slide it aside by himself.

Maomao went to the coffin Gaoshun had freed, dragging her foot as she moved. "You can see a nail mark here," she observed. "I suspect this is the coffin Suirei was in. She lay here, awaiting rescue."

By the time her help arrived, Suirei was breathing again. After she was free, they would have switched the coffins, and then Suirei would have escaped the mortuary dressed like one of those who delivered the dead. People went out of their way to avoid paying attention to those who did such unclean work, and the uncommonly tall Suirei could easily have passed for a man.

Now Maomao asked the doctor, "Did you know there are medicines that can cause a person to appear dead?"

He opened his mouth, briefly stupefied, but finally he said, "I've heard tell. But I have no idea how to make them."

It would have been easy to dismiss the idea of a "resurrection medicine" as pure fantasy, but that wasn't wholly true. Certain substances existed that could produce an effect very much like coming back from the dead.

"I'm sorry to hear that," Maomao said, "for I don't know the details myself. However, I *have* heard that the ingredients include thornapple and blowfish poison."

Once—just once—her old man had told her a story. In a far country, he said, there was a medicine that could kill a person and then bring them back to life. It required several other toxins in addition to the thornapple and blowfish poison. These substances, each normally immensely poisonous, somehow neutralized each other, so that after a brief period the subject began to breathe again.

Naturally, Maomao's father had never made this drug, and he wasn't about to tell Maomao how to do it. Even the fact that she knew about the thornapple and the blowfish was only because she had secretly read her father's book. He'd evidently never imagined she could read the writing of that far, strange country. It was his own fault for underestimating her, or at least her obsession with poisons. She'd wheedled the occasional customer from those lands to teach her, and gradually assembled a working knowledge of the language. Unfortunately, her father discovered the subterfuge before she had read the entire thing, and he had simply burned the book.

"Do you really think Suirei would have used such an uncertain method?" the doctor asked.

"What did she have to lose? She was facing the death penalty. If I were in her shoes, it's a bet I would gladly take."

"I don't think it would take impending doom to make you do it." Why did Jinshi seem so eager to butt in? Maomao ignored him lest he derail the conversation.

"The fact that there's no body here suggests she won her bet. If no one had thought to look until after the cremation, her victory would have been complete."

I just didn't let her get away with it, Maomao thought. She smiled as she stared at the coffin. Inside was an anonymous woman, dead of who knew what. It didn't seem like much to smile about. *She was sloppy.* Maomao wasn't so soft as to bewail the death of a complete stranger. There were more important things to worry about.

The laughter bubbled up from deep in her belly, *heh heh heh.* Something was rising from within her, something that threatened to take over her entire body. "If she is alive, then I'd love to meet her," Maomao said to no one in particular. No, not so she could arrest the woman. Another reason entirely.

It was the wit Suirei must have had to make so many cases look like accidents, and the nerve to pull them off. And above all, she'd had the guts to wager her own life in hopes of fooling them all. What a waste it would be, Maomao thought, for such a person to simply kick the bucket. Yes, there had been casualties because of her, but Maomao couldn't deny what she was feeling.

The resurrection drug. I must *know how to make it!*

The thought almost overwhelmed her. Maybe that was why she was suddenly cackling. The three men in the room looked at her doubtfully.

At length Maomao cleared her throat and looked at the doctor. "Pardon me, but might I trouble you to sew up my leg? I seem to have reopened the wound." Maomao brushed her leg as if she hadn't been dragging it around all this time. The bandages were soaked with blood.

"Tell us that *before* you disappear into hilarity! Before!" Jinshi exclaimed, his agitated voice filling the mortuary.

CHAPTER 14

Gaoshun

Jinshi had finished his bath and was savoring a cup of wine. It seemed as if everything that came up these days was a fresh headache. He was at something of a loss. As if everything else vying for his attention hadn't been enough, just the other day, he had nearly been killed.

After what they had learned in the mortuary, the matter of Suirei had been taken care of with the utmost circumspection. That was the most convenient for everyone. He queried the mortuary workers who had supposedly brought in coffins while Suirei's body had been there, but strangely, they claimed not to have received any such requests.

About the court lady Suirei herself, much remained uncertain. The reason she had been so close with the doctor was because her guardian had been the physician's own teacher. Apparently, this teacher had seen Suirei's talent for medicine and had adopted her as his daughter some years ago, but little more was known than that.

Jinshi saw that this situation wasn't likely to go away anytime soon, but that was nothing new. There were many problems that went unresolved, simply piling up. The most he could do with such issues was to bear them in mind for the future. He had to focus on what he could do at this moment.

Jinshi was surprised by the crackling of charcoal, but when he looked outside, he saw the world had gone white with snow. It was getting chilly. He picked his robe up from off the couch where it lay and slipped it on.

A metallic tinkling came from the entrance. The building was designed so that it could be heard from almost anywhere. Jinshi knew who it was likely to be.

As he'd expected, his aide, with his perpetually furrowed brow, entered the room.

"She's safely back," Gaoshun said.

"Sorry to put you to such trouble all the time."

Jinshi had instructed Gaoshun to see Maomao back whenever the hour got late. It had been in saving Jinshi, after all, that she had hurt her leg. He worried that if he left her to her own devices, the wound would open again.

That wasn't the only thing that concerned him, though. There was also the eccentric Lakan. As far as Jinshi could tell, the man was telling the truth about being Maomao's biological father, but Maomao's attitude on the subject made it more than clear that their relationship was not the usual one. The general consensus in the palace was that you could never be sure what Lakan might do, and Jinshi preferred to take no chances.

Lakan had had something to do with Maomao's reaching the altar during the ritual, as well. No doubt the soldier who'd struck her was by now deeply regretting his actions.

One of Jinshi's saving graces was that unlike some *other* people of the court, Gaoshun could read him well enough to know when to leave him alone to do his work. This was, after all, the man who had been assigned to Jinshi as a tutor practically from the moment he was weaned. Notwithstanding a brief separation when Gaoshun had been sent to do other work, he was certainly among those who knew Jinshi best. When he considered that Gaoshun's own wife had been his wet nurse, Jinshi saw that he might never outlive his debt to this man.

"We'll be at the rear palace tomorrow."

"Yes, sir." Gaoshun brought out two bowls and a pot. It was full of a sickly sweet liquid. They had to drink it every day in order for it to have its full effect.

Gaoshun poured the contents of the pot into the two silver bowls, and then he took the first sip. It was a role Maomao might have eagerly assumed, but there would have been no point in having her taste it. It had no effect on women. Gaoshun frowned even deeper as he drank the stuff down, and then he waited a few moments.

"I think it's all right. Nothing unusual."

Nothing unusual—except the flavor was always unusual. The mixture contained a powdered variety of potato imported from another land, one with a very particular side effect.

The potato flour was just one of several ingredients Jinshi and Gaoshun had to take on a daily basis.

"Very well." Jinshi picked up his bowl, pinched his nose, and drained it in a single long gulp. He wiped flecks of the liquid from his mouth with the back of his hand, then accepted a cup of cold water from Suiren. Five years drinking this stuff, and he'd never gotten used to it.

"You shouldn't hold your nose like that when people are watching," Suiren said.

"I know that."

"It makes you look like such a little boy when you do."

"I *know* that." Jinshi sat down on the couch, pouting. His tone of voice, the way he spoke, the way he walked and moved: he had to constantly pay attention to all of it.

The eunuch Jinshi was twenty-four years of age. He straightened up, striving to put on his best official face, but the taste of the medicine still lingered in his mouth, making his lip curl.

Gaoshun frowned. "You needn't drink it, sir, if you detest it so."

"This is what makes me who I am. As a eunuch."

It had been five years since the current emperor had taken over the rear palace. Five years—now nearly six—that Jinshi had continued to wear this twisted mask. Year after year taking the medicine that made him not a man. He did it even though the emperor had told him he could do as he wished around the lower-ranked consorts, and any ladies less prestigious than they.

Gaoshun touched a hand to the furrows in his brow. "If you do this long enough, you'll never regain the function."

Jinshi spat out his water at that. He put his hand to his mouth with a reproachful look at Gaoshun. Gaoshun looked back at him, as if to communicate that every now and again he would have his say.

"Well, the same is true of you!" Jinshi said.

"Not so. Why, just last month, a grandchild was born to me." Gaoshun's point seemed to be that his children were already grown; he had no need to produce more offspring.

"How old are you again?"

"Thirty-seven."

If Jinshi had his facts straight, Gaoshun had married at sixteen, and the couple had had one child each year for the next three years. Jinshi's milk brothers. He was particularly close with Gaoshun's youngest son. In fact, the lad had made himself helpful just the other day, during the food-poisoning case involving the seaweed. The young man who had accompanied Maomao to the official's house—that had been him.

"Which of the two elder brothers is it?"

"My eldest son. And I think my youngest could stand to find himself a wife sometime soon."

"He's only nineteen."

"Yes. Just the same as you, *milord*."

Gaoshun specifically refrained from using the name *Jinshi*. *Jinshi* was a twenty-four-year-old man who had become a eunuch five years earlier. He couldn't possibly be nineteen.

Gaoshun clearly thought he was making some sort of point, Jinshi observed. Maybe he felt Jinshi should hurry up and get himself some female companions, as the emperor had done. Jinshi crossed his legs and looked at Gaoshun as innocently as he could.

"I want to hold my grandchild. Soon." *So let's finish this assignment quickly,* he seemed to be saying.

"I'll see what I can do."

Gaoshun accepted some hot tea from Suiren and took a sip. Jinshi, ignoring his aide's baleful look, drank the rest of his water.

———◇———

Another routine round of visits to the emperor's ladies had gone without a hitch. Consort Loulan seemed to be integrating into the rear palace without any trouble. The move to bring her in had been somewhat forceful, so it wouldn't have been surprising if her presence had caused discord, but neither Consort Gyokuyou or Consort Lihua were short-tempered enough to let the new girl get to them. Yes, there had been the contretemps between the two of them after the births of their respective children, but that had been exceptional. Since then they had maintained a distant but cordial relationship.

As for Consort Lishu, she was much too retiring to be the one to start any fights. It was always possible her ladies-in-waiting could goad her into it, though; he would have to keep an eye on the situation.

The residence of the former consort Ah-Duo had become a sorry sight to him under its new occupant. Under the old mistress, there had been not a frivolous furnishing to be seen, but now that the new one had moved in, the pavilion had become an eye-watering riot of ostentatious displays.

Consort Loulan's father was a man of whom the former emperor—or rather, more precisely, the former empress dowager—had been quite fond. It was under him that the number of palace women had ballooned to fully three thousand.

At present, Consort Gyokuyou was foremost in His Majesty's affections, and Consort Lihua next, but as ruler he could not limit his nocturnal visits only to those concubines he most favored. If the rear palace helped maintain the balance of power within the Imperial court, it could likewise upset that balance. The emperor couldn't afford to mishandle Loulan, and he was (Jinshi was given to understand) taking care to visit her at least once every ten days.

This could not but dismay the other consorts. Yes, His Majesty was visiting them more often than Loulan, yet who knew who would conceive a child and when, and who wouldn't?

Even so, compatibility did mean something, and it was clear that Loulan didn't excite the emperor's interest in the same way as some of his other ladies. Looking at her, Jinshi thought perhaps he could understand why. Back when the apothecary's daughter had given her "class," Loulan had been bedecked with a most unexpected accessory: an outlandish ornament featuring the plumes of a bird from the southern lands. But although sometimes Loulan dressed herself in the style of the southern lands, other times she was clad in an outfit from the northern tribes. No sooner had she put on the garments of the east than she traded them for a dress from the west. And each time, her hair and makeup changed to complement her outfit. It was enough to make the emperor feel like he was seeing a different person every time he visited. Under those circumstances, he claimed, it was hard for him to get in the mood.

Consort Lishu was another who posed a challenge to "mood," but for different reasons. The emperor viscerally rejected his father's preferences, and refused to touch, let alone bed, a girl who could still have passed for a child.

The empress dowager's belly bore a great scar, for she had given birth to His Present Majesty very young, her body too small for the task. The birth canal had been too narrow, the child delivered by slitting her open. It had been questionable whether the mother would survive the delivery, but she and her child had both emerged safely.

The surgery, it seemed, had been performed by a doctor recently returned from foreign lands. His skill had been so superlative, in fact, that although she was scarred, the empress dowager's ability to bear children was left intact, and more than ten years later she conceived and bore again. To the end of his life, these were the only offspring the former emperor ever had.

There was, however, a complication. The physician who had attended the first delivery for the empress dowager (then a consort) found himself attending almost exclusively on Her Majesty, precisely because of his actions during that first, difficult delivery. A child born to the consort of the crown prince at the same time was neglected, with tragic consequences.

How could Jinshi not wonder what things might be like now if the current emperor's first child had lived?

He shook his head: there was nothing to gain from meaningless fantasies. And he further thought that His Majesty ought to hurry up and get about the business of producing a *new* crown prince. On this point, he and Gaoshun were of the same mind. After the "lecture," the emperor's visits had increased substantially. The *fruits* of Maomao's labors might come sooner than expected.

During Jinshi's visit, Consort Gyokuyou's chief lady-in-waiting, Hongniang, had confessed something to him with concern. The emperor had called at the Jade Pavilion yet again the day before, and her mistress was looking quite fatigued. Hongniang worried for her. The disheveled appearance of her jet-black hair bespoke the great effort to which the lady-in-waiting was putting herself. Gaoshun seemed to relate to her. Hongniang, for her part, didn't seem averse to Gaoshun at all, but as he already had a wife to look after and henpeck him (each as necessary), they would have to disabuse her of any interest sooner or later.

All this led Jinshi to believe he had the perfect solution. Gyokuyou agreed without a second thought. Hongniang made a point to look put-upon, but quietly seemed to welcome the idea. She said as much to the three ladies-in-waiting who had been eavesdropping at the door.

It seemed Jinshi had made the right choice.

"The rear palace, sir?"

"That's right. Back to your favorite job."

Maomao was polishing a silver eating vessel to a mirrorlike shine. When she was certain it didn't have so much as a smudge on it, she put it back on the shelf. Her leg still wasn't better, so she did a lot of her work sitting in a chair, but Suiren made sure that she *did* have work to do. A real stickler, that woman was.

Jinshi was eating a tangerine. Very literally: he wasn't even peeling it himself. Suiren did that, carefully removing the thin rind and setting each piece on a plate in front of him. What a spoiled brat.

The old attendant seemed to have a habit of indulging Jinshi. She would bundle him in a cotton jacket when it was cold, or cool down his tea because it was hot. An adult man should've been embarrassed to be treated that way.

"It would appear Consort Gyokuyou has ceased to walk the path of the moon."

The "path of the moon" was a polite term for menstruation. *So she might be pregnant,* Maomao thought. Two separate attempts had been made to poison the consort while she was pregnant with Princess Lingli. The culprit had never been found. Maomao could understand why Jinshi might be uneasy.

"And when am I to begin my new assignment?"

"Would today be possible?"

"Possible? I would positively prefer it."

As men were not allowed in the rear palace, she would be free of any possibility of bumping into the one person she didn't want to meet—whose name she didn't even want to hear. Perhaps Jinshi had arranged this change of workplace out of consideration for her, or perhaps it was simply an opportune coincidence for him. Maomao decided she didn't care which.

She thought she was exercising admirable self-restraint, but then Suiren said, "Ah, good news, my dear?" Apparently Maomao wasn't hiding it as well as she thought.

"Not to speak of," she said.

"Too bad for me. I thought I'd finally found a protégé worthy of my training."

Maomao, a touch terrified by the grinning Suiren, determined to finish her work as quickly as she could.

CHAPTER 15

Rear Palace Redux

I used to think I didn't like this place, but I guess I was wrong, Maomao thought with surprise. She was finding life in the rear palace, now that she was finally back, quite congenial. She'd grown up in another place full of women, so maybe the rear palace simply clicked with her.

Her days once again consisted of tasting food, mixing medicines, and taking little walks. Her leg still wasn't healed, and she'd been given explicit instructions not to go out too much, but in her opinion she was fine so long as she avoided anything strenuous that might open the wound again. Frankly, her left arm proved she was nowhere near delicate.

The question of Gyokuyou's pregnancy still wasn't definitively settled. When she had been pregnant with Princess Lingli, she hadn't suffered from any severe morning sickness, and her food preferences had hardly changed. Other than the delay in her menstruation, there was no evidence one way or the other.

Nonetheless, a gag order was imposed on the Jade Pavilion, so as not to take any chances. If there were any who didn't wish to see Consort Gyokuyou with child, they would certainly want to strike during the early stages, when the pregnancy would be most vulnerable. Poison was just one of many concerns.

For good measure, the sex-crazed old man (i.e., the emperor) was discouraged from nocturnal activities at the Jade Pavilion for the time being. Normally this wouldn't have been a problem, but ever since Consort Gyokuyou had begun to put the things she learned at the consorts' seminar into practice, "normal" no longer seemed to apply. There was no telling what might happen.

Maybe I should have taken it a little easier on the lessons, Maomao thought. But no. Then Gyokuyou and even the emperor would have wound up dissatisfied. Even if the end result of her approach had been to terrify Consort Lishu and cause Consort Lihua's women to view Maomao as even more of a monster.

Maomao naturally hesitated to raise the subject with the emperor herself—it was hardly something for a person of her status to bring up with His Majesty—so she communicated through Jinshi instead. Though she couldn't quite make the suggestion explicitly, her hope was that the ruler would continue to visit Gyokuyou exactly as often as he had before, no more and no less. After all, while Gyokuyou wasn't His Majesty's only consort, if he were to suddenly visit her less often, some observant soul might sniff out the truth.

To her surprise, the emperor continued to visit as faithfully as he ever had, playing with his adorable daughter and passing the time in idle conversation with Gyokuyou. Maomao was reminded, as she had been by Ah-Duo's story, that perhaps she shouldn't dismiss the emperor as simply sex-crazed. Or again, perhaps His Majesty grasped the implications of his actions better than she gave him credit for. Some people regarded the current ruler as a sort of sage-king, and while some of this was because almost anyone would have looked competent after the buffoon that the previous emperor had been, Maomao did believe that the current ruler had his wits about him.

Not that it really matters to me, she thought. As long as he let life go on and didn't exact outrageous taxes, she was happy. Some said the real difference between a foolish ruler and a brilliant one was that a foolish ruler thought the people were inexhaustible, while a brilliant one realized that they had their limits. If that was so, well, the present emperor was certainly the latter. Still, she saw the lonesome faces he occasionally pulled, so she decided to pass along the rest of her teaching materials. They would help him pass the time, if nothing else. (It needn't be said exactly what kind of teaching materials they were.) She'd made sure to have a number of different books on hand, just in case, but unfortunately none of the ladies-in-waiting had been interested in them.

He'll just have to make do with two dimensions . . . Maomao placed the materials where they would be unobtrusive but noticeable, and luckily it seemed he spotted them.

When, a few days later, she was ordered to prepare more such "materials," she decided that maybe "sex-crazed" was the right way to describe him after all.

There was a penchant for rumormongering in the rear palace, most likely attributable to the boredom generated by the endless routine and the perennial shortage of the opposite sex. Thus when the ladies-in-waiting didn't have much to do, they found themselves chatting in the kitchen. For snacks they had the castoffs from the latest tea party—today it was *longxutang*, dragon's beard candy, a treat made of delicate fibers that melted in the mouth. This one had tea leaves mixed in, giving it a faint aroma.

"I couldn't believe that outfit, could you?" Yinghua, one of the Jade Pavilion's ladies-in-waiting, said around a mouthful of candy. She was a self-possessed woman, more than willing to say what she thought.

"It's true. But that thing she wore a little while ago, I thought that was nice. Western clothing is so cool, isn't it?" said Guiyuan in a mild tone. She was smiling, happy just to be enjoying a sweet treat.

"Clothes like that choose their own wearers," Ailan observed. "But hers have never looked bad on her." The lanky lady-in-waiting wasn't big on sweets and was simply sipping some tea at the moment.

Yinghua, looking wounded by her friends' faithlessness, turned to her last refuge, Maomao. "Yeah, sure," Maomao said, nodding and privately thinking how she hated to get dragged into these spats. That was as far as her engagement in the conversation went.

Yinghua, her hopes of reinforcement disappointed, puffed out her cheeks. "Well, I thought Consort Ah-Duo was *much* cooler." She took an angry sip of tea without ever pulling her cheeks back in. Guiyuan and Ailan grinned at each other.

"Well! It turns out you were on Team Ah-Duo all this time, Yinghua!"

"I—I was not!" Yinghua exclaimed.

Ailan just smirked. "You don't have to hide it. I know we serve Lady Gyokuyou, but no one would blame you for feeling the way you do."

"I don't feel that way!"

Maomao listened to the girls chatter as she drank the rest of her tea. She much preferred savory treats; the cottony candy was too sweet for her. She would have loved to have some salty rice crackers to refresh her palate.

As for who exactly Yinghua and the other girls were talking about, it was the newly arrived consort, Loulan. She had one unusual quality, which was more than enough to inspire conversation. Which quality? Her clothes. Virtually every time she appeared, she wore an outfit with a different personality. One day she might be in a western dress; the next, she would be outfitted like a rider from one of the tribes.

I wonder what the story is, Maomao thought. Maybe she just had too much money. If she kept changing outfits at that pace, pretty soon her pavilion would be crammed with clothing. The formerly austere Garnet Pavilion had already changed beyond recognition, as if the new resident were intent on banishing the spirit of Ah-Duo.

It was both the right and the wrong thing to do. On the one hand, the rear palace was a world in which one got ahead by standing out; but on the other, the nail that stuck up, as they said, would be pounded down. Loulan might have found herself to be such a nail under normal circumstances, but her father was an important advisor from the days of the former emperor, so there was, as it were, no hammer big enough for the job.

That explains a lot, Maomao thought. That would be more than enough reason to drive Ah-Duo out. Considering Loulan's age, it might even have seemed a bit belated.

Then Maomao had a thought. Might it not have been more convenient in some ways for the emperor had Ah-Duo remained in the rear palace? Because she could never be a mother of the country, her eyes had been fixed straight ahead. She was so perceptive and intelligent one might wish she had been born a man. And now, at a stroke, the emperor had lost an excellent advisor and gained a young woman who might influence not only the rear palace but the greater court itself. Perhaps it hadn't seemed to him the most advantageous trade.

He couldn't simply ignore her, but it wouldn't necessarily be to his benefit to get too friendly with Loulan and have her conceive a child. A consort's backer was really only powerful during a child's minority. Once the boy became emperor—even had a child of his own—such a person could find himself altogether extraneous.

So what did that mean? Maomao entertained the possibilities as she helped herself to another cupful from the little teapot.

CHAPTER 16

Paper

When Maomao made her first visit in quite some time to the rear palace's medical office, she found its resident eunuch as mellow as ever.

"Ah, haven't seen you in a while, young lady," the quack doctor said, happily pouring tea. "It's gotten much warmer these days, hasn't it?" He politely brought her a drink, using a medical treatise in lieu of a tray. Maomao snatched the tea and the treatise both at once, wishing she could give him a piece of her mind for so blatantly abusing such a priceless object.

As ever, the quack was the only one in the office. She couldn't believe how little work he actually seemed to do in here. He was lucky he still had a job.

"Oh, it's still plenty chilly," Maomao said, placing a laundry basket on top of his desk.

Yes, there was still a chill in the air. It was cold enough that the butterbur hesitated to show their faces. Maybe the doctor only felt it had gotten warmer because he was so plump.

Maomao would have to pick plenty of herbs as the new season took hold, but there was something she wanted to do before that happened, and that was what had brought her here today. This wouldn't normally have been an urgent task, but she was who she was—and the quack was who he was.

"Gracious, young lady, you only just got here. What are you doing?" the doctor asked as Maomao pulled something out of the laundry basket.

"What a question." From the basket Maomao produced a set of cleaning supplies and as much bamboo charcoal as she had been able to stuff in there. "We're going to clean. This room." Her eyes flashed. Apparently two months of Suiren's discipline had rubbed off on her. With nothing to do in the Jade Pavilion, Maomao had come to the one place where she had almost free rein. She'd always thought the medical office was a bit of a pigsty. Now the fire was lit, and there was no putting it out.

"How's that?" the doctor asked, but his sudden frown couldn't save him.

The quack wasn't a bad person; indeed, he was quite kindhearted. But that, Maomao knew, was an entirely separate thing from being good at his job.

The next room over from the main office contained cabinets full of medicines. Three walls towered high with drawers, a veritable paradise for Maomao, but it wasn't all joy and sunshine. Yes, there might be a great many medicines there, but it was the quack who got to use them. Those he didn't use regularly would get dusty or might be eaten by bugs. And then there was a dried herb's greatest enemy: humidity. Let down your guard for a second, and the materials would rot. The warmer it got, the more humid it would become. They had to clean things up now, before that happened, or it would be too late.

It wasn't that Maomao particularly liked cleaning. Neither did she have any special reason to help out here, as all too often when she visited the medical office, it was just to kill time. But still, she felt she must. The sense of duty thrummed in her. (As did the nagging feeling that she'd been thoroughly corrupted by Suiren.)

"You don't have to do all this, young lady. Surely someone else can take care of the cleaning," the doctor said, sounding deeply unmotivated. The tone of his voice caused Maomao to involuntarily look at him in a way she normally reserved for Jinshi. Put simply, it was as if she were looking into a puddle full of mosquito larvae.

"Heek!" The doctor quivered right down to his loach mustache. Any gravitas he might have had vanished.

Darn it, stop that, Maomao chided herself. He might be a quack, but he was still her superior. She had to at least *act* respectful toward him. Otherwise he might not put out rice crackers the next time she showed up. There were too many sweet snacks around the rear palace, not enough salt.

"Yes, we could ask someone else," Maomao said, "but what if they accidentally switched some medicines around while they were working? What would we do then?"

The doctor was quiet. It wasn't exactly proper for Maomao to show up at her leisure and decide to clean, but he was quiet about that too. He could hardly chase her out. The doctor who had been close with Suirei had indeed, they'd heard, been punished for the missing thorn-apple. According to Gaoshun, though, the man was too talented to let go. He merely suffered a reduction in salary.

Maomao started in on the dusty shelves, opening the drawers one by one and running a cloth through them. She threw out anything that had obviously gone bad and wrote the name of each item on a wooden tag. Whatever medicine remained she put in new paper pouches, then returned them each to their proper places.

Whenever there was something that required particularly strenuous activity, she got the quack to do it. Her leg still wasn't completely healed. And the doctor was a bit overweight, anyway; the exercise would be good for him.

He certainly uses fine paper here, she observed. Most paper used among the populace was of a low-quality, disposable type. Paper that would last was too expensive for ordinary people. Instead, commoners did most of their writing on wooden strips. There was plenty of firewood floating around, much of it already cut thin enough to start a blaze with. That was what the people used. And when they were done, it doubled as a convenient source of firewood.

The nation had actually exported paper once upon a time, but the former emperor—or rather, his mother, the former empress dowager—had forbidden the felling of the trees used to make the finest paper. The restriction had been eased somewhat since then, but not enough to meet demand. Why had the empress dowager forbidden the trees to be cut down? There had been no one heedless enough of their life to ask at the time. But considering that the harvesting of those trees was still limited, Maomao figured there must be some sort of reason.

The upshot was that these days, with the exception of the very finest stuff, paper was made of other trees, or grasses, or old cloth. Such resources were less readily available than trees and took time to process, making them more expensive—and all the time and trouble caused producers to try to find shortcuts, leading to a low-quality product. Thus paper had acquired a reputation among the populace for being exorbitantly expensive but not actually worthwhile, and it had failed to gain traction despite being more convenient than wood.

Maomao exhaled: "Phew . . ."

"All finished, young lady?" the doctor asked hopefully.

"No, only about half done."

A disappointed silence followed. Maomao, though, saw that half the work was about as much as she could hope to do in a day considering the sheer scale of the task, and decided to deal with the rest the next day. She left the charcoal sitting in the room to help absorb the humidity. She still didn't have enough of it, though, and requested that the doctor requisition more.

The doctor massaged his shoulders as he went about fixing a snack. He brought over fruit juice poured from a ceramic bottle. "A sweet treat, that's the thing when you're feeling tired," he said, using a bamboo spoon to scoop mashed chestnut and sweet potato onto some paper. He handed one of the portions to Maomao.

Old guy has rich tastes! Sweet potato was hard to get ahold of at this time of year, making such a snack a particular indulgence. And on top

of that, he served it on high-quality paper as if doing so were completely unremarkable.

Maomao cleared the sweet potato in a single bite, then looked at the paper, now stained with round fingerprints. The material had a noticeable sheen.

"This is excellent paper you're using," she remarked.

"Oh, you can tell?" It had been an offhand comment, but it seemed to have gotten the doctor's attention. "My family produces this. We even supply it here to the court. Impressive, no?"

"It is indeed."

That would explain how he happened to have some lying around. It wasn't just flattery, either. Maomao could see that this really was material of high quality. Her old man had always picked the best of the worst when choosing from among the selection of disposable paper for his medicine packets. Quality material was desirable to prevent the infiltration of humidity or the spillage of powder, but costs had to be kept down somewhere—and for the sake of the patients, it couldn't be in the medicines themselves. But savings had to be made, lest supplies consume all of the profit and then some.

Maybe I could get him to sell me some, Maomao mused. *You know, at a friendly discount.* Ah, the unfair advantage. She sipped her juice as she thought and it coursed, sweet and lukewarm, down her throat. *Not for me*, she thought, and decided to heat some water for tea. A fire was always kept burning in the medical office, very convenient at times like this.

"The whole village pitches in to make it. There was a time when we actually thought about throwing in the towel, but thankfully, we managed to scrape by somehow."

Maomao hadn't asked for the doctor's life story, but he seemed in a talkative mood today. In the past, making paper had been enough to earn a profit, so his family had concentrated on cutting down the local trees and shaving them as finely as possible to supply product. It was more lucrative to sell abroad than domestically, so their paper became an increasingly important trade good. In his childhood, the village had been so wealthy that the quack doctor could ask for sweets anytime he wanted and eat as many as he liked.

For one reason or another, though—perhaps they simply got too big—the village incurred the wrath of the former empress dowager, who forbade them to cut down the trees they used to make their paper. They were forced to find other materials to produce with, but that inevitably meant a decline in the quality of their product. Now the trading houses were mad at them and had ceased to do business with them.

The village's salad days were over. The headman—who, in fact, was the quack doctor's father—was beset by villagers demanding he do something. He saw the writing on the proverbial wall, that they could no longer go on making paper as they had. However, not everyone in the village was able or willing to see this reality, and a great deal of anger focused on the headman and his family.

Maomao listened patiently, pouring boiled water from a teapot into a cup.

"It broke my heart when my older sister came here to the rear palace."

The village had been established in an ideal place for making paper, but not for much else. They decided to relocate the village but lacked the resources. Around that time, the rear palace was looking for more palace women, and so the doctor's older sister answered the call.

"She laughed and said the next time I saw her she would be a mother to the country, but in the end, I never saw her again."

What exactly to do with themselves remained an issue on the new land. More resources were needed, and then the quack's younger sister volunteered to follow the older into the rear palace.

"And finally I decided to go. There was really no other choice," the quack said. As the rear palace expanded, there was inevitably a need for more eunuchs. They were in shorter supply than women, though, and thus commanded a higher price.

He's had it tougher than I realized, Maomao thought as she drank her tea.

The more one cleaned, the more one saw things that needed cleaning. Maomao successfully finished with the medicine cabinets on the second day, but now the next room over bothered her. The quack did some basic cleaning, it appeared, but he didn't seem to have an eye for detail. Maomao spent the third day brushing cobwebs off the ceiling and carefully wiping down the walls, and after that she wanted to organize the equipment. The quack had quite a bit of it, she'd discovered, and anything he didn't much use he stuffed into one of the other rooms.

What a waste, she thought as she surveyed that next room. She'd been given to understand that it wasn't being used, but for Maomao, it was a treasure trove. She and the quack tackled the scads of medical treatises, Maomao with a glowing smile on her face and the doctor looking rather glum. In this way, over the quack's pouting, they spent seven full days cleaning. Maomao had also been doing food tasting for

Consort Gyokuyou during that time, but nothing out of the ordinary had occurred.

It was around then, as the doctor was grudgingly polishing a mortar and pestle, that another eunuch showed up at the medical office. The quack had received a letter.

"Well, now, what have we here?" the doctor said. He took the letter eagerly, spying a chance to do some slacking off.

"Who's it from?" Maomao asked. In her mind, she was purely being polite, but the doctor replied, "It's from my younger sister." He showed her the letter, which was written on crackly, uneven paper that made Maomao wonder if it was produced from seaweed. It was very much the sort of low-quality product the average person might use.

I thought he said his family made paper. Maybe the sister figured a botched batch was good enough for writing to a family member.

As he perused the letter, though, the doctor's face took on a look of shock, his eyes boring into the page. Maomao sidled up beside him, curious what was going on, but at just that moment the quack's shoulders slumped. He slid weakly into a chair, hung his head, and let the letter drop onto the table. A few words jumped out at Maomao:

"Our Imperial commission may be withdrawn."

But the doctor had been bragging to Maomao just the other day about how his family supplied the court with paper!

"I wonder what could be the matter," the doctor said, almost to himself. "And we were just now able to start producing more supply . . ."

An Imperial commission—or lack thereof—could have major consequences for the family's income. The hoity-toity types who bought high-quality paper could never resist the idea that they were using the same stuff as the emperor.

"Producing more?" Maomao asked. "They haven't started cutting corners, have they?" She fingered the rough paper of the letter.

"They would never. They've been more excited to work than ever since they got that ox. Nowadays it does all the things we always used to need people to do. Why should that change anything?"

Making paper involved a great deal of physical labor. The work ought to be easier with an ox to do all the heavy lifting.

"And yet if this sample is anything to judge by, I can see why the court wouldn't be interested." Maomao picked up the letter and fluttered it at the quack. Low-quality paper would disintegrate if it got the slightest bit wet. Moreover, the uneven surface resulted in hideous written characters.

The doctor was silent, as if in tacit admission that he knew the workmanship was poor. Finally he leaned so far forward his head was on the table. "I just don't know what's wrong."

Maomao, recognizing that now was not the time for cleaning, studied the paper intently. Much of the paper circulating among the commoners was of questionable purity, made of strands of fiber from many different plants. Because the fibers weren't cut carefully, the glue hardened inconsistently, causing the paper to fall to tatters. Her inspection, though, showed that the fibers of this sample were of uniform size and diligently measured thickness. Yet the surface was uneven, and a gentle tug was enough to tear off a corner of the letter.

Maomao tilted her head in curiosity, reading the letter once more. It said that the family was still employing the age-old methods of making the paper and using the same materials they always had. The younger sister implored her brother to advise them what to do, but sadly, the half-man who was her brother seemed at his wit's end.

"She mentions a time-tested way of making paper. Exactly what methods do you use?" Maomao finished drying the mortar and pestle and returned them to the shelf. Then she put on a kettle to help them relax.

"The same ones everyone else does," the quack replied. "The difference is, our family is very particular about how we break down the materials and how we make the glue. I can't say more than that."

Not so talkative on this subject, huh? Maomao thought. She pulled a container of tea leaves off the shelf. She was rifling through it, trying to decide which would be good, when some arrowroot practically jumped out at her. She grabbed it and tossed it in a teacup. Then she put the kettle back on the fire to boil.

"Are you also particular about your water?" she asked.

"Mm. We use spring water heated to a very precise temperature to get the glue to set just right. I can't tell you more, though. That's a trade secret."

That was the quack doctor she knew, Maomao thought, as she set down another teacup. She filled it with hot water, then stirred it assiduously with a spoon before it could cool, producing a viscous gruel. Arrowroot tea.

"And the glue, do you boil it with water left over from washing rice?"

"No, we take the trouble to dissolve wheat flour into it, the way you're supposed to. Otherwise it doesn't stick well." The moment he'd spoken, the doctor slapped his hand over his mouth, but it made scant difference to Maomao whether they used rice water or wheat flour or whatever else. She placed the arrowroot tea in front of the doctor.

"In that case, where do you keep the ox?" she said.

"I'm afraid I don't know that." He looked at her as if to ask *Why arrowroot?* but nonetheless started lapping at the hot liquid. It stuck to the teacup, making it tricky to drink. "Young lady, I do believe you've mistaken the proportions here. It's impossible to drink this."

Maomao passed him a spoon. "My apologies. I'm happy to tell you how to make it drinkable. Want to give it a try?"

"What should I do?"

Maomao placed the spoon briefly in her mouth, then stuck it into the tea and stirred vigorously. Then she did it again, and then again.

"Somewhat uncouth," the quack remarked with a frown, but he did as she showed him. As he repeatedly put the spoon in his mouth and then stirred, a change began to take place. "It's getting less starchy," he observed.

"I should think so."

"In fact, it's practically watery now." The doctor looked quite impressed.

"Arrowroot and glue are rather similar," Maomao offered.

"I suppose you could say that . . . I wonder if saliva thins out glue the same way it does arrowroot."

"Indeed."

The doctor's mouth opened. "Indeed what?"

He wasn't as quick on the uptake as Maomao would have liked. *I'm practically rubbing his nose in it,* she thought, but she decided to give him one more hint.

"Oxen, I believe, produce a great deal of slobber."

"Yes, now that you mention it, I suppose that's true."

"What if you were to find out where the ox is drinking its water? Just to be sure."

Maomao, resolved not to say anything further, cleaned up the teacups, and promptly went back to the Jade Pavilion. The quack must have finally caught on, for he dashed off a letter and hurried out of the medical office to send it.

Maomao contemplated what she would do when she was done cleaning.

But it's when things seem most quiet that disaster often lurks.

CHAPTER 17

How to Buy Out a Contract

"So, how much does it cost to buy out a courtesan's contract?" Lihaku asked. He and Maomao were sitting in the room that connected the rear palace to the outside world. When Maomao heard Lihaku's question, her mouth dropped open. Since he'd summoned her personally rather than sending a letter, she'd assumed he had some new information to give her about the incident. But *this* was what he wanted to know?

I just knew he was a big, dumb mutt.

Lihaku clutched his head until finally, unable to take it anymore, he pounded the desk between them and exclaimed, "You've *got* to tell me, young lady!" The eunuchs guarding the entrances on either end of the room observed the commotion but clearly considered the entire thing a headache.

Evidently, on a recent visit to the Verdigris House, Lihaku had heard some talk of someone buying out one of the ladies' contracts. One of the three princesses, no less. Lihaku, who was very passionate indeed about Pairin, one of said princesses, couldn't let the subject go.

"There are any number of answers to that question," Maomao said.

"For one of the very best courtesans, then."

"I hear you," Maomao said, studying him from under lidded eyes. She requested a brush and an inkstone from one of the guards, and Lihaku provided some paper. "Market price can change in a heartbeat, of course, so consider this to be merely a guesstimate," she said. Then she wrote the number *200* on the paper. This was roughly the amount of silver your average farmer could expect to earn in a year. A nice, cheap courtesan could be had for about twice that amount. Lihaku nodded along.

"That excludes celebration money, though," Maomao informed him. A courtesan's actual buyout price could be influenced by factors like how long was left on her contract and how much money she might be expected to earn during that time, but one could also find oneself paying almost double that amount again on top of the buyout. For it was the custom of the pleasure district to see its ladies off with the grandest of celebrations.

"Give it to me straight. How much can I expect to pay in all?"

Maomao was somewhat stymied by Lihaku's soulful look. *It's not an easy question to answer,* she thought. Pairin had earned herself many customers, and a commensurate amount of money, since making her debut at the establishment. She didn't owe the brothel anything for clothes or hair ornaments, and in fact her term of service as such had been up long ago. She remained at the Verdigris House—and kept earning—because her sexual preferences happened to make her perfect for courtesans' work. If a woman's buyout price were purely about offsetting her debts, well, then Pairin's would have been virtually nil.

How old is she this year, again? Maomao wondered. Pairin was the oldest of the three princesses, to which group she had belonged since before Maomao was born. Yet her skin was still lustrous, and she had honed her specialty, dancing, over many years. Her youthful looks even sometimes prompted rumors that she stayed young by sucking the essence out of men. There were practices—the so-called *fangzhongshu,* or "arts of the bedchamber"—that supposedly allowed both men and women to maintain their vital essence by making love, and Maomao had occasionally wondered idly if Pairin had learned those abilities.

Judging strictly by age, Pairin's value should have been naught, but her beauty remained undiminished, as did her energies. At the same time, the old madam wouldn't want her three princesses to stagnate. She would be looking to move the oldest of them—Pairin—along one of these days. Maomao had heard her muttering about it on her last visit home.

Pairin had been a model courtesan, supporting the Verdigris House when it had teetered on the brink, but she couldn't rest on these laurels forever, nor could the Verdigris House rest on her. It would have to foster a new generation of famous faces while it was in the ascendant, lest its current crop suddenly turn out one day to be old and dusty.

Maomao scratched the back of her neck and grunted thoughtfully. "If anyone was going to buy Sis—I mean Pairin—out, it would be one of two people." She searched her memory. It was likely to be someone

Pairin knew well. The Verdigris House didn't take that many new customers.

One of the candidates was the head of a prosperous merchant business, a lavish spender who had been so good as to continue patronizing the Verdigris House even when it had fallen on hard times. A decent old man. He'd often given Maomao candy when she was little. He frequently came not to stay the night as such, but to have a drink of wine and enjoy watching a dance or two. He'd spoken of buying Pairin out more than once. The greedy old woman had managed to put him off the subject each time, but if he were to raise the possibility again now, she might be more receptive.

The other possibility was a high-ranking official who was a regular client. Still young, only just past thirty, Maomao didn't know exactly what kind of official he was, but when she thought back to the jeweled ornament she'd seen on the hilt of his sword some years ago, she realized that at that time he had already ranked higher than Lihaku did now. Surely the man had been promoted since then, as well. He seemed to be quite a match for Pairin as far as nocturnal activities went; she was always in excellent spirits after a night with him.

Just one thing nagged Maomao about this second suitor. Compared to the indefatigable Pairin, he often seemed a bit . . . *tired*. She worried about how Pairin would get along after being bought out by either of these men.

Pairin was a beautiful woman and a superb dancer, but at the same time, she was renowned for never coming off second best in bed. It was even said that when she got too frustrated, her appetites could extend not just to the menservants of the brothel, but to the other courtesans and apprentices as well . . . In short, she was insatiable.

That was what caused the madam to consider not just the possibility of selling Pairin's contract, but alternatively of letting her take over the Verdigris House. It was also conceivable that Pairin might simply leave the brothel, but her personality made that seem unlikely.

Even though it would probably be the most peaceful solution for her, Maomao thought. Formally she would retire, but she could be allowed to take customers in special cases, while on her own time she could love freely. She would have far more liberty than she'd ever had before, which would presumably please her to no end.

Hmmm . . . Maomao eyeballed Lihaku again. She took him to be in his mid-twenties. He was toned and muscled, his brawny arms just the sort of thing Pairin liked. Not to mention that when he had come to the Verdigris House that first time, he and Pairin had gone into her room and not come out for the whole two days Maomao was home, yet Lihaku hadn't appeared spent afterward.

"Master Lihaku, how much money do you make?"

"That question seems kind of forward," Lihaku said, a bit apprehensively.

"Around eight hundred silver a year?"

"Hey, don't go around trying to put numbers on people." Lihaku was frowning, but not very hard. A little low, she saw.

"Twelve hundred, then?"

This time he didn't say anything. That suggested a number in the middle—about a thousand silver per year, say. A fairly good income at his age. To buy out a high-ranking courtesan, though, one ideally wanted to have at least ten thousand silver on hand. After all, such women could command a hundred silver for a cup of tea, or three hundred for a night's company. Lihaku had returned to spend two or three more nights with Pairin since that first visit. He would have to stretch his salary to support that habit, but Maomao suspected the old madam herself was behind this. Most likely using Lihaku to help ensure Pairin didn't become too frustrated.

"Not enough?" Lihaku asked.

"I'm afraid not."

"What if I promised to pay the money back after I make it in the world?"

"They'd never allow it. They'll probably expect at least ten thousand in hard cash."

"T-ten thousand?!"

Lihaku was rooted to his spot. Maomao wasn't sure what to do. If he could somehow raise the money, he wouldn't be such a bad suitor for Pairin. She would no doubt appreciate his tremendous endurance.

Yes, she would appreciate it—but did that constitute love? Maomao wasn't sure. *Hmmm,* she thought again. She looked at Lihaku, who was clearly depressed, and let out a breath.

He seemed to be thinking along the same lines she was. He looked at Maomao with uncertainty and said, "If, hypothetically, I was able to get together ten thousand silver, would I be able to buy out her contract?"

"Are you asking whether Sis would simply turn you down out of hand?" Maomao said coolly. The moment she spoke, Lihaku's eyes became a little more bloodshot, and he ground his teeth. She'd only mentioned the possibility. She hadn't said it would happen.

Okay then, just one thing to do, she thought. Maomao rose and stood in front of Lihaku. "Please get up for a moment, sir."

"All right . . ." Lihaku said dejectedly. Maybe a disappointed dog is an obedient one, for he promptly did as Maomao said.

"Good. Now take off your shirt, raise your arms to shoulder height, and flex."

"All right." Lihaku began to do as he was told, but he seemed to be causing some alarm among the eunuchs on guard. They stopped him before he could remove his shirt.

"Don't worry, nothing untoward is going on," Maomao said. "I just want to have a look at him." Despite her assurances, the eunuchs didn't move.

Still openly disappointed, Lihaku sat formally on the chair.

"If I take it off, she won't reject me?"

"If I know nothing else, I know Pairin's tastes."

"I'll take it off," Lihaku said promptly, and then he did so. He quelled the objections of the eunuchs by displaying his accessory of office.

Maomao circled around the posing Lihaku, examining him from every angle. Occasionally she would form a square with her palms and pointer fingers and peer at him through it critically. He had the carefully crafted body of a military officer. Nothing slumped or sagged, and muscles covered virtually everything. His right arm was slightly larger than his left, suggesting he was right-handed. Pairin was ravenous and would devour almost anything if she had no other choice, but like anyone else, she had her preferences. If she'd been here at this moment, she would have been licking her lips.

"Very well. Now the bottom half."

"The bottom half?" Lihaku said plaintively.

"I insist." Maomao's expression was perfectly serious.

Lihaku shuffled out of his trousers, though he didn't look thrilled about it, until he was standing there in nothing but a loincloth. Maomao's face didn't change. She continued to study him with almost scientific rigor.

Lihaku's legs and hips were as sturdy as the rest of him, demonstrating that there were no imbalances in his training regimen. There was no fat on his thighs, and the muscles flowed smoothly toward the joints of his knees, then swelled out again to his calves.

These really are exceptional muscles, Maomao thought. He didn't have the wine-bolstered belly of so many who frequented the brothel. His skin was a healthy color. *Just Sis's type.*

Maomao had Lihaku strike pose after pose, starting to think he just might have what it took. As Lihaku started to warm to the exercise, he took the positions with ever more vigor.

Finally, Maomao was ready to inspect the most important part. "Now, if you'll remove your l—" she started, but she was interrupted by the door banging open. Lihaku, who had looked downright enthusiastic an instant ago, blanched. The eunuchs looked like they thought they might be given the death penalty.

As for Maomao, her mouth simply hung open.

"*What* are you all doing in here?" The overseer of the rear palace (a vein standing out prominently on his temple) was standing in the doorway, accompanied by his aide. A bevy of palace women who were hanging around hoping to get close to Jinshi scattered and even fainted as if they had seen something unbearable.

"Good day to you, Master Jinshi," Maomao said mildly.

———◇———

218

Some things in the world were mysterious, Maomao thought. For example, why was she sitting so formally just then? And why was Jinshi looking at her with such a chill in his eyes?

Lihaku had hurried home, still barely dressed. Maomao thought the whole scene was ridiculous. She also felt it was vaguely unfair, but having the soldier stay seemed like it would somehow have made things even more complicated than they already were, so perhaps it was just as well for him to go.

"What were you doing?" Jinshi reiterated. Maomao looked up at him, privately observing that the beautiful were truly fearsome when roused to anger. Jinshi had crossed his arms and was standing imposingly in front of her. Behind him, Gaoshun stood with his hands together and the impassive expression of a monk contemplating Emptiness. The eunuchs, looking weary, had resumed their positions by the doors, though they stole occasional glances at their glorious chieftain.

"He simply came to me for advice," Maomao said. She'd informed Hongniang at the Jade Pavilion, per protocol. She'd finished the laundry in the morning, and as there were no tea parties planned for today, a food taster would not be necessary. Maomao had no work duties to attend to until evening.

"Advice, eh? Then what was he doing looking like *that*?"

Ah, Maomao thought, so that was the issue. Despite the fact that there had been guards present, it was admittedly beyond problematic for a man from outside the rear palace to be seen in such a state. She vowed to resolve what was obviously a misunderstanding.

"It was nothing inappropriate, sir. I never touched him; I was only taking a good look." She tried to emphasize that point: she hadn't laid a finger on him. That was what she wanted Jinshi to take away from this.

Jinshi, though, reacted poorly; his eyes went wide and he looked like he might fall over backward. Gaoshun, meanwhile, seemed to be advancing from the contemplation of Emptiness to the realization of Liberation. Maomao wondered why he was looking at her with the unperturbed compassion of a bodhisattva.

"*A good look*, you say?"

"Yes, sir. I was only looking."

"To what end?"

"I should think that was obvious. I needed to make sure his body would be satisfying, and examining it in the flesh was the only way."

In a conversation about who would buy out Pairin's contract, Maomao wanted to be sure to take her sister's feelings into special consideration. Pairin was a woman who loved often and much, and it would be ideal, in Maomao's opinion, if she could go to a man she truly cared for. If Maomao had thought Lihaku was too far removed from being Pairin's type, she certainly wouldn't have offered him any further advice. She wasn't such a soft touch as that.

Maomao had grown up at the Verdigris House, at least until she had been torn away from her old man. In her youth, it had been the three princesses—Pairin, Meimei, and Joka—along with the old madam who had seen to her upbringing.

Pairin was unique in that although she had never borne a child, her breasts still produced milk, and it was this milk that had fed Maomao as an infant. When Maomao was born, Pairin had only just graduated from her apprenticeship, but she was already plenty voluptuous. Maomao always thought of Pairin as "Sis," but in reality it was something more like "Mom." Incidentally, she took this informal tone with Pairin lest Meimei and Joka get mad at her.

Maomao suspected that if Pairin went to one of the two long-standing prospects, she was unlikely to have the life she truly wanted. Even so, Maomao wasn't sure it would be best for her to simply go on and end up like the old madam.

Many former courtesans gave up on having children. The constant use of contraceptive drugs and abortifacients robbed their wombs of the strength to foster a child. Maomao didn't know if this was the case for Pairin or not. But when she remembered her youngest days, being rocked to sleep in Pairin's arms, she thought it would be a shame for Pairin never to have children of her own. She was a woman of immense sexual appetites, but her maternal instinct was just as strong.

Lihaku was thoroughly smitten with the courtesan Pairin. He was well aware that as a courtesan, he wasn't the only man to whom she offered her services. Yet as much as Lihaku could be a bit of a big puppy sometimes, at heart he was a serious and diligent man, and his determination to rise in the world for the sake of a woman was both silly and endearing.

Lihaku's single-mindedness meant his ardor was unlikely to cool suddenly, and even if he should fall out of love one day, Maomao suspected she could help handle arrangements surrounding any breakup. What was most important was that he had impeccable endurance.

And just as she was appraising this specimen, Jinshi had arrived. As the one responsible for overseeing affairs in the rear palace, he probably wasn't thrilled to have one of its women meeting with a random man from the outside. He chose, Maomao thought, the oddest times to be passionate about his work.

"His body—satisfying?!"

"Yes, sir. Appearance is just one part of a person, yet one may certainly hope it might be to one's liking."

As far as she had seen, Maomao could give passing marks to Lihaku's body. She was already trying to decide how she would explain to Pairin that she hadn't gotten a chance to evaluate the last and most important part of all.

Maomao had told Lihaku that it would take ten thousand in silver to buy Pairin out, but depending on how the matter was approached, he might get away paying as little as half that. It would depend in particular on how Pairin felt about him.

"Is outward appearance that important?" Jinshi finally stopped looming over her and took a seat instead. His foot tapped the floor restlessly; he was clearly still irritated.

"I should say so," Maomao replied, reflecting that she found it oddly vexing that Jinshi of all people should ask this question.

"I must admit I never expected to hear that from you. So? What did you make of his looks?"

He's just full of questions, Maomao thought. But it was an underling's burden to answer every inquiry of those above her.

"His body shows excellent proportions. He's lean all around. It's clear he has a superb physical foundation, and I believe it's fair to assume he's quite dedicated. He must work at his training and physical conditioning each and every day. If I had to guess, I would suspect he's quite capable even by military standards."

Jinshi was agog at Maomao's proclamation. She almost thought he found her response surprising. His expression swiftly soured until he looked downright irate.

"Can you really tell what kind of person someone is based solely on how their body looks?"

"More or less. The fruits of habit appear in the flesh, if you will."

When providing medicine to a customer who was reluctant to talk about themselves, it was important to be able to discern who you were dealing with. Any apothecary worth their salt would acquire the skill whether they consciously intended to or not.

"And would you be able to evaluate me by my body?"

"Huh?" Maomao said in spite of herself. She almost thought there was a trace of sullenness on Jinshi's face.

Wait . . .

Could it be he was *jealous* of Lihaku? That would explain why he had looked increasingly displeased over the course of their conversation. It was all because Maomao had been too lavish in her praise of the other man's physical qualities.

I can't believe this guy, she thought with a mental sigh. *He just has to be reassured that he's the more attractive one.*

Jinshi had a beautiful face. So beautiful, in fact, that had he been a woman, he could have had the country wrapped around his little finger; and one suspected that even as a male, it wouldn't have been impossible. And yet, despite having a countenance that was beyond compare, now he wanted to gloat about his body too?

I mean, I guess that's fine by me, Maomao thought. The glimpse she had gotten of Jinshi's body had shown someone surprisingly muscular and toned. She didn't have to study it closely to see that he was quite attractive. But so what? Was he trying to suggest she should recommend *him* to Pairin if she thought he outstripped Lihaku in physical beauty? Come to think of it, had she ever even mentioned Pairin to Jinshi?

While Maomao thought all this over, Jinshi leaned his elbows on the table and watched her intently, his lips pursed. The eunuchs standing guard looked absolutely cowed, yet nonetheless entranced by his stormy visage. As for Gaoshun, he looked at Maomao with all the tranquility of an image of nirvana.

Maomao felt a bit bad for Jinshi, but she would have to be clear about this here and now: Jinshi lacked the one thing Pairin considered more important than any other in a man. No matter how exquisite his other physical features might be, without that crucial thing, it would be no use even talking about it.

"I did see your body, Master Jinshi, but I'm afraid there's simply no point," Maomao said, albeit reluctantly. The atmosphere in the room iced over immediately. Gaoshun went from looking like a saint in nirvana to looking like the criminal Kandata as the spider's thread broke. "I'm quite sorry to have to tell you this, sir," Maomao went on, "but you simply aren't a match for my elder sister."

"Huh?" This time it was Jinshi's turn to sound completely flummoxed.

Gaoshun pressed his forehead against the wall.

Lihaku could only wonder what in the world was going on. The eunuch who had given him the glaring of a lifetime over his little blunder the day before was now here in front of him—and on his unimpeachably lovely face was a smile.

The man's name was Jinshi, Lihaku recalled. Jinshi seemed a bit younger than Lihaku, but he was also in the emperor's confidence.

With that gorgeous face, rumors occasionally cropped up of a dalliance between Jinshi and the emperor, but at the very least Jinshi seemed serious about his job; there was nothing to complain about in that respect. The way he could cause virtually anyone, man or woman, to fall head over heels for him could be a bit of an issue, but otherwise, in Lihaku's opinion, there was nothing objectionable about him. As for Lihaku, though, he wasn't the type to be interested in another man, no matter how lovely.

All the same, when that man showed up practically out of the blue and started staring intently at him, Lihaku was a little bit lost for what to do. He was just glad there was no one else around to see them. They were in the officers' building, which was rarely very populated. One particularly eccentric commander made his base of operations here, a person with whom everyone else preferred to have the minimum of contact.

Word was that the eccentric had been out and about quite a bit recently, and Lihaku thought maybe this eunuch had been press-ganged into helping with something around here. Lihaku had submitted his paperwork and tried to get out of the building as quickly as he could so as not to get dragged into anything himself, but just as he had been leaving Lakan's office, he had bumped into this eunuch. And now he was facing that mystifying smile.

Speaking of mystifying, the aide standing behind Jinshi was the man who had requested Lihaku to be his go-between at the brothel. Allegedly, he was an old acquaintance of one of Lihaku's superiors. He'd wondered how the man knew the freckled palace woman Maomao, but now it was starting to make sense.

"Might I have a moment of your time?" Jinshi asked. It was a polite request, but Lihaku was hardly in a position to refuse. Although the other man was younger than him, the jeweled ornament hanging at his hip showed a more esteemed color than Lihaku's. If he didn't do as he was asked, there was no telling if he would ever get the promotion he sought.

"As you wish," was all he said, and then he followed after the eunuchs.

They were in a courtyard of the palace, a place the officers often went to enjoy the refreshing breeze on summer nights. Admittedly, Lihaku wasn't a frequent visitor. He had never been terribly attuned to aesthetics. In this season the chill in the air went beyond refreshing; it was getting downright cold. Between the time of year and the time of day, they could count on not being disturbed.

In summer, flowers called bigleaf hydrangeas would have been putting out blooms as large as embroidered handballs. Apparently they were unusual flowers that had been brought from an island country to the east, and depending on the day the blossoms might be red or they might be blue. The commander had gone out of his way to have them planted here. The blooms bore some resemblance to lilacs, but at the moment they simply looked like stubby bushes. Lihaku sometimes wondered if they gave the man a bit *too* much discretion, but one heard tell that even the general had trouble asserting himself with the monocled man, so maybe there wasn't much to be done.

Jinshi took a seat in an open-air pavilion, then gestured for Lihaku to do the same. Left with no other choice, he sat down facing the eunuch.

Jinshi set his chin on his clasped hands and fixed Lihaku with a radiant smile. His aide, behind him, seemed entirely used to this, but Lihaku found himself somewhat unsettled. It was ridiculous, but the smile was so brilliant that he almost wanted to look away. He realized now that all the talk of how Jinshi could have brought the country to its knees if he were a woman was more than idle gossip. But he was a man. Even if he was missing something normally considered important to one.

One could be deceived by his nymphlike smile and silken hair, but his stature and the broadness of his shoulders gave him away. He didn't look too frail even compared to his own aide, who looked distinctly like a military man, and anyone who was misled by the delicate smile into thinking they might have their way with this person would seem likely to find out otherwise, and painfully. Every motion he made was entrancingly elegant, yet also utterly efficient and precise. Lihaku had thought so even when simply following along behind the eunuch. He'd also thought the man looked somehow familiar, but he couldn't place him. The thought nagged at him, even though he'd only ever caught glimpses of Jinshi. He'd never really seen him face-to-face. What did a person of such high station want with him?

"My attendant informs me that you, my boy, have your heart set on somebody."

Would it be overthinking it, Lihaku wondered, if he felt the crack about "my boy" was a somewhat unnecessary twist of the knife? It took him a second to understand who Jinshi meant by his attendant, but he realized that in this context it could only be the scraggly, freckled girl. Come to think of it, she had apparently done a stint in the outer palace—Lihaku realized she'd been working for this eunuch, of all people. He put his hand to his chin unconsciously.

He'd always thought it would take someone of very particular tastes to hire that woman as their personal servant. He never would have imagined this gorgeous eunuch would have those tastes.

Even recognizing that the situation in which Jinshi had found them would require some explanation, though, Lihaku was a bit taken aback to realize she had told Jinshi of his desire to buy out Pairin's contract. Maybe that was what inspired the eunuch to smile so intently at him. At his young age, for him to aspire to buy out one of the most beautiful, most revered courtesans in all the land was humorous indeed.

And frankly, Lihaku didn't mind if Jinshi thought he was a buffoon. Let him laugh at Lihaku—but if he intended to make light of Lihaku's beloved Pairin, then things might be different.

Pairin was a good woman. Not just a good courtesan—a good woman. He pictured her, smiling at him in bed. Saw her dancing, holding up the hem of her robe with two fingers. Thought of the way she served tea with attention to every detail.

Some might say that was just what a courtesan was supposed to do, and with such people there would be no room for further discussion. But Lihaku didn't mind. He didn't care if it was real or not. As long as he believed in it, it didn't matter.

He'd seen more than one of his colleagues lose themselves in women and gambling, and to those around him, perhaps he just looked like another such lost cause. Those who would tell him that Pairin was no good for him no doubt had his best interests at heart. And for that he was grateful—but he wished they would butt out.

Lihaku went to the Verdigris House of his own volition. Frequently he didn't even see Pairin but was simply served tea in the front room by an apprentice. And that was fine with him. It was part of Pairin's business to be as unreachable as a flower on a distant peak. If she charged a month's silver for a cup of tea, who was anyone to say that was greedy? Pairin poured all of herself into being a courtesan; she was living merchandise. Any who claimed she was too expensive simply didn't understand.

That was why if the eunuch across from Lihaku tried to belittle Pairin, Lihaku was prepared to get physical. He knew perfectly well that it might cost him his head, but he could live with that, so to speak. He had never compromised his principles, his beliefs. This way of life, as straightforward and unrelenting as a charging animal, had always suited him. If those around him thought he had gone mad for some woman, let them.

For the moment, he controlled himself with an effort, pressing his trembling hands together and looking at Jinshi. "And what if I do, sir?"

He was careful not to add "It's none of your business," or anything else unnecessarily antagonistic. Jinshi appeared to pay no mind to Lihaku's dark look, and the heavenly smile remained unmoved. What Jinshi said next shocked Lihaku. "What would you do if I said I would shoulder the cost of purchasing her contract for you?"

Lihaku caught his breath, jumped to his feet, and pounded the table. The granite surface sent some of the force back at him. Only when the shiver had passed through his entire body was he at last able to speak. "What do you mean by that?"

"Precisely what I said. How much would it take to buy her out? Twenty thousand? Do you think that would be enough?"

It was as if the number meant nothing to Jinshi, but it made Lihaku gulp. Twenty thousand was not an amount to simply give away. Certainly not to an officer one barely knew. Had Jinshi already spoken to Maomao about the probable cost? Or was the sum truly an afterthought to this man? Lihaku put his head in his hands.

The thought did go through his mind: if this man spoke of twenty thousand as if it were nothing, then half that would be less than nothing to him. But he resolved not to get lost in a naive fantasy.

"I'm overjoyed by your words, sir," he said, "but I must wonder what would prompt such generosity toward someone you hardly know."

Offers that were too good to be true always had a sting in the tail. Even a child knew that, and Lihaku wasn't foolish enough to forget this basic rule. He sat back in his chair and looked at the man across from him. The eunuch's expression showed no change despite having offered this staggering amount of money, although his aide, behind him, looked slightly exasperated.

"My cat is most wary, yet not only was she willing to speak to you, she seems to be earnestly considering you as a possible match for a woman she thinks of as an older sister."

The "cat" must have been Maomao—it was the meaning of her name—and when Lihaku thought about it, he realized that she could indeed be catlike. She could be as suspicious of others as a stray cat, but when there was food to be had she would come just close enough to get it, take as much as she could, and then she would be gone again.

Lihaku had never wanted a cat. If he was going to have an animal, he would have liked a dog, something that could hunt with him.

Despite the eunuch's choice of metaphor, though, and despite Maomao's attitude, apparently she trusted Lihaku to at least some extent. True, the disinterest in her eyes had made it clear that she thought it was annoying to have to answer his questions, but answer them she did. Ultimately, it had led to this conversation.

"You're saying that when a mistrustful cat takes to somebody, that's reason enough to have faith in them," Lihaku said, earning a slight flinch from Jinshi. He wondered if he'd said something wrong, but the soft smile was back on Jinshi's face so quickly that Lihaku wondered if it had been his imagination.

"I did a bit of asking around about you," Jinshi said. "I learned that you're the son of a provincial official. To rise up the ranks in the capital must have taken quite a bit of work."

"A fair amount."

There were cliques and factions anywhere you went. His father had been an official, yes, but only a regional civil administrator. That had meant an uphill battle for Lihaku, and a good deal of time before anyone really took him seriously.

"They say you were discovered by a commander with an eye for talent and entrusted with a unit of your own."

"Yes, sir," Lihaku said hesitantly. He wondered just how much this man had learned about him. Outwardly, Lihaku was supposed to have been promoted after the commander of a small unit left the service.

"And who wouldn't want to be on good terms with a promising young soldier?" Jinshi continued.

Many might, but rarely to the tune of twenty thousand silver.

Lihaku only really needed half that amount—or actually, if one factored in his own contributions and all he could scare up, even just a quarter of it. One quarter, or five thousand in silver. Would this man really just give it to him? Lihaku was nearly sick with wishing for it—but he shook his head.

He looked at Jinshi seriously and said, "I truly do appreciate your vote of confidence, and I confess I'm almost beside myself wanting to accept your offer, but I can't take your silver. To you, she may be simply another courtesan, but to me she is a woman. A woman I wish to take to wife. And if I don't do that with my own money, then what kind of man am I?"

Lihaku managed to say all this to Jinshi, though it wearied him having to be constantly alert to the tenor of his language.

He'd thought Jinshi might be peeved by his refusal, but that nymphlike smile didn't change. He even thought it might have softened a little. Then the smile turned into laughter. "I see! I'm afraid I've been quite rude." The eunuch stood, utterly elegant as he ran his fingers through his hair. Looking like he had stepped out of a painting of a classical beauty, he stood there with a satisfied smile on his face. "I think there may be something I will wish to speak to you about later. You wouldn't mind?"

"Whatever you wish, sir." Lihaku stood up as well; he pressed a fist respectfully into his open palm and bowed. The gorgeous eunuch responded with a short nod, and then he and his aide went home. Lihaku watched Jinshi go, almost befuddled by his elegance, until they were out of sight.

Finally he murmured, "What was that all about?" and scratched his head, truly puzzled. His heart dropped a little when he felt the bald patch that still remained where his hair had been scorched off. Then he sat down again, mumbling, "What am I going to do . . . ?"

He would have to try to show his best side for his superiors at their next training session. Or maybe he could take on more work. No, no, there was something more important. He would send a letter to the woman he hoped to be joined to someday. He wouldn't simply, unilaterally take her. He wanted to know how she felt as well. Whatever she said in reply might be only for politeness's sake, but he would place his faith in it. That would be what sustained him.

"A'right." Lihaku stuck his hands into his sleeves and set off from the courtyard at a brisk trot. He wondered what kind of branch would make the best accompaniment for his letter.

"Maomao, you've got a letter." Guiyuan held out a bundle of wood writing strips. Maomao took it and undid the tie, to find the strips were covered in a light, flowing hand. It was a reply to the message she'd sent to the Verdigris House several days earlier.

"The old lady can say what she wants, but I'm still earning plenty."

The letter was from Pairin. Maomao could practically see her sensuous older sister puffing out her ample chest.

"Besides, I'm still waiting for a prince on his white horse to come and get me."

In one far country, white horses were what princes were said to ride when they came to rescue trapped young maidens. Pairin was still a woman, and she had a woman's dreams. Maybe it was a bit late to call her a young maiden—she'd already been with more gentlemen than could be counted on both hands—but she didn't give up on the fantasy. Maybe that stubbornness was part of what had preserved her youth for so long.

I sort of suspected, Maomao thought. If the prospect was someone who pleased her, she didn't even need that ten thousand silver. He just had to play the part of her "prince." The role demanded absolute physical strength and endurance, along with something that most men had but eunuchs didn't. Add a dash of theatricality and a little bit of money with which to celebrate, and that would do the trick. No, it wouldn't be necessary to buy Pairin out as such, but the community wouldn't sit by and watch her go without marking the occasion.

The old madam herself had once said to Pairin, "If you want to retire, I won't stop you. But we're going to have the party to end all parties." It was quite a striking remark from a woman who was normally so tightfisted. When Pairin left the stage, it would be commemorated as befitted one of the pleasure quarter's most beautiful blossoms. A courtesan had her pride, after all. Thus, for a man who suitably impressed Pairin, even the old madam wouldn't try to wring out too much. But surely five thousand or so for the celebration. Anyone who couldn't come up with at least that much money wasn't fit for Pairin—and if they had the money but refused to spend it, that would show them even worse.

Yeah, even if ten thousand is out of reach, five thousand ought to do it. If Lihaku continued his steady rise up the ranks, he should be able to save up that much within a matter of years. The rest would be up to luck. If Pairin were to be brainwashed by the old woman, that would spell the end. Lihaku just had to get her out of there before that happened.

There was no part for Maomao to play in any of this. There was just one thing that worried her. *Surely he wouldn't go into debt to get the money, would he?* she thought. If he took a loan to get the cash, the madam would sniff it out, and that would be it. *"How can I let Pairin go to a man mired in debt?"* she would demand. Maomao was fairly confident Lihaku wouldn't do anything so silly, but she couldn't be sure.

With these thoughts running through her head, she found herself at the end of the letter—where she discovered something very troubling.

"A certain someone was coming around talking about buying out a contract. I think the apprentices got the wrong idea."

A certain someone. Right, Maomao thought. It was unusual for Pairin to be so indirect, but Maomao knew perfectly well who she was talking about.

Maomao tied the letter closed again and put it on a shelf in her room. When she emerged into the hallway, she discovered that Jinshi was visiting the Jade Pavilion for the first time in several days. He'd looked downright stormy the last time they'd parted, but today he seemed in high spirits. Maomao went to the kitchen to prepare tea, wondering what might have him so pleased.

CHAPTER 18

Blue Roses

The cold was gradually loosening its grip on the world, and the first hints of spring were in the air. As Maomao stood out drying some bedding, she felt like she might succumb to the temptation of the warm, pleasant sun, but she shook her head (*Mustn't sleep on the job!*) and forced herself to focus on her work.

Time did pass quickly when one's days were full and satisfying. Even though somehow, the two months she had spent in Jinshi's employ had felt interminably long.

She still longed sometimes for the packed shelves of medicines in the outer-palace physician's office, but she could rectify that issue here. She could work through the quack doctor to get the rear palace medical office up to speed. Meanwhile, she could lean on Gaoshun to get her anything she needed from the archives. It would have been even better if she could have left the rear palace at will, but, well, one couldn't have everything. So long as she was serving there, she couldn't expect to come and go as she pleased.

Consort Gyokuyou's pregnancy was becoming more and more certain. Her menses still hadn't resumed, and now she was experiencing fatigue as well. Her temperature was slightly elevated, and it seemed she was evacuating more often than usual. Princess Lingli would occasionally put her cheek to Gyokuyou's belly and grin, as if to intimate that she knew there was something in there.

Can babies tell? Maomao wondered. Lingli was waving bye-bye to Gyokuyou's belly as Hongniang took her away for her afternoon nap.

Children were most mysterious creatures.

The princess had begun to toddle around on her own. The emperor gave Lingli a pair of little red shoes, while she in turn gave the ladies-in-waiting their share of headaches. She had become more expressive as well. If you gave her a nice, soft bun, she would smile broadly in return. The ladies-in-waiting of the Jade Pavilion had no children of their own but apparently did have the maternal instinct, for they doted endlessly on the little princess.

Hongniang became given to saying "Perhaps I'll have one of my own sooner or later," but the other women, including Maomao, weren't sure how to respond. Hongniang looked concerned when she said this, yet no one expected the devoted head lady-in-waiting to retire from her post. Even had a suitable offer come along, the other women would most likely have done anything to stop Hongniang from leaving. It was she who allowed the Jade Pavilion to function with such a small staff.

Ah, being too talented could have challenges of its own.

Maomao took to entertaining Princess Lingli when she had no other work to do. The injury to her leg was another factor. Rather than having the busy and able-bodied other ladies-in-waiting watch the princess on top of all their other duties, wasn't it more efficient to have the woman with nothing to do but taste food look after her?

Thus, on this day, Maomao found herself once more playing with Princess Lingli, who was making piles of wooden blocks (purposely constructed with light materials) and then knocking them down. She also showed some interest in illustrated books, so Maomao would copy the pictures out of books she got Gaoshun to borrow for her, writing the words below each one. Lingli was still just two years old, but Maomao had heard it was never too early to get them started. Sadly, Hongniang put a premature end to her educational efforts when she confiscated the pictures.

"Draw flowers like a normal person," she instructed, pointing to the flowers in the courtyard. Apparently, no matter how excellent the renderings might have been, pictures of poisonous mushrooms were off-limits.

That was how Maomao passed the time until, one day, a gorgeous eunuch appeared for the first time in quite a while, bringing trouble with him.

B lue roses, sir?" Maomao asked, looking at the eunuch with some fatigue.

"Oh, yes. Everyone's quite interested, you see."

Jinshi looked like he was in something of a bind. To the palace women, he looked beautiful even in his distress, and at this moment, three pairs of eyes were watching through the crack in the door. Maomao chose to ignore them. Shortly thereafter, Hongniang, looking rather exasperated herself, grabbed the owners of the eyes—quite nimbly, we might add; two with her right hand, one with her left—by the ears and dragged them away. Maomao chose to ignore that too.

"Such capable handling," Gaoshun commented, a remark Maomao would keep to herself.

Back to the subject at hand.

"Everyone would like to admire some of these flowers," Jinshi said. And for some reason, he was the one who was supposed to come up with them.

I knew this was going to be trouble, Maomao thought.

"You want me to find some?" she asked.

"I thought you might know something about them."

"I'm an apothecary, not a botanist."

"It just seemed like something that might be in your wheelhouse . . ." Jinshi offered weakly.

"Oh, very convincing, sir," Consort Gyokuyou said gaily from where she was lounging on a couch. The princess was beside her, sipping on some juice.

Someone somewhere (Jinshi professed not to know who) had suggested that one of Gyokuyou's ladies might know something about the subject. That at least explained why he was here.

Was it the quack? Maomao wondered. It wasn't impossible. The good-natured old fart had a bad habit of overestimating the abilities of others. It was profoundly frustrating.

Maomao wasn't entirely bereft of knowledge about roses. She knew the petals yielded an oil that served as a skin beautifier—the courtesans had used it periodically. She had earned herself some pocket change by steaming the petals of wild roses, with their powerful aroma, to make the stuff.

"I'm given to understand such flowers once bloomed on the palace grounds," Jinshi said, folding his arms. Hongniang, evidently done disciplining the three eavesdroppers, entered with fresh tea.

"Someone was seeing things, surely." *Arrgh, my calf itches*, Maomao thought. Her wound was driving her crazy as it healed. Small blessings: her feet were hidden under the table, so she could scratch it with the toes of her other foot. But somehow, that seemed to inspire itches elsewhere.

"I only heard one person say it, but upon investigation I discovered a number of people who testified to it." Jinshi's expression was hard to read.

"Was opium ever widely used here?"

"It would be the end of the damn country if the likes of opium got around!"

Consort Gyokuyou and Hongniang looked at Jinshi, wide-eyed at the sudden change of tone. Gaoshun furrowed his brow and coughed politely. The anger lingered on Jinshi's face for another beat, but the next second, the celestial smile had returned. Maomao looked at him almost pleadingly. She just didn't deal well with that smile. Gyokuyou was watching them with considerable amusement, though Maomao herself wasn't amused in the least.

"Can't you possibly?" Jinshi said.

Yeesh! Personal space! Maomao thought. He kept leaning in, but she didn't want him any closer than he already was. Finally, she heaved a sigh. "What is it you want me to do, sir?"

"I'd like them to be ready by the garden party next month."

It was time for the spring party. Had it really been that long since the last one? Maomao's emotions were just threatening to get the better of her when she had a thought. *Huh? Next month?*

"Master Jinshi, were you aware?"

"Of what?" He looked at her, curious.

He didn't understand. Of course not. There wouldn't be blue roses, couldn't be blue roses, and it wasn't a problem of color.

"It's going to be at least two more months before any roses come into bloom."

His silence was her proof: he'd had no idea. *Of course.* She was starting to get one of her bad feelings. He was going to press the matter, and she wasn't going to like it.

"I'll turn them down . . . somehow." Jinshi's shoulders slumped.

"May I ask you one thing, sir?" Maomao said. Jinshi looked at her hopefully. "Would this request happen to have come from a certain military commander?" It was the only thing she could think of, considering the circumstances. *That would explain the itching,* she thought. She'd had her suspicions; and her body had reacted in a show of absolute denial of this name she didn't wish to hear.

"Indeed. Laka—"

Jinshi slapped his hands over his mouth before he could get the name out. Gyokuyou and Hongniang looked at him, mystified.

He was speaking, of course, about *him.*

No way around it, then, Maomao thought. If he was involved, then she bore a certain responsibility.

"I don't know if I can help you," she said, "but I'll try."

"Are you sure?"

"I'm sure. But there are a few things—and a place—that I'll need."

It would have been too infuriating simply to run away from the challenge. She would have liked nothing better than to snatch the monocle off that leering face and smash it.

The spring garden party would take place among the peonies. It would ordinarily have been held a little earlier, but people kept complaining about the cold, so it had been moved back. Maybe they should have done that sooner, but precedent was a hard thing to change.

A red carpet had been laid out and long tables surrounded by chairs set up in the garden. The musical performers restlessly tuned their instruments, ready to start anytime they were needed. Women rushed back and forth making sure everything was in order, while young military men stroked their as-yet underdeveloped beards and enjoyed the sight.

A curtain had been set up behind them all as a blind, and someone behind it was making a fuss. A slim girl—practically emaciated, in fact—was holding a giant vase of flowers. Cradled in it were colorful roses—even though it was still too early in the year for them.

"You really did it," Jinshi said, gazing at the roses, whose buds had not yet opened. The flowers were red, and yellow, and white, and pink, and yes, blue—as well as black, purple, and even green. When Maomao had promised to try to create blue roses, no one had imagined this panoply of colors. Jinshi was set back on his heels, wondering how she had done it.

"I can tell you, it wasn't easy. I didn't even get them to bloom,"

Maomao said with genuine regret. She wasn't sorry to have come up short for Jinshi so much as she was disappointed not to have been able to make things go exactly as she had envisioned them. Jinshi already knew she was like that—but it still irked him.

It irked him so much.

"No, this will be just fine." He picked up a rose, water dribbling from its stem. "Hmm?" Something seemed off. For the moment, though, he didn't care; he put the rose back in the vase.

He remained surprised that, though she had only agreed to blue roses, Maomao had produced a veritable rainbow. However she had done it, she looked like she might collapse from sheer fatigue. He entrusted her to the care of the ladies-in-waiting of the Jade Pavilion, while he took the vase and set it by the seat of honor. Even as buds, not blossoms, the roses were more than enough to steal the peonies' thunder. Everyone seemed to notice them, and everyone was amazed.

Murmurs spread among the gathered officials, along with some derisive snorts: this wasn't possible.

Jinshi was a eunuch in His Majesty's good graces. What was more, though he understood that it sounded like hubris to say it, he knew that his looks were enough to take most anyone's breath away. But for all that, he still had his enemies. One would have to be all but bereft of ambition to enjoy the prospect of a young eunuch throwing his weight around with the emperor—and most officials were anything but. Jinshi never let his nymphlike smile slide, making sure his posture was perfectly straight as he approached the dais. The emperor with his prodigious beard sat there, surrounded by beautiful women.

The gazes that focused on Jinshi concealed many different thoughts and feelings. Lust was fine by him—there were endless ways to use it.

Jealousy likewise. Very simple to exploit. Whatever someone might be feeling, so long as you knew what it was, there were ways to handle it.

Far more problematic when a person was hard to read. Jinshi looked at the official who sat to the emperor's left. Full cheeks—and eyes that never gave away what he was thinking. If Jinshi was a little uncomfortable around him, who could blame him?

As far as this man was concerned, Jinshi was just a young upstart, and a eunuch at that. At one moment, he could seem to be studying Jinshi intently. The next, it was as if he were looking at empty air. The man's smile was ambiguous, defying exact interpretation.

He was Shishou, the father of one of the consorts currently at the rear palace—Loulan. He'd had the Imperial affection during the previous reign—not of the emperor, but of his mother, the empress dowager—and he continued to lord it over the current ruler.

It was not a good thing.

Even so, Jinshi never let his smile slip . . .

At least, not intentionally.

Then his gaze went from Shishou on the emperor's left to the man sitting to the emperor's right, and their eyes met. This man wore a monocle in one of his fox-like eyes, and he was eating a chicken wing with no concern for decorum. He seemed to think he was being subtle about it, but he would take a bite, stash the food in his sleeve, then take another little bite before concealing it again.

At the moment, this was the man Jinshi considered most dangerous—Lakan. He appeared to be studying the head of the high official standing beside him. Then, as if the chicken wing wasn't bad enough, he reached over and plucked away the official's cap. What could he be thinking?

For some reason, a wad of black fluff was attached to the cap's underside. Lakan feigned a look of astonishment. When they realized they could see the man's bare head, three officials across from him fell silent.

It was a cruel prank, exposing the man's (admittedly well-made) wig. A few people chuckled at the childish mischief, some were openly exasperated, and a few had their hands full trying to control a rush of anger. Jinshi wasn't the only one who couldn't maintain an impassive expression.

It wouldn't do for him to burst into laughter, however, so he somehow mastered his face and instead knelt on the carpet. He offered the vase of roses to the emperor, who stroked his beard and nodded with undisguised pleasure. Jinshi prevented himself from sighing as he respectfully withdrew.

Lakan inspected the roses theatrically, this time with a raisin in his fingers. Jinshi couldn't help wondering why nothing ever came of his failures of civility.

"You mustn't go to the Crystal Pavilion anymore."

Maomao's head rested on Yinghua's knees. They were in an open-air pavilion some distance from the banquet. Yinghua had been quite worried about Maomao, and she was keeping a close eye on her.

With her pregnancy beginning to show, Consort Gyokuyou had excused herself from this event on the pretext that she was giving her place to Loulan, the new Pure Consort, for whom this was in effect a public debut.

Why had Maomao grown so gaunt as to alarm Yinghua? It seemed every time she went to the Crystal Pavilion, she ended up ravaged by fatigue.

That was where she had been for the past month or so. She'd had Jinshi make the arrangements. The ladies-in-waiting of the Crystal Pavilion continued to look at her as if they thought she was some sort of evil spirit, but she paid them no mind. There was something she needed there in order to make her blue roses.

The "place" she had requested of Jinshi was the Crystal Pavilion's sauna, which she'd asked to have built when Consort Lihua had been convalescing. Maomao knew that despite the consort's high status, Lihua could be a very generous person, so she'd figured it couldn't hurt to ask if she might borrow the bath. And indeed, Lihua had agreed without hesitation.

Maomao still felt bad using the place for free, though, so she'd brought along a book she'd recently obtained from the Verdigris House. "This is His Majesty's favorite reading material," she said as she gave it to Lihua. The emperor had requested new and different "texts," so one of them might as well come from Lihua.

When the consort realized what kind of book it was, she calmly put it away in her private chambers, maintaining her elegant demeanor the entire time. Her ladies-in-waiting whispered among themselves as they watched their lady go to her room. Maomao regarded them with a detached gaze. No one would ever imagine that such an aristocratic woman would have a book like that tucked in her sleeve.

Having thus earned the goodwill of the mistress of the house, Mao-

mao received permission to construct a small shed in the courtyard, into which the steam from the sauna would flow. The building looked rather strange: it had large windows, including one right on the roof. Like the sauna itself, it was expensive—well, expensive for Jinshi, who paid for it out of his own purse. No skin off Maomao's nose. Still, she couldn't help wondering just how much of a salary he must draw to afford things like this.

Into the building she brought roses. Not just one, or a few, but dozens, hundreds. She cultivated them amid the warmth from the steam, making sure they got plenty of light and taking them outside when the weather was good. On any evening cold enough to threaten frost, she would stay up with the flowers all night, pouring water over hot stones to keep them warm.

More than once, all the to-ing and fro-ing caused the wound on her leg to open. When Gaoshun discovered this, he insisted on assigning another maid to be Maomao's minder. Xiaolan, of all people, was the one who arrived. (How had Gaoshun known about her?) It had proven simple enough to motivate Xiaolan: when she found out that not only would she get to skip her chores but be given snacks, too, she was thrilled to do it. She was probably the one thing that kept Maomao from collapsing from overwork.

Maomao's goal in all this elaborate maneuvering was to confuse the roses. Flowers bloom according to their season, but once in a while, for whatever reason, they can be seen to bloom at a different time of year. That was what Maomao was hoping for: to trick the roses into thinking it was time to bloom.

She'd brought in the massive number of plants on the understanding that not every one would put out buds. She'd picked a species that bloomed on the early side, and not every rose in her collection was of the same variety. With just a month to work, she couldn't guarantee success—so she was overjoyed when she saw the first buds. She'd known that would be the real challenge, far more difficult than achieving the right color. She'd gotten several eunuch helpers from Jinshi, but the subtleties of maintaining the correct temperature were something she alone could oversee. If there was the slightest mistake and the roses died, it would all be for naught.

From time to time, the women of the Crystal Pavilion would hover around, either out of open curiosity, or a desire to test their nerve against the sheer fright of seeing Maomao. They began to irritate her, so Maomao decided to arrange for something else to hold their attention. But what? The idea came to her when she was staring at her fingers, considering what to do.

She took some rouge and painted it on her fingernails, then buffed them carefully with a cloth. It was a simple manicure, the sort of thing they did all the time in the pleasure district, but it was uncommon in the rear palace. Such decoration would get in the way of work—but it immediately drew the interest of the ladies of the Crystal Pavilion, who didn't do much work to begin with. Maomao made sure the other women "happened" to catch sight of her nails, sending them scrambling to their own rooms to dig out their rouge.

That worked out very nicely, Maomao thought, and then she had a very slightly naughty idea. She decided to suggest a manicure to Consort Lihua as well.

The rear palace had its own trends, and the trendsetters were frequently the ladies who had the eye of the emperor. And since even a maid, if she became His Majesty's bedmate, could be elevated to the status of consort, it was only natural that the women of the rear palace should all want to imitate anything that might please the emperor.

At the moment, it was unquestionably Loulan who was at the cutting edge of fashion in the rear palace, but she changed her clothes so often that none of her looks could take hold as a genuine trend. When Maomao went back to the Jade Pavilion to do Gyokuyou's food tasting, she showed her manicure to the Precious Consort and the other ladies-in-waiting. Hongniang was vociferous about the inefficiency of it, but the others were all very impressed.

Wish I had some balsam plants or woodsorrel. Balsam, which was sometimes simply referred to as "nail reddener," could be ground up together with woodsorrel (sometimes called "cat's paw" in Maomao's language) and applied to the fingernails. The woodsorrel helped bring out the red color of the balsam.

About the same time a craze for manicures began to take hold in the rear palace, the buds of the roses started to swell and then put forth blossoms, a profusion of white petals. All the roses Maomao had chosen were white.

W hat in the world did you do?" Jinshi asked as he came back after presenting the flowers. There was a deep furrow in his brow, and Gaoshun, behind him, looked equally intrigued. Yinghua had gone, dismissed by Jinshi. Although Maomao was publicly Consort Gyokuyou's lady-in-waiting, Jinshi was still technically her direct employer.

"I dyed them."

"Dyed them? But there's nothing on them," Jinshi said, plucking at a petal.

"Not on the outside," Maomao said. "I dyed them from the inside." She picked up one of the blue roses and pointed to where the stem was cut. Droplets of blue liquid clung to it.

She had put the white roses in colored water. It was as simple as that. The flowers absorbed the water, color and all, through their stems, dying the petals a whole rainbow of hues. However, when they were arranged in a vase together, all the flowers except the white ones had to be specially treated, lest the colors mingle together and turn the blossoms an unpleasant black.

Thus, although the roses appeared to be arranged all in a single vase, the base of each stem had been padded with a bit of cotton impregnated with color and secured with oil paper. Maomao had left the paper there until the moment the flowers were to be presented.

That really was all there was to it.

The gimmick being so simple, it was conceivable that somebody might figure it out and say something, but Maomao had a way of dealing with that too. The night before the banquet, when His Majesty visited the Jade Pavilion, she had told him exactly what she had done. Everyone likes to be the first to learn a secret, and with the pleasure of having been let in on the game, His Majesty seemed apt to remain in good spirits no matter what anyone said to him.

Jinshi, it seemed, had withdrawn before the emperor had a chance to tell him the story.

"In other words, the last time there were blue roses around here, it was because someone or other had enough time to kill that they could spend every day infusing the roses with blue water," Maomao said, looking toward the garden of roses.

"But why on earth would someone go to all that trouble?"

"Who knows? Wanted to impress a woman, maybe," Maomao said flatly. Then she produced a narrow, oblong, paulownia-wood box from the folds of her robe. It looked like the box in which she kept her caterpillar fungus, but it was something she'd had sent along when she'd requested the "special" books.

"Now, that's unusual," Jinshi said, peering at the box. "Do you color your nails?"

"I do, though I can't say it suits me." Being exposed to so many drugs and poisons and doing so much scrubbing and washing had left her hands in a sorry state. The pinky finger on her left hand was slightly deformed. Painting it red wouldn't change the unnatural shape, but it helped.

Jinshi was looking a little too interested, so she regarded him the way she so often did: like he was a fish gawping at the surface of the water.

Oops, can't be doing that, she reminded herself, shaking her head. If a little peek was enough to set her off, she'd never last with him. Anyway, she still had work to do.

"Master Gaoshun. Do you have what I asked for?"

"Yes. Exactly as you requested."

"Thank you very much."

The stage was set. She was going to give that bastard the scare of his life.

CHAPTER 19

Red Nails

The disgustingly multicolored roses stole the show at the garden party. Lakan looked at them vacantly. The musical performance had virtually lulled him to sleep. He was holding someone's cap with a ball of fuzz attached to it in his hand, and he didn't even know where he had gotten it.

Oh well, Lakan thought, and placed the cap next to him on the table. The official beside him greedily snatched it up and arranged it on his own head. He seemed to be looking reproachfully at Lakan, but the strategist didn't really know why. He decided to take out his monocle, polish it with a handkerchief, and then put it back on the other eye.

The roses were positioned in the very center of the banquet, as if to show off the poor taste of whoever had arranged them.

He was at a banquet; he remembered that much. Music furled around him, and silk streamers waved. He was presented with a meal that was clearly the height of luxury, and he could smell wine everywhere.

It so happened that Lakan had never been very good at remembering things that didn't interest him. He recalled what had happened, but not the attendant emotions. He felt completely divorced from those.

Before he knew it, the proceedings were over, and two consorts, one dressed in black and the other in blue, were receiving roses from the emperor matching the colors they wore. Lakan heard whispers around him indicating how beautiful the women were, but he wouldn't know. Whether people's faces were beautiful or ugly was something else he'd never had a connection to.

God, this was boring. Wasn't *he* here? Why go to all the trouble of provoking him if he wasn't even going to come?

He was left with no choice but to find someone else to tease. He could at least let off a little steam. He looked around: there were plenty of people still here.

He hated crowds.

Most people's faces just looked like go stones to him. He could differentiate between men and women, for men's faces looked like black stones, and women's like white ones, but they all had nondescript, expressionless caricatures of faces on them. Some of the people he knew particularly well in the military had graduated to looking like shogi tiles, but that was all. The grunts all look like pawns, and as their ranks went up they started to look like lances or knights, the game's more powerful pieces.

The job of a military commander was simple: to arrange the pieces where each was most suited. A place for everything and everything in its place; that was what won most battles. It wasn't difficult! That was all Lakan had to do, and his job was finished. He might be a talentless hack himself, but if he could distribute his pieces correctly, those around him would take care of his work. That was how Lakan felt about the matter, anyway.

Even that man whom everyone said was as beautiful as a celestial nymph—Lakan had to take their word for it. He couldn't tell. All he knew was that he had to find a gold general with a promoted silver in tow.

And finding people was something he was used to.

Argh, but his eyes hurt worse than usual today. The red stuck in them. Everyone had red pigment on the tips of their fingers.

This so-called "red polish" was supposed to be all the rage among the palace women these days. The red polish that *he* recalled, floating back from his memories, had never been so garish. It had been thinner, lighter. The red of balsam.

The word tugged on his heartstrings, reminding him of the name of a courtesan. Even as the thought floated through his mind, a diminutive palace woman appeared directly in his line of sight. She looked small and frail, but determined, like woodsorrel.

She turned hollow eyes on him. When she saw he was looking at her, she turned as if to say, *Come with me.*

Out beyond the peony garden, a shogi board had been set up in a small open-air pavilion. On top of the board was a paulownia-wood box, inside which rested something that looked like the withered remains of a rose.

"Might I ask you for a game?" the girl said, but her voice was flat, affectless, as she picked up the pieces.

Nearby was the gold general, with his promoted silver close at hand.

What possible reason could he have to refuse? How could he turn down a request from this dear little girl—his dear little girl?

Lakan grinned cunningly.

What in the world did she hope to achieve?

Maomao had asked Jinshi to go home if it was at all possible; he, in turn, had ignored her. She looked deeply displeased but accepted it on the condition that he be quiet. Then she had issued her unspoken invitation to the commander, after which she began lining up the shogi pieces.

Her face was utterly without emotion; even her usual cold reticence seemed warm and humane in comparison. She would scratch the back of her hand from time to time; maybe she had a bugbite.

"So, who'll go first?" Lakan asked. His eyes, one of them behind a monocle, gleamed with genuine joy. It only went to show how obsessed he was with this game.

"Before we decide that, let us lay out the rules—and the wager," Maomao said.

"That should be easy enough."

Jinshi stared over Maomao's shoulder at the board. Lakan fixed an unsettling grin on him, but this was one contest he wasn't going to lose. He poured ever more honey into his own smile.

It would be a standard contest of three games out of five. Jinshi simply didn't understand. The commander had never been beaten at shogi. Maomao's very choice of game was madness. From the way Gaoshun's brow was furrowed, it seemed he shared Jinshi's opinion. What could be going through Maomao's head?

"What pieces do you want for your handicap? A rook, perhaps? Or a bishop?" Lakan said.

"I don't need a handicap," Maomao replied. Jinshi, though, thought Lakan had been very sporting to offer one, and that Maomao should have politely accepted it.

"Very well. If I win, you'll become my child."

Jinshi nearly objected aloud to this, but Gaoshun stopped him. They had promised not to speak.

"I'm currently employed, so you would have to wait until my term of service expires."

"Employed?" The fox-like eyes glanced in Jinshi's direction. He never let his smile slip, though he had to resist a twitching in his cheeks. "Are you really?"

"Yes, and the paperwork says so."

And so it did—at least, that was what the paper Maomao had seen said. But suppose it had been the old madam—her guardian, after a fashion—who had actually signed it? The man who was effectively Maomao's adoptive father had pinched the brush right out of Mao-mao's hand.

"Well, I hope it's all in order. But more importantly . . ." Lakan studied her. ". . . what will *you* ask for?"

"Yes, the wager I request." Maomao closed her eyes. "Perhaps I could ask you to purchase one courtesan from the Verdigris House?"

Lakan stroked his chin. "I must say, of everything I thought you might ask for, I didn't expect that."

Maomao remained completely impassive. "The madam is looking to clear out those who are getting on in years. I won't stipulate who you must buy out."

"So it's come to that." Lakan looked absolutely exasperated somehow. And then he grinned. "But if that's what you request, then that's what I must accept. Is that all you ask for?"

Maomao regarded Lakan coldly. "Perhaps I could also stipulate two additional rules."

"Name them."

"All right." Maomao produced a bottle of wine she'd asked Gaoshun to prepare. She poured equal amounts into five separate cups. The smell suggested it was distinctly potent stuff.

Then Maomao produced some medicine packets from her sleeve and sprinkled one into three of the cups. They each contained similar-looking powder. She gave each cup a gentle tilt, dissolving the powder, then quickly shuffled the five cups around until it was impossible to say which were which.

"After each game, the winner will pick one of these cups, and the loser must drink from it. The loser doesn't have to drain the entire cup; a mouthful will do."

Jinshi was getting a very, very bad feeling about this. He moved from directly behind Maomao over to one side. He had the impression that her face had taken on a slight flush. Previously so emotionless, her lips now flirted with a smile.

He knew what caused Maomao to make that face. He wanted to know what the powder was but didn't dare ask. He was angry at himself for not being able to ask.

Lakan voiced the question instead. "What was that powder you put in them?"

"A drug. Medicinal, in small quantities." But, Maomao added, all three cups together would be tremendously poisonous. She managed to say this with a smile on her face, strange girl that she was. "The other rule I request," she said, "is that if a person abandons a game for any reason, it will be considered a loss. Those are my two rules."

She gently rocked the cups that might or might not have been poisoned. Her hand was stained red, and on that hand the pinky finger was deformed.

Lakan stared intently at that finger.

M aomao thought of the most terrible things, Jinshi reflected. Even knowing it would be all right as long as one didn't drink all three cups, she seemed cavalier about it. Was she trying to gain a psychological advantage? True, any ordinary opponent might have been shaken by the extra pressure. But this wasn't an ordinary opponent; it was the master strategist himself, widely regarded as a superlative player. It would take more than a little scare tactic to bend him out of shape.

As anyone might have predicted, Maomao lost the first two games in a row.

Jinshi had thought maybe she at least knew the ins and outs of the game, but it became clear that she knew the rules at best and had no real experience of actual play. She had already drunk down two of the cups; quite eagerly, in fact.

For the umpteenth time, Jinshi asked himself what she could be thinking.

The third game had only just begun, but the outcome already seemed apparent. When Maomao drank that third cup, she might poison herself. The chances of picking one of the drugged cups were three out of five the first time, and after the second game, two out of four. After this last game, the chance would be one out of three. In other words, there was a one-in-ten chance that she was about to poison herself horribly.

Jinshi wasn't sure which was more frightening: the thought that Maomao might poison herself, or the realization that he knew she might drink the poison and be just fine. He wasn't sure if Lakan knew how resilient Maomao was when it came to toxic substances.

He looked at Gaoshun, wondering what they would do when the winner was decided. At that moment, there came a voice: "Check." But the voice didn't belong to Lakan; it was Maomao's.

Jinshi and Gaoshun both looked at the board to discover Maomao's gold general closing in on Lakan's king. The way she had used her pieces was pathetic, amateurish—but there was no denying that the king had been trapped with no escape.

"Well, heck. I yield." Lakan put his hands up.

"A win is a win, even if you gave it to me, yes?" Maomao said.

"So it is. God knows I can't poison my own daughter, even if I do it by mistake."

Maomao's expression hadn't changed as she drank the two cups; it was impossible to know whether there had been drugs in them or not. Lakan gazed at his expressionless daughter with a somewhat cowed smile. "That drug you used—does it have any taste?" he asked.

"It's quite salty. You'll know at the first sip."

"Fine, then. Which one will you pick for me?"

"Take whichever one you like."

So that was it: Lakan could afford to lose two games. If either of the drinks he took tasted salty, he would know Maomao was out of danger. The percentages were the same, but this was a much safer method. Nothing escaped this man.

Lakan took the cup in the center and brought it to his lips.

"Oof. Salty."

Jinshi hung his head. To his ears, the words signaled that it would all be over with the next game. He wondered what he would do now . . .

"And . . . warm." He looked up when he heard that. Lakan's face was bright red, and he was swaying unsteadily. Then the blood drained from his face, and suddenly he slumped over, pale as a sheet.

Gaoshun rushed over and propped Lakan up.

"What the hell is wrong with you?" Jinshi demanded. "You said one dose of that drug was safe!" No matter how much she hated Lakan, he couldn't believe she would actually poison him.

"I did. And it is," Maomao replied, appearing thoroughly vexed. She picked up a carafe of water nearby and brought it over to Gaoshun and Lakan. She pried Lakan's eyes open to make sure he wasn't comatose, then dumped water into his mouth, forcing him to drink. She wasn't exactly gentle.

"Master Jinshi," Gaoshun said, perplexed. "He appears to be . . . drunk."

"Alcohol is the king of all drugs," Maomao commented. She had, she said, simply added a bit of salt and sugar to help the body absorb it. She was attending to Lakan, albeit with a minimum of enthusiasm.

Despite her distaste for him, she was evidently going to do justice to her vocation as an apothecary. "And this man is not a drinker," she said.

With that, Jinshi finally understood what she had been plotting all along. He realized that he had only ever seen Lakan drink juice, never alcohol.

"All right," Maomao said, scratching the back of her head and looking at Jinshi. "Let's drag him off to the brothel so he can pick a flower."

She sounded practically disinterested. Jinshi could only offer a stunned "Right."

CHAPTER 20

Balsam and Woodsorrel

An old memory came back to him. So many scenes in black and white—this one alone boasted some faint red. It seemed he had trouble seeing things others saw easily, but this alone shone bright and clear.

Red. Red were the fingers that held the go stones or shogi tiles.

His toned, rippling muscles would have been the envy of anyone. Only one person seemed unimpressed by them: that great lady, the esteemed courtesan Fengxian.

He was sometimes obliged to visit brothels when out socially with others, but to be blunt, they were of little interest to him. He couldn't drink alcohol, and dancing or erhu performances didn't excite him. No matter how beautifully a woman dressed, she looked like nothing more than a plain white go stone to him.

He had been this way for a long time: he couldn't tell one human face from another. But even this was an improvement. It was bad enough to confuse one's mother with his wet nurse, but he couldn't even tell men apart from women.

His father, feeling that there was nothing he could do for his child, had begun seeing a young lover. His mother promptly began plotting to get back her husband—though he had abandoned his child because the boy couldn't identify his own father's face!

Thus, despite being born the eldest son of a prominent family, Lakan had lived his life with an unusual amount of freedom—a blessing, as far as he was concerned. He lost himself in go and shogi, which he learned by playing game after game; he kept his ear to the ground for rumors, and once in a while he pulled a little prank.

That time he made blue roses bloom in the palace? That was something he'd tried after hearing his uncle talk about it. His uncle wasn't always the most pleasant person, but was, the young man felt, the only one who understood him. It was his uncle who told him to focus not on people's faces, but on their voices, their body language, their silhouettes. It made life a little easier when he started to assign shogi pieces to those he was closest to; over time he reached a point where only those he had no interest in were go stones, while those he was starting to become more intimate with appeared as shogi tiles.

When his uncle began to appear as a dragon king—a promoted rook—the young man knew for certain that his uncle was a person of great accomplishment.

To him, go and shogi were simply games, extensions of his leisure. He never imagined that they would reveal his true aptitudes. His family background afforded him another stroke of luck: although he had no special martial talents, he was promptly made a captain. He knew he didn't have to be strong and powerful, though; if he used his subordinates wisely, the profit would come. Shogi with human pieces was the most interesting game of all.

He continued undefeated in both his games and his work until a spiteful colleague introduced him to the famed courtesan. Fengxian had never lost to anyone at her brothel, and he had never lost to anyone in the army. Whichever of them had their streak broken in this game, the spectators would enjoy themselves.

He discovered then that he had been like a frog living at the bottom of a well. Fengxian all but broke him over her knee. Even though she held the white stones, meaning she had the disadvantage of playing second, she amassed a crushing amount of territory. She took the stones in her delicately painted fingers and systematically cut him down to size.

He could hardly remember the last time he had lost a game. He didn't feel anger so much as a sort of awe at the remorseless wound she had inflicted on him. Fengxian resented that he had taken her lightly: he surmised as much from the way she never said a word, the way even her movements were dismissive, as if the game hardly warranted her attention.

Entirely without meaning to, he started laughing, so hard he clutched his sides. The onlookers murmured; they thought he had gone insane. He laughed so hard his eyes blurred with tears, but when he looked at the merciless courtesan, he saw not the usual white go stone, but the face of a woman in an ill humor. The look in her eyes would let no one get close to her. Like her namesake, the balsam, Fengxian seemed as if she might burst at the slightest touch.

Was this what human faces looked like?

It was the first time he had experienced something other people took for granted.

Fengxian whispered something to an apprentice who was attending her. The little girl pattered away and returned with a shogi board. The courtesan, so lofty that she wouldn't even allow a man to hear her voice at their first meeting, was challenging him to another game.

This time, he wouldn't lose.

He rolled up his sleeves and began setting out his pieces.

The woman named Fengxian had her pride as a courtesan if nothing else. Perhaps it was because she had been born in a brothel. She sometimes said that she had no mother, only a woman who bore her—for in the pleasure district, courtesans could not be mothers.

Their acquaintance continued for years and years, and during their meetings they would focus on one thing only: playing go or shogi. Gradually, though, they saw each other less frequently. As accomplished courtesans grew more popular, they also became more reluctant to take customers, and Fengxian was no exception.

Fengxian was intelligent, but flinty and hard; this might not have appealed to most people, but there was a small cadre of diehards who ate it up. Perhaps there's no accounting for taste.

Her price kept going up, until it was all he could do to see her once every few months.

Once when he went to the brothel to see her after a long absence, he found her painting her nails, looking as disinterested as ever. Red balsam flowers and some thin grass sat on a plate in front of her. When he asked what the latter was, she replied, "It's cat's paw." A plant with medicinal properties, evidently, useful to counteract bugbites and some poisons.

Interestingly, balsam and cat's paw shared an unusual characteristic: if you so much as touched the ripe seed pods, they would burst and send seeds everywhere. He picked up one of the yellow flowers, thinking that maybe he would try touching one the next time he had a chance, just to see what happened—when Fengxian said, "When will you come next?"

How strange—this from the woman who only ever sent the most impersonal notices to remind him her services were available.

"Another three months on."

"Very well."

Fengxian told an apprentice to clean up her manicure supplies, then began setting up a game of shogi.

It was about that time that he first heard talk of Fengxian's contract being bought out. Sometimes the price had little to do with a courtesan's perceived value: some people would drive up the amount simply because they didn't like one of the other bidders.

He had managed to earn some promotions in the military, but meanwhile, his position as heir to his family's fortune had been usurped by a younger half brother, and the bidding ultimately became impossible for him to keep up with.

So, what to do?

An awful idea entered his head, but he immediately snuffed it out. It would have been unimaginable to actually do it.

270

———◇———

A nother three months, another trip to the brothel, and now Fengxian sat before him with two game boards ready to play, one of go, one of shogi.

The first words out of her mouth were: "Perhaps a wager today?"

If you win, I'll give you anything you like. And if I win, I'll take something I want.

"Choose your game."

It was shogi at which he held the upper hand—yet when he sat, it was in front of the go board.

Fengxian dismissed her apprentice, saying she wished to focus on the game.

H e didn't know which of them had been victorious, but the next thing he knew their hands were intertwined. There were no sweet nothings from Fengxian. Nor did he feel compelled to offer any vapid words of sentiment. In that respect, perhaps, they were alike.

He heard Fengxian, cradled in his arms, whisper, "I want to play go."

Personally, he had been thinking about some shogi.

T he misfortune began after that. The uncle with whom he had been so close was dismissed from his position. The man never had known how to play the game, and Lakan's father declared the uncle a disgrace to the family. The uncle's misadventure had not in fact done any harm to the family, but Lakan now found himself persona non grata for having been too close to him. He was told to go on a long trip and not come back for a while.

He could have ignored this, but it would only have been a headache later. His father was in the military, too, making him not just a parent but a superior officer. At last, he wrote to the brothel saying he would return in half a year's time. This was after he had received a letter saying the contract buyout had fallen through.

Thus, for a time, he labored under the impression that all would be well.

Little did he imagine that it would be some three years before he came back.

When he finally returned home, he found a mountain of letters had been tossed carelessly into his dust-choked room. The branches tied to them were withered and dry, making the passage of time painfully evident.

His gaze fell on one letter that showed signs of having been opened. It was full of all the familiar banalities—but in the corner of the letter, there was a dark-red stain. He glanced into the half-open pouch beside the letter. It, too, was stained.

He opened the pouch to discover what looked like two small twigs, or maybe lumps of clay. One of them was tiny; it looked delicate enough to crush in his hand.

He was too late realizing what they were: he had ten of them himself. The trend known as "pinky swear" came to mind . . .

He rewrapped the two twigs and shoved them back into the pouch, then raced for the pleasure district as fast as his horse would carry him.

When he reached the brothel, which he found looking substantially more dilapidated than when he had seen it last, there were only go stones there. There was no one who resembled balsam, although a woman came at him with a broom. It was the old madam; he could tell by her voice.

Fengxian was no longer there: that was the only thing the madam said to him. A courtesan who'd been abandoned by two important prospects, had dragged the name of her establishment through the mud, and was no longer trusted by anyone had no choice but to turn tricks like a common harlot. Did he not grasp what happened to such women?

A little thought might have revealed the answer, but his head was full of go and shogi and nothing else, and he had been unable to arrive at the truth. Throwing himself on the ground and crying, heedless of onlookers, wouldn't turn back time.

It was all his fault for being so impulsive. All of it.

Lakan sat up abruptly in bed, gripping his still-throbbing head. He recognized the room he was in. Somewhere with a fragrant but not overpowering incense.

"Are you awake now, sir?" someone said gently. A face like a white go stone appeared before him. He recognized her from the voice.

"What am I doing here, Meimei?"

Yes, he knew this courtesan of the Verdigris House. She'd been Fengxian's apprentice long ago. She was the one Fengxian had ordered out of the room, in fact, if he recalled correctly. He'd seen her as an apprentice tentatively toying with go stones from time to time, and so he had humored her with the occasional game. She always acted all embarrassed when he told her she was a pretty good player.

"A messenger from some noble brought you here and left you. My word, but you were a mess. I don't know whether your face was more red or blue!"

Meimei was more or less the only courtesan at the Verdigris House who would entertain him. It was always her room to which he was shown on his visits.

"I sure didn't think I'd end up this way." He'd assumed that if his daughter was drinking it, the alcohol couldn't be that strong. Then again, Lakan had never been very conversant with different types of alcoholic drink. Just a single swallow of that stuff had been enough to set his throat on fire. He grabbed a carafe of water from the bedside and drank lustily.

A bitter flavor spread through his mouth, and he spat the water out before he knew what he was doing. "Wh-what is this swill?!"

"Maomao prepared it," Meimei said. He presumed she was smiling, for she covered her mouth with her sleeve. The drink was probably intended as a hangover cure, but the way it was delivered implied a touch of malice. Was it strange that, even so, he couldn't keep a grin from his face?

Beside the carafe was a paulownia-wood box.

"Well, would you look at that . . ."

He had sent it along with a letter a long time ago, jokingly, as if it were loot. He opened it to find a single dried rose. He hadn't realized it would retain its shape so well despite having dried out. He thought of his daughter, who reminded him of woodsorrel—cat's paw.

After those long-ago events, he had come knocking on the door of the Verdigris House again and again, each time to be met with the madam's recriminations. There's no baby here, go on home, she would shout as she thrashed him with the broom. She could be terrifying indeed.

Once, as he was sitting, exhausted, with blood dribbling down the side of his head, he noticed a child rooting around nearby. There had been grasses with some sort of yellow flowers growing by the building. When he asked the child what she was doing, she said she was going to turn the grass into medicine. Instead of the go stone he expected to see, he perceived an emotionless face.

The girl set off running with two handfuls of grass. She was heading for someone who walked with a limp like an old man. And *his* face, which might have been expected to look like a go stone, instead looked like a shogi tile. And not simply a pawn or a knight, but a dragon king, a powerful and important piece.

He knew now who it was who had opened the one letter out of all those he had received, and the dirty pouch. For here was his uncle Luomen, who had disappeared after being banished from the rear palace. The girl with the cat's paw went trotting about after him; he called her Maomao.

Lakan pulled out the dirty pouch. It was even more worn than it used to be, since he carried it with him at all times. He knew the two twig-like objects would still be inside, wrapped in paper.

Maomao's hand had looked unsteady as she moved her tiles. Partly that could have been because she didn't play the game much. But partly it was because she was playing with her left hand. When he had looked at the red-colored fingertips, he had noted that her pinky finger on that hand was deformed.

He couldn't blame her for hating him. Not considering all he had done. But even so, he wanted to put himself near her. He was tired of a life of nothing but go stones and shogi tiles. That had given him the incentive he had needed to steal back his birthright, to expel his half brother, and to adopt his nephew as his own. Then, in the course of much negotiating with the old madam and over some ten years, he had successfully paid off an amount of money equivalent to two times the damages.

It must have been around that time that he was finally allowed back into the rooms. Meimei naturally took on the role. Perhaps she was paying him back for teaching her shogi all those years before.

Lakan continued to visit, time and time again, because the only thing he wanted was to be with his daughter. Unfortunately, one talent Lakan decidedly lacked was the ability to grasp how other people were feeling, and again and again the things he did seemed to backfire.

He tucked the pouch back among the folds of his robe. Maybe it was time to give up, at least this time. Somehow—call it stubbornness—he couldn't bring himself to let the matter drop completely.

And besides, he didn't like the man in her company. He stood much too close to her, and during their match, he had touched her shoulders no fewer than three times. Lakan had been peevishly pleased to see his daughter brush the hand away each time, though.

All right, how to make himself feel a little better? Lakan picked up the carafe and drank down the foul-tasting medicine. However disgusting it might have been, his daughter had made it herself.

Maybe he would spend some time deciding how to knock the bug off his flower. His thoughts were interrupted when the door flew open with a slam.

"Finally had enough sleep, have we?" a go stone cried hoarsely. He could tell from the voice that it was the old madam. "So you're looking to buy one of my girls, are you? You ought to know by now that a couple of thousand silver isn't going to cut it."

Still a skinflint, as ever. Lakan held his pounding head, but a wry smile appeared on his face. He put on the monocle (which he only wore for effect). "Try ten thousand. And if that's not enough, how about twenty or thirty? Admittedly, a hundred might be a bit of a stretch." Lakan winced inwardly as he spoke. They weren't small sums, even in his position. He would have to beg from his nephew for a while; the boy had some side businesses he ran.

"Well, all right. Come this way and make it snappy. I'll even let you choose, whichever one you like." He let the madam lead him into the main room of the brothel, in which there stood a whole row of gaudily attired go stones. Even Meimei was mixed in among them.

"Hoh, I could even pick one of the Three Princesses?"

"I said whichever one you liked, and I meant it," the madam veritably spat. "But you can expect to pay for it."

Even with this dispensation to choose freely, Lakan faced a unique problem. However fancy the girls' dresses, to him they all looked like nothing more than go stones. He could practically hear the women smiling. He could smell their sweet fragrances. And the kaleidoscope of colors that was their outfits nearly blinded him. But that was all. He felt nothing more than that. None of them moved Lakan's heart.

He had been told to choose, though, so choose he must. Once he had purchased the girl, he could do as he pleased with her. He had enough money to keep a lady, and if she was unhappy with that, then he would give her some cash and set her free to do as she wished. Fine, surely that would be fine.

With that in mind, he turned toward Meimei. He supposed it was guilt that induced her to be so kind to him. If she hadn't left them that day, perhaps none of this would have happened. It would be well and good, he thought, to reward her decency.

At that moment, Meimei spoke. "Master Lakan." He could hear a small smile in her voice. "You must know I have my courtesan's pride. If I am your desire, then I will have no hesitation." So saying, she pattered over to the great window that looked onto the courtyard and opened it. The curtain fluttered, and a few stray flower petals drifted into the room. "But if you're going to choose, then choose with your eyes open."

"Meimei, I didn't give you permission to open that window!" the madam exclaimed, rushing to close it again.

But Lakan had already heard it, distantly. Laughter. Like a courtesan's chuckle, but somehow more innocent. He thought he caught the words of a child's song.

His eyes widened.

"What is it?" the madam asked suspiciously. Lakan gazed out the ornate window. The singing drifted to them in snatches. "What are you doing?!" Becoming increasingly agitated, she tried to grab his hand.

But she was too late. He jumped out the window and hit the ground running, dashing single-mindedly toward the source of the voice. He had never regretted his failure to exercise more bitterly than he did at this moment. Yet he ran on, even as his legs threatened to buckle underneath him.

For all the times he had been to the Verdigris House, he had never been to this particular part of it: a small building, almost a storage shed, at a distance from the main house. He could hear the song coming from within.

Trying to keep his heart from pounding clear out of his chest, Lakan opened the door. He caught a distinctive odor of medicine.

Inside was an emaciated woman. Her hair ringed her head but had no luster, and her arms lay atop her like withered branches. She reeked of illness. And there was something else: her left ring finger was deformed. Lakan could only stare in amazement. He realized then that he felt something on his cheeks.

The madam rushed up. "What are you doing? This is a sickroom!" She grabbed his hand and tried to drag him away, but Lakan didn't move. He was staring, fixated on the emaciated woman. "Come on, get out of here. Come choose one of my girls."

"Yes. Right. Must make a choice." Lakan sat down slowly, making no effort to wipe away the overflowing droplets. The woman didn't seem to notice him; she only smiled and sang her little song. There was no longer any trace of the imperious bearing or the mocking look. Her heart had reverted to that of an innocent child. Yet despite her wasted state, to Lakan, she looked more beautiful than anyone in the world.

"This woman, madam. I want this woman."

"Don't be stupid. Get back in there and pick."

Lakan, though, reached into the folds of his robe, feeling around until he found a heavy pouch. He pulled it out and placed it in the woman's hand. It appeared to catch her interest; she opened it and looked inside with stiff, stilted motions. With trembling fingers, she pulled out a go stone.

Perhaps it was only his imagination that made him think he saw a momentary flush on her face. Lakan grinned. "This is the woman I'm going to buy out, and I don't care how much it costs. Ten thousand, twenty, it doesn't matter."

There was nothing the old madam could say to that. Meimei came up behind her, her dress dragging on the floor as she entered the room to sit across from the sick woman. She took the woman's bony hand. "If only you had said what you wanted to begin with, Elder Sister. Why didn't you speak up sooner?" Meimei seemed to be crying; he could tell when he heard the sob. "Why not let it be over before I started to hope?"

Lakan didn't understand why Meimei was crying. He was busy studying the woman, who looked affably at the go stone.

She was as beautiful as balsam.

I am so tired . . .

Maomao was reminded how exhausting it was to deal with people she wasn't used to. She'd helped get the soused fox-eyed man to a sleeping chamber, and now was all but stumbling home. She'd already parted ways with Jinshi and Gaoshun, who had business of their own to attend to. They'd left her with another official—the one who had accompanied her during the food-poisoning investigation.

Basen, that was his name. She'd only had to meet him several times to start remembering it. He was easy to work with: he wasn't effusive, but he did his job attentively and thoroughly. It was a good combination for Maomao, who rarely felt compelled to start a conversation if someone else didn't do it first.

Seeing *him* again, though, had reminded Maomao that sometimes there were people you simply didn't get along with. Things you simply couldn't accept. Even if the other person had never had any malice.

As she trudged along, Maomao spied a glittering entourage. At the center of it, attended by a palace woman holding a parasol for her, was a woman in a lavish dress—Consort Loulan.

Maomao heard someone cluck their tongue. She realized Basen was beside her, watching the group through lidded eyes. He didn't seem to like it very much. Maomao briefly wondered why, but then she saw a portly court official standing and waiting for Loulan. He was flanked by men who looked like aides, and there was a train of people behind him.

When Loulan saw the portly man, she hid her mouth with a folding fan and began speaking to him in an obviously friendly manner. Notwithstanding all the ladies-in-waiting who were present, Maomao wondered if it was really all right for any consort to be speaking so intimately with a man who wasn't His Majesty.

A venomous whisper from Basen, however, answered her question. "Damned schemers, father and daughter both."

So that must be Loulan's father, the one who had pushed to have her admitted to the rear palace. Maomao had heard rumors that the man had been an influential advisor of the former emperor, but that the current ruler, who preferred to promote people on demonstrated merit, regarded him about as favorably as a black eye.

Nonetheless, Maomao shot Basen a look. She wished he wouldn't bad-mouth a high official out loud, even if she was the only one around. If anyone chanced to hear them, they might think she was a willing party to the conversation.

He's still young, I guess. Looking at him, it occurred to her that he wasn't much older than she was.

It had been decided that Maomao wouldn't go back to the rear palace that night, but would stay at Jinshi's residence instead.

"And here I was under the impression you despised him," Jinshi said slowly, his arms crossed. He'd gotten there before she had and had been waiting for her.

Maomao was sipping some congee Suiren had prepared. It was bad manners to talk while one ate, but she was more interested in catching up on the nutrition she'd missed during her time at the Crystal Pavilion. Suiren, shocked to see Maomao so thin when she reappeared after her stint away from Jinshi's residence, hadn't stopped at congee but was producing one dish after another. In this, too, she was like the women of the Jade Pavilion, not begrudging any task because she was a lady-in-waiting.

"I don't despise him. It's precisely because he did what he did—and *who* he did—that I'm here at all."

"*Who* he—?" Jinshi seemed to be wondering if there wasn't a more delicate way to put that.

Not sure what he wants me to say, Maomao thought. She was only telling the truth.

"I don't know how you imagine the pleasure district works, but no courtesan has a child unless she wants to."

All courtesans routinely took contraceptive medicines or abortifacients. Even if a child was conceived, there were any number of ways to end the pregnancy early on. If they gave birth, it meant they wanted to.

"In fact, one might almost think it had been planned."

By paying attention to when a woman had her flow of blood, it was simple enough to take an educated guess when she was likely to conceive. A courtesan need only send a letter changing her partner's visit to a convenient day.

"By the commander?" Jinshi asked as he took a bite of a snack Suiren brought him.

"Women are cunning creatures," Maomao replied. Thus, when her aim had gone awry, she'd lost control of herself. She had been so far gone that she had even been willing to injure herself, and worse . . .

That dream the other day.

It really had happened. Not satisfied with just severing her own finger, the courtesan who had given birth to Maomao had taken her child's to add to her letter as well.

No one at the brothel ever spoke to Maomao about the courtesan who had borne her. She was well aware that the old madam had ordered everyone to stay silent on the subject. But just the atmosphere of the place, along with a modicum of curiosity, was enough to make the truth clear.

Maomao was the reason the Verdigris House had nearly gone under.

She also learned that her father was an eccentric man who loved go and shogi—and that all that had happened could be laid at the feet of one headstrong and selfish courtesan.

She learned one other thing, as well: the identity of this woman, whom Maomao had always been told was no longer there. The identity of the woman who, until the humiliation of her missing nose drove her insane, had always refused to go anywhere near Maomao.

That fool of a man. There were better courtesans! Why didn't he just buy one of them out? That's what he should have done . . .

"Master Jinshi, does that man ever speak to you anywhere but your office?"

Jinshi thought for a second. "Now that you mention it, no, he doesn't." The most he ever did, Jinshi said, was give him a quick nod of the head when they passed each other in the hallway. The only time the man ever cornered him with chatter was when he showed up at Jinshi's office.

"Once in a while," Maomao said, "you'll meet someone who can't discern people's faces. That man is one of them."

This was something Maomao's old man had told her. She'd only half believed it herself, but when he'd told her that *he* was like that, it had somehow seemed to make sense.

"Can't discern?" Jinshi said. "What do you mean?"

"Simply what I said. They can't seem to put faces together. They know what an eye is, or a mouth, and can perceive these different bits, but they don't register them in aggregate as distinct faces."

Her old man had been solemn as he told her this. He was communicating that even *he* deserved sympathy, for he had suffered much in his life because of this thing he couldn't control. Nonetheless, while her old man was compassionate, he did grasp the broader situation, and he never tried to stop the old madam from chasing the other man out of the brothel with her broom. He knew that wrong was wrong.

"For some reason, he does seem to recognize me and my adoptive father. I think that's where that stubborn obsession of his comes from."

One day, out of the blue, a strange man had appeared and tried to lead her away. The madam had shown up shortly after and beaten him with a broom, and the sight of the bruised and bloodied man had inspired fear in her young heart. Anyone would be scared by a man who reached out to them grinning even as blood poured from his face.

He showed up periodically after that, always doing something unexpected before being sent home a bloody mess. It had taught her not to be surprised by anything, or at any rate by very few things. The man kept calling himself her father, but as far as Maomao was concerned her father was her "old man," not that raving eccentric. He was, at best, the stud who had sired her.

He was trying to displace Maomao's old man, Luomen, and be her father instead, but Maomao was having none of it. This was one point on which she wouldn't bend. Everyone at the brothel told her that the woman who had given birth to her was gone—it was less trouble that way. And even if she was alive, what did Maomao care? Maomao had her old man; she was Luomen's daughter. And she was perfectly happy that way.

That man wasn't the only one responsible for her. In fact, she was grateful to him on that count. She had no memories of her *mother*— only of a terrifying demon.

As for how Maomao felt toward Lakan—she might hate him, but she didn't resent him. He was clumsy about some things, but not malicious, even if he was sometimes a bit overdramatic in his reactions. If there was a question of forgiveness to be answered, well, there was at least one person who had more reason to resent him than Maomao did.

Maybe the madam's forgiven him by now, she thought.

She wondered if the man had noticed the letter in the box with the rose in it. It was the biggest concession Maomao was capable of making to her sire. Well, if he never noticed, that was fine. Let him buy out her pleasant courtesan-sister. That might be the happiest outcome all around.

"I can't help thinking it certainly *looked* like you hated him."

"That's simply because you don't know him very well yet, Master Jinshi."

When Maomao had been trying to get into the ritual, it was Lakan who had helped her. She suspected he'd had an intuition that something was going to happen. He'd never needed to look at scenes and gather evidence the way Maomao did in order to predict impending events. He seemed to simply have a nose for them. And his guesses were rarely wrong.

"Has he never wheedled you into looking into a matter you otherwise wouldn't?" Maomao asked.

Jinshi fell quiet at that, but from the way he then whispered, "So *that's* what that was," she presumed she had guessed correctly. Perhaps he was also the reason Lihaku had been so quick to investigate Suirei, and that the Board of Justice had responded so efficiently to her.

The one hitch with that man was that as much as trouble as he put everyone else to, he never seemed to want to lift a finger himself. Just imagine what might happen if he were willing to take a public stand every once in a while.

Maybe that resurrection drug would already be within reach. The thought pained her immensely.

He didn't understand what genius he was blessed with. This whole country held few people whom her old man would praise so openly and with such fervor. Maomao recognized this feeling: it was jealousy.

"It might be impossible to make a friend of him, but I'd suggest you not make him an enemy either." She almost spat the words—then held up her left hand and looked at the pinky finger. "Master Jinshi, do you know something?"

"What is it?"

"If you cut off a fingertip, it will grow back."

"Must you say that while I'm eating?" He gave her an uncharacteristic glare, their usual positions reversed.

"One more thing, then."

"Yes, what?"

"If that man with his monocle ever told you to 'Call me Papa,' how would you feel?"

Jinshi paused for a moment and looked deeply disturbed: another unusual expression for him.

"My goodness," Suiren said, putting her hand to her mouth.

"I suppose I would want to tear that stupid monocle off his face and shatter it."

"I expect so."

Jinshi seemed to understand what Maomao was getting at. He

whispered a question, something about whether it was rough to be a father. Standing beside him, a twinge of grief passed over Gaoshun's face. Perhaps something about the conversation struck a nerve.

"Is something the matter?" Maomao asked, and Gaoshun gazed up at the ceiling.

"No. Only bear in mind that no father in the world wishes to be reviled," he said softly.

Well now, Maomao thought, but she only brought her spoon to her mouth, determined to finish the last of her congee.

Epilogue

Several days after Maomao returned to the rear palace, a letter from Meimei arrived, along with a package. The letter spelled out exactly whose contract had been bought out, and by whom. It must have been raining or something when she wrote, for the page was streaked with droplets.

In the small case that accompanied the letter was a lovely scarf of the kind courtesans used on celebratory occasions. Maomao was about to close the case again but thought better of it. Instead she went over to a chest of clothing, one of the furnishings in her small room, and started digging for something at the very bottom.

The lights of the pleasure quarter glittered in the distance. Maomao thought they looked even brighter and more numerous than usual. From her place atop the outer wall of the rear palace, she could hear jangling bells—courtesans dancing with their scarves, she imagined. They would wear their most beautiful outfits, wave long, flowing cloths, and scatter flower petals.

Being bought out of a contract was a cause for celebration. When all the city bloomed for one woman alone, the other flowers would dance to see her off. There would be wine and feasting, singing and dancing. The pleasure district never slept, so the carousing would go on all night.

As for Maomao, she had the gossamer scarf Meimei had sent her wrapped around her shoulders. She grasped it with her fingers. Her left leg still wasn't at its best, but she thought she could manage this. She removed her overrobe and dabbed a touch of rouge on her lips. That, too, she had received from Meimei.

It feels like some kind of joke. Maomao thought of Princess Fuyou, who had been given to a military officer, an old friend of hers, in marriage the year before. Had she forgotten all about her days in the rear palace by now? Or did she sometimes remember how she once danced on these walls, night after night?

Now Maomao would do the same thing as the princess. Clad in the lovely dress her sisters had foisted on her, she called to mind the first steps of the dance she'd been taught so long ago. The rouge she'd received from her sister Meimei was on her lips. Small bells were attached to her sleeves, so she jingled with each movement. Small stones were sewn into the long skirt so that it would billow out each time Maomao spun.

Her skirt circled around her, her scarf traced an arc, and her sleeves slipped through the air. She'd let her hair down tonight, decorating it with a single rose, a small flower dyed blue.

The scarf danced; the skirt rose in time; sleeves and hair fluttered together.

Didn't think it would come back to me so easily, she mused, surprised to find the dance the old woman had taught her still within.

Her scarf billowed again—and then Maomao found herself looking directly at a very unwelcome companion. That was when she tripped on her skirt.

She fell face-first, and as she tried to protect herself from striking the ground with her nose, she tumbled—straight toward the edge of the wall. She just managed to stop herself, and someone pulled her up.

"Wh-*what* are you doing here?" the unexpected visitor asked, breathing hard. His hair, which had been carefully bound, was a mess now.

"I should ask you the same question, Master Jinshi," Maomao said, brushing off her dress. "Why are *you* here?"

He fixed her with an exasperated look. She was safely away from the edge of the wall now, but for some reason he was still holding on to her hand. "Where else was I supposed to be? When I got word a strange woman was dancing on the wall again, I had to come deal with the matter."

Huh, and I thought I'd kept a low profile. Now Maomao thought about it, though, maybe it shouldn't have been so surprising that she was noticed. Still, did this mean the guards still believed in ghosts?

"I'll thank you not to add to my workload," Jinshi said, placing his hand on Maomao's head.

"Surely you didn't have to come yourself, Master Jinshi. Couldn't you have sent someone else?" She slid her head aside, out from under his hand.

"A very kind guard recognized your face and contacted me directly," Jinshi said. Maomao touched her face. "You may think what you're doing is innocuous, but remember that it won't look that way to those who see you."

"As you say," Maomao replied. Somewhat embarrassed, she scratched her cheek. This whole endeavor was harder than she'd thought.

"That's my story," Jinshi said. "Now it's your turn. What are you doing here?"

After a moment, Maomao replied, "In the pleasure quarter, we dance to send off a courtesan who's been bought out of her contract. My celebratory outfit arrived this very day."

In truth, she'd wished to send off the courtesan who'd given her the clothes. Meimei had stuck with Maomao faithfully as she struggled to learn to dance. "I want you to be able to dance properly when I leave," her sister had always said.

Jinshi was looking at her intently. "What is it, sir?" she asked.

"I just didn't know you could dance."

"It's a basic subject of education where I grew up. I couldn't *not* learn it. Although admittedly, I never got good enough to perform for a paying customer."

Still, she told him, sometimes when celebrating a woman's departure, what mattered was the number of dancers more than their quality. When she said that, Jinshi looked out toward the distant lights of the pleasure district. "The rumors are already starting beyond these walls. The stories of how that eccentric bought out a courtesan."

"I imagine so."

"What's more, he's put in for leave. He plans to take off for ten straight days."

"He does know how to cause trouble."

Maomao suspected that tomorrow, another new rumor would begin as well. She didn't know how much the old kook had spent on this banquet, but judging by the number of lanterns she could see from her perch on the wall, it far outstripped what anyone would spend on the average courtesan. Meimei's letter made it sound like there would be feasting and celebrating enough for a solid week. So the tongues would wag: who had known that it wasn't only the Three Princesses at the Verdigris House? That there had been another such courtesan there?

I still think he should have taken Meimei, Maomao thought. The sick woman, ravaged by her illness, surely didn't have long. She certainly lacked her memories of those long-ago days; all she knew was how to sing children's songs and set go stones beside each other.

But that man had found her, after the old lady had hidden her for all those years.

I wish he hadn't, Maomao thought. Then he could have picked her wonderful sister. Meimei was overflowing with talent and still beautiful; she would have made an excellent wife. *But she's strange in her own ways.*

It was Meimei who had first let the man the madam so reviled into her room. Maybe she thought it was the only thing to do with the strange person who continually came pursuing Maomao. Once he was with Meimei, he hadn't *done* anything, but only talked endlessly of Maomao and the woman who had borne her. Sometimes he would seat himself in front of a go board, but they never played a game together.

Instead the man would play out one old game after another from memory.

That, at least, was what Meimei told her. Maomao couldn't know for sure. Maybe Meimei was just being considerate of her. But it really didn't matter to Maomao. She would have been happy enough to see Meimei go to that man. His personality aside, at least he had plenty of money. Her sister wouldn't have wanted for anything in her life. Maomao wanted to know what there was not to like about her sister.

"I can't help wondering who in the world he bought out," Jinshi said. He'd known of the wager, but evidently hadn't imagined the celebrations would be so momentous. He was surprised to discover the man was even more eccentric than he had realized.

"Yes, I wonder who it could be."

"Do you know?"

In response, Maomao only closed her eyes.

"You *do* know, don't you?"

"No woman he chose could be more gorgeous than you are, Master Jinshi."

"That's not what I asked."

He doesn't deny it, though, she thought. She suspected Jinshi wasn't the only one wondering. The whole palace—probably the whole capital—would be asking the same question. The courtesan for whom all this fuss was being made must be resplendently dressed, but she would never appear in public. There would be only rumors, and they would only grow. People would ask themselves what woman could have so caught the eye of a man like him, how beautiful she must be.

And won't the old hag be pleased, Maomao thought. People would be talking about the Verdigris House for quite a while to come. More than a few officials would come knocking on the door—purely out of curiosity, of course.

Maomao's whole body felt hot. Maybe it was because she hadn't danced in so long. Her feet in particular tingled, and when she looked down, she saw her skirt was tinged with red.

"Oh, shit," she said and grabbed up her skirt.

"Wh-what are you doing?!" Jinshi cried, his voice scratching.

Maomao looked at her leg and made a face. The heat had become pain. Her experiments with medicines had dulled her perception of such sensations. She'd been convinced the wound in her leg had healed pretty thoroughly, but her dancing had torn it right open again.

"Huh, guess it opened up again . . ."

"You act like it did that on its own!"

"Don't worry, I'll sew it right back up." Maomao rooted among her discarded overgarments and came up with some disinfectant alcohol and a needle and thread.

"Why are you so prepared for this exact situation?!"

"You never know." Maomao was just about to make the first stitch when Jinshi grabbed the needle. "You can't sew, sir," she said.

"Don't do it here!" No sooner had he spoken than he hefted Maomao into his arms and made his way deftly down the wall without so much as a ladder. Maomao was so stunned she didn't even think to struggle. When they reached the ground, she assumed he would put her down, but instead he continued to carry her, though he shifted her somewhat in his arms.

"What are you doing that for?" she asked.

"It was getting hard to hold you."

"Then put me down."

"And let you make it worse?" Jinshi pursed his lips. He had his arms around Maomao, and she found it most uncomfortable how close her face was to his.

How do I end up in these situations? she thought, but she said, "What if someone sees us, sir?"

"No one will see us. It's too dark. Besides—" He lifted her slightly and adjusted his grip so she wouldn't fall. "—this is the second time I've held you like this."

The second time? she thought. *Oh!*

It must have been the day she'd injured her leg. She'd been unconscious. Someone had carried her away from the scene. It would make a lot of sense if it had been Jinshi. Which would mean he had picked her up in front of an entire ceremony's worth of people . . .

There was something more important, though, something she'd been forgetting. She'd meant to say it for so long, and she deeply regretted not having said it before. She pressed a handkerchief to the blood that dribbled down her calf.

"Master Jinshi," she began. "I know this is hardly an ideal moment, but if I may, there's something I've been meaning to say to you for quite a long time."

"Why so formal all of a sudden?" Jinshi asked, somewhat perplexed.

"Sir, I simply *must* say it."

He slowed his pace. "Well, then, out with it!"

"Very well," Maomao said, looking Jinshi full in the face. "Sir . . . Please give me my ox bezoar."

Jinshi's head connected with Maomao's with a *thwack*, and she saw stars.

A headbutt! Right out of the blue! It crossed her mind that perhaps he'd only been leading her on the entire time.

"Sir, don't tell me . . . You don't have it?"

"Please. Surely you have a *little* more respect for me than that." As Maomao looked at him questioningly, the slightest of smiles crossed Jinshi's face.

The rapid change in the eunuch's expression from annoyance to amusement reminded her how immature he could seem. But then again, she found him easier to talk to that way, she thought, as she rocked in his arms.

No one knew quite where the rumor had started—but word was that some profligate noble from the great country that occupied the middle of the continent was buying up every kind of rare and unusual medicament he could find. It was during an afternoon tea party that Maomao first heard that Jinshi's office was so full of get-well flowers he could hardly get inside. She only took a bite of her peach bun and commented, "Huh."